ONE MORE RODEO
Lynnette Kent

Harlequin Books

TORONTO • NEW YORK • LONDON
AMSTERDAM • PARIS • SYDNEY • HAMBURG
STOCKHOLM • ATHENS • TOKYO • MILAN
MADRID • WARSAW • BUDAPEST • AUCKLAND

ISBN 0-373-70765-7

ONE MORE RODEO

Copyright © 1997 by Cheryl B. Bacon.

All rights reserved. Except for use in any review, the reproduction or utilization of this work in whole or in part in any form by any electronic, mechanical or other means, now known or hereafter invented, including xerography, photocopying and recording, or in any information storage or retrieval system, is forbidden without the written permission of the publisher, Harlequin Enterprises Limited, 225 Duncan Mill Road, Don Mills, Ontario, Canada M3B 3K9.

All characters in this book have no existence outside the imagination of the author and have no relation whatsoever to anyone bearing the same name or names. They are not even distantly inspired by any individual known or unknown to the author, and all incidents are pure invention.

This edition published by arrangement with Harlequin Books S.A.

® and TM are trademarks of the publisher. Trademarks indicated with ® are registered in the United States Patent and Trademark Office, the Canadian Trade Marks Office and in other countries.

Printed in U.S.A.

Dear Reader,

For as long as I've been reading books, I've wanted to write them. I never settled on just what kind of story to write, though, until a few years ago when my husband suggested I write what I so love to read. A romance novel.

His words opened a door in my mind, or—perhaps—in my heart. Characters came into my life through that door, people from different places and different walks of life, all with stories to tell and relationships that needed working out. As a new author for Superromance, I'm delighted to introduce you to some of these special friends.

Mickey York and Jeff Buchanan of *One More Rodeo* are two of my favorites. I think most of us have stood on the threshold of a big event in our lives, wondering if we were making the right decision. Many of us probably asked later, "What if I'd changed my mind? Where would I be now?" Not everyone gets a chance to revisit his or her past. My hope is that those of us who do—like Mickey and Jeff—will find wisdom and courage to make the best choice the second time around.

I look forward to hearing from readers. Please feel free to write me at P.O. Box 17195, Fayetteville, NC 28314.

Wishing you all the best,

Lynnette Kent

Jeff's heart slammed to a stop, then started up again, triple-time

He stepped inside the diner and stared at the lone customer. She sat in the end booth, with her back to the door and to him. But that plait of sable hair, a braid starting at the crown of her head and ending in a soft brush between her shoulders, was as familiar as his own cowlick. A long time ago she'd shown him how to weave it, and he could still remember the fineness of it in his fingers.

And that was only one of a thousand things he remembered about Mickey York.

What the *hell* was she doing here?

He didn't intend to ask. Drawing a deep breath, he blew it out quietly and turned to leave.

"Evenin', Doc!" Delia Francis, the waitress, had a voice that could etch glass. "What can we do for you?"

He froze. To his right, he saw Mickey start to move. Time crawled; it seemed to take forever for her to shift in her seat, to lift her chin, to meet his eyes with her shocked blue gaze. Even as he watched, the color drained from her face.

Well, good. He didn't expect her to like this situation any more than he did.

"Hey, there, Mickey. It's been a long time."

An understatement if ever there was one!

Without friendship, achievement rings hollow. This book is dedicated to all the friends who sustain me when I falter and celebrate with me when good news arrives. And especially to Von and Pam, with love and gratitude.

PROLOGUE

Las Vegas—December

SIX SECONDS.

Six heartbeats of eternity stretched between her and the prize. She could endure anything for six seconds.

A cowboy yelled into her ear above the noise of the crowd and the band. "You set, Mickey?"

She nodded once and gripped tighter, leaned back another inch and set her feet.

Six seconds.

"Go!"

The big gate swung back and the horse, Attitude, leaped sideways out of the chute, coming down rear end first.

Stay back, stay square.

Attitude's front hooves bit the dirt.

Use the spurs. Make it look good.

The dance started with a lift of the big hindquarters, like a rocket's thrust, then a jerk down and a thud as the strong forelegs caught them both. Mickey braced her arm against the crazy, rocking give-and-take that rattled her teeth and jarred her bones.

On the third buck, Attitude twisted to the left. Mickey's hat flew off to the right.

Oh no you don't—you're not getting rid of me!

Mickey shifted with the turn, dug her heels in and

raked back, asking for another jump. Attitude got the message. He lifted his haunches and kicked out, landing on his forelegs, then touched down in back and kicked out again. Higher.

Yes! Come on, you ugly animal, let's give 'em everything we've got! Yes!

Like wind and rain united into the power of a hurricane, Mickey joined Attitude in their elemental effort, driven by a force impossible to explain or even understand. They worked as a team, communicating in a way she'd never been able to describe with words. She only knew that when a ride was this good, she wished it could go on forever.

But then came the one sound that could pierce the storm—the timer's horn. Six seconds had ended.

She twisted her wrist and loosened her grip, then bent forward and slid a leg backward, reaching for the pickup man beside her. Attitude gave a final jerk and they separated; the horse rampaged across the arena as Mickey hit the dirt on her knees.

Yes!

The audience surged to its feet as she rose. She lifted both arms, fists clenched, in a gesture of triumph. The clown retrieved Mickey's hat and handed it to her, giving her a thumbs-up as she walked slowly back toward the chute. With a wink at him, Mickey put it on, then turned to give the screaming crowd another wave, all the while waiting for the verdict.

Finally, the band music faded, letting the announcer come through loud and clear. "Yes, ladies and gentlemen, that's right. World champion Mickey York scored a near-perfect ninety-six points on the ride you just saw to win her third world championship in bareback riding. Let's give her a big hand!"

He hardly needed to ask. The spectators had gone wild. A grin cracking her cheeks, Mickey walked into the middle of the arena to take a bow, and then another. She scanned the crowd as she stood there. A face in the middle of the stands—blond hair and dark eyes under a working cowboy's gray hat—caught her eye. But it was nobody she knew. This was just another bunch of strangers who loved a good show, and she'd given them one. That's why she was here.

It was almost all she had left.

On the way to her truck after the awards ceremony, she was mobbed by a crowd of giggling teenage girls. She kept walking until she could load her gear before giving everyone an autograph and a smile. One or two asked for pointers and she gave those, too. Heaven knows, she'd gotten enough advice in her time. This was one debt she could repay.

Finally, the last of the crowd left, the lights went out, the rodeo closed down. Tired, aching, sore, the world-champion bareback rider made her way to her truck, shoved her trophy saddle over onto the passenger side of the seat and climbed in stiffly. She heard the engraved gold belt buckle she'd won clank against the floor as she turned the key. Chilly air streamed from the dashboard vents, and wouldn't get one degree warmer, no matter how long the engine ran. Maybe when tonight's check came, she would use the money to get the heater fixed. Meantime, she'd be making the drive from Las Vegas to Colorado with her coat and gloves on.

And what a long, lonely drive it would be.

But that was rodeo life. She'd been a part of it since she could walk; some of her earliest recollections were of watching her dad compete in the national finals for calf-roping. And she'd never forget how proud he was when she won her first barrel race. She hadn't been a great student, couldn't play the piano like her sisters or cook like her mom, but she could always get a grin from her dad when she got on the back of a horse. The wilder the ride, the bigger the smile.

With a grin of her own at the memory, Mickey pumped the gas pedal and released the brake. If you wanted to succeed at something, if you made it your life and sacrificed everything for it, well, she figured, then you took the good times with the bad. Without complaining.

Or, at least, not much. Wintry air shimmied down her back, and she shivered. Turning up her coat collar, she flipped the radio knob, tuned it to a country station and settled more comfortably into her seat.

Fourteen hours to Denver. Time to get started for home.

CHAPTER ONE

Wyoming—the following June

"IS SHE A BEAUTY, or what?"

At the rancher's question, Jeff Buchanan finished shrugging into his shirt and moved stiffly to the stall. Inside, a newborn Appaloosa foal searched out her first meal, serenaded by her mother's soft, whickering sighs.

"Yes, sir," he agreed softly. "I'd say that's one of the prettiest fillies I've had the pleasure of bringing into the world." When he lifted his hands to start buttoning, fatigue dragged at his muscles. "It wasn't easy, though. Damn, I'm tired!"

Mitch Snyder clapped him on the back. "But it's worth it. That horse is gonna earn me some serious money one day. I don't even mind payin' your bill on this one, Doc!"

Jeff only grinned and didn't mention that Snyder still owed him on last year's foaling fees. It had been a hard winter and a late spring, but now that warm weather was here to stay, he figured the ranchers who'd fallen behind would start paying up. They always did.

"Dr. Buchanan?" Jeff looked over his shoulder to see Annie Snyder, her father's first pride and joy, holding up a big mug of steaming coffee. "Mama said to bring you a drink."

"Why, thanks, Annie." He took the cup carefully,

not sure his aching hands would hold it steady. "I can't think of anything I'd enjoy more right now." Except maybe twelve hours of sleep. "How's the riding going?"

The rising star's account of her triumphs and tragedies on the barrel-racing circuit delayed him a good ten minutes. Finally shooed back to the house by her dad, Annie only agreed to leave once Jeff promised he'd come out soon to watch her ride. And then it was another ten minutes of listening to Mitch go over the finer attributes of his newest prize before Jeff was allowed to climb into his truck and head for home.

The trip from Snyder's ranch into Flying Rock took the better part of an hour. Wyoming back roads were hardly crowded during the day; at night, without even an occasional pair of headlights for distraction, Jeff had to fight the drooping of his eyelids through every mile of velvet darkness. When he reached the edge of town, he drew in a deep breath of relief. Five more minutes and he could hit the sack.

Just then, a rumble under his belt buckle reminded him that he'd missed dinner. He pressed his fingers against his eyes, rubbing hard. There were leftovers in the refrigerator, but he didn't think he had the energy even to open the door. Right now, rest seemed more important than food. He'd just have to fall asleep hungry.

Driving down Main Street, he noticed lights still on in the diner. A beat-up truck with Colorado plates was parked out front; through the dusty windows he could see a customer's head against the back of a booth. His stomach growled again, louder. Maybe a piece of Emmitt's chocolate pie wouldn't be such a bad idea, with a cup of decaf... Yeah, a little comfort food would help him rest better.

Jeff pulled the Suburban to a stop beside the battered red pickup. A glance in the truck's window showed him a well-worn saddle lying on the passenger seat.

A rodeo junkie, he concluded, walking by. *Stopping for a midnight snack on the drive to a Saturday show.* Interstate 25 ran six miles west of town, a river of asphalt flowing between big competitions in Sheridan, Cheyenne and Denver, with a hundred smaller shows along the way. Some cowboys tried to hit every one, spending all their time and money driving from one ride to the next. He remembered that lifestyle all too well...and was thankful every day to be free of it.

The bell on the diner's front door jingled as he pushed on the handle. Stepping in, he appeased his curiosity with a look at the town's late-night visitor.

His heart slammed to a stop, then started up again, triple time.

She sat in the end booth next to the door, with her back to him. But that pleat of sable hair, a braid starting at the crown of her head and ending in a soft brush between her shoulder blades, was as familiar as his own cowlick. A long time ago, she'd shown him how to braid her hair, and he could still feel the fineness of it in his fingers.

And that was only one of a thousand things he remembered about Mickey York.

What the *hell* was she doing here?

Jeff didn't intend to ask. Drawing a deep breath, he blew it out quietly and turned to leave.

"'Evenin', Doc!" Delia Francis, the waitress, had a voice that could etch glass. "What can we do for you?"

He froze like a burglar caught in the act, then pivoted slowly back, feeling guilty. And hating it.

To his right, he saw Mickey start to move. Time crawled; his pulse pounded through the eternity she took to shift in her seat and lift her chin, to meet his eyes with a shocked blue gaze. He watched the color drain from her face.

Well, good. He didn't expect her to like this situation any more than he did. But he wasn't going to let her presence drive him away. Whatever had been the case in the past, Flying Rock was *his* town now. His home.

Not that it mattered. Mickey was, he had no doubt, just passing through. She'd demonstrated ten years ago that nothing here—including him—would make her stay.

Belatedly, he shifted his stare to acknowledge the waitress's question. "Hi, Delia. How are you? Can I get some pie and a cup of decaf?"

"Sure, honey. You want whipped cream?"

Jeff grinned, though he thought his cheeks might crumble with the effort. "Don't I always?" Then, with a short sigh, he looked again at the woman beside him. "Hey, there, Mickey. It's been a long time."

An understatement if ever there was one.

He took satisfaction from the fact that she had to clear her throat before she spoke. "Hello, Jeff. How...how's it going?"

"Great, thanks." Forcing himself to move, he managed to step fairly easily around the corner of the booth until he could lean against the side of the seat facing her. "How's everything with you?"

Her lashes fluttered down, making star-shaped shadows on her cheeks. "Good. Real good." She was twirling her fork in the chocolate ruins of her pie. A familiar sight—Mickey always played with her food when she was nervous. He strangled the memory as he surveyed what he could see of her—her pale face, the flashy purple performance shirt, and her boots, propped on the seat opposite. Very impressive, those boots—navy blue leather, hand-worked with red tulips. She must be winning big.

As usual.

"Nice footgear," he commented, his thoughts ricocheting in a hundred different directions. "A little pricey for rodeo work, aren't they?"

Her gaze flashed to his face; he thought he could read panic, maybe even fear, in those usually sparkling eyes. "I…I got to the arena in Cheyenne late and didn't have time to change. I just made my ride, as it was."

"It happens." In all the time he'd known her, she'd never been late for a ride. He wondered what could have held her up.

But he wasn't about to ask. "How's your mom?"

"Fine, just fine," She sounded a little breathless. "She's visiting Kayla in San Diego."

He shifted his weight, aware of stiffening muscles and an urgent need to sit down. But not with Mickey. "That's what I heard. Does she get to Denver to see you pretty often?"

"Uh, no, not really. I'm…um…not there too much, you know. I usually go to see her when she's in Phoenix with Barb."

"We still miss your folks around here," he told her. "Nothing's been the same with them gone." But then, life never turned out the way it should. Mickey had taught him that lesson herself. "The ranch is in great shape, though. Dexter Hightower, the new owner, is a good man. He made things easy for your mom, and paid more than fair market value when he bought the Triple A."

She nodded, dropping her gaze back to the mountains and valleys of chocolate on her plate. "I know. She told me."

"I wanted a chance to talk to you when your dad died." He dropped his voice, covering a strange tightness in his throat. "But I couldn't find you."

Five years ago, that was. Bob York's heart attack had been unexpected, swift, devastating. Mickey hadn't stayed in town more than two days for the funeral. And she hadn't returned his calls.

Surprise, surprise.

"Well," she said, still not looking at him, "I didn't hang around for long. Mom moved out to California to be with her sister, Aunt Sarah, and I had a show to do, you know how it is..."

Despite his resolve to stay calm, his hands fisted at his sides as his temper surged. "Yeah, I know how it is." Mickey always had another show. Another place to be, another highway to drive. Always somewhere to run, a way to avoid the past...

A plate clanked on the counter behind him. "Here's your pie, Jeff." Delia said loudly. "Extra whipped cream, as usual." Even from the kitchen, the woman didn't miss much. And she wouldn't keep it quiet. Everybody in town knew what had happened between him and Mickey. Tonight's little epilogue would be the highlight of conversation by the end of tomorrow.

So he decided he'd rather retain his dignity than get the answer to a decade-old question. Straightening, he loosened his hands and nodded in Mickey's direction. "Well, it's been good to see you again. We heard about your win at the nationals last December. Congratulations, you deserve it. Take care of yourself.''

He stopped talking before he started babbling, touched two fingers to the brim of his hat and turned away. If Mickey said something in reply, he didn't hear it.

Delia, bless her, had put his plate at the very end of the counter. As far away now as he could get from the woman in the booth, he propped a hip on the stool, kept his back to her and took a sip of coffee. The strong, bitter taste steadied him, while the illusion of caffeine helped focus his thoughts.

"What you doin' out so late on a Friday night, Doc?" Delia sank into the chair she kept behind the counter and propped her feet on an empty lettuce crate. "Somebody have an emergency?"

"Yeah, over at the Snyder ranch. His Appaloosa mare had some trouble foaling." Jeff made a pretence of eating the pie he'd ordered, though it tasted like dirt to him tonight. "But we got her through it—cutest filly you'd want to see. How's that rascal Ranger? Is the swelling going down?"

The silence behind him remained absolute. He wondered what she could be doing, but he was damned if he'd turn around to see.

Delia shook her head in disgust. "Yeah, his jaw's back to normal. You'd think any dog dumb enough to tangle with a rattler once would learn his lesson after he got bit. But, noooooo…Danny had to shoot one the other day just before Ranger jumped on it. Dumb dog.''

Jeff smiled. "There's always some excitement at your place, Delia." *Like life with Mickey.* He banished the thought. "How are you feeling these days? You've got—what?—six weeks left until the baby comes? Are you going to make it?''

"Do I have a choice?"

They laughed together. "Probably not, but you're looking good, all the same."

"For a beached whale."

"You know better than that," Jeff said patiently, grateful for the distraction. "Pregnant mothers are the most beautiful women in the world."

The clatter of dropped silverware, coming from the booth by the door, covered Delia's cynical snort. "Sure, Doc," the waitress said when the place was quiet again. "Just call me Sleeping Beauty!"

STUPID. With exaggerated care, Mickey placed the fork and knife she'd fumbled across the rim of the plate in front of her. Stupid, to let Jeff's words upset her.

Even more stupid, being here at all. Every instinct she possessed had voted against stopping in Flying Rock tonight. Why the devil hadn't she listened?

Because she was exhausted. And hungry. And because she couldn't focus on anything but the throbbing in her leg. Whatever harm she'd done getting off that bronc back in Cheyenne, four hours of driving hadn't improved the situation. A few minutes with her foot propped up, a good meal and a chance to relax...that's all she'd expected when she came into town. No reunions to endure, no explanations to give, no excuses to make. She wouldn't see anyone she knew. People here just didn't prowl around at midnight. Not in Flying Rock, Wyoming.

And then who should walk in but Jeff Buchanan...the one man she would have given everything she owned to avoid. She had spent a great deal of time and money during the past ten years just to make sure their paths never crossed. Today, her luck had finally run out.

Of course, he obviously felt the same. After the barest civilities, he was sitting there with his back to her, as if she wasn't even in the place, talking to Delia about babies. All Mickey could see of him was the brim of his gray Stetson, the square width of his shoulders, and the tilt of his narrow hips as he perched on the stool with one long, lean leg stretched out to the side. He hadn't even favored her with a smile when they talked, though she could conjure up from memory the way the grooves in his cheeks deepened when he grinned, the way his dark chocolate eyes glinted when he laughed…

"Are you still thinking it's a boy?" she heard him ask. "After three, I believe you're due for a girl."

Who would have expected him to be interested in such things? Oh, sure, they'd talked about children back then, in a "someday" sort of way. After the wedding, after vet school, after she'd milked every ounce of success from the rodeo circuit.

Think again, Mickey told herself miserably. *It was only you who saw it as a someday thing.* Jeff had wanted a family sooner—that was a big part of the problem. She tightened her grip on the edge of the table as she remembered those days, remembered the fear and desperation she'd felt as she faced a future she wasn't ready for.

And—as usual—her reaction had only made everything worse. Tragically, unforgivably worse.

In her preoccupation, she missed Delia's answer to his question. But then Jeff said, "Either way, I hope Danny knows how lucky he is. He's got the finest set of kids a man could hope for. Those twins are pistols, that's for sure. As for Kevin, I'd take him off your hands in a minute. I hope one day I'll have a boy like that of my own.''

Something inside Mickey's chest crumpled, like the fender of an old truck driven into a concrete wall. The longing in Jeff's words, probably not obvious to Delia, came through clearly to the woman who'd once known every nuance of his voice.

''You will, Jeff,'' Delia said. The ache in Mickey's chest swelled to agony. ''Just find the right woman and you'll have it all.''

No. She couldn't bear this for another second. Shaking, sweating, Mickey used her hands to slide her left leg over on the seat, then supported her knee while she lowered her foot slowly to the floor. She pushed against the table and the back of the booth to stand, taking all her weight on the good leg. From a wad of money in her pocket she thumbed out enough to cover the cost of the meal plus a tip. Twice over.

She cleared her throat. ''I've gotta be going. Keep the change, Delia. Thanks for a great meal.''

Now the hard part. *Take a deep breath, make it short and sweet.* ''It was good to see you again, Jeff. Take care.'' She said it with a glance toward that end of the diner, too fast to meet anyone's eyes, and turned away.

The stool squeaked as Jeff rotated to face her. By then she had almost reached the door, every ounce of concentration focused on not screaming when she put weight on her foot in an effort to walk normally. She wouldn't let him know she was hurting; it wasn't as if her injuries were any of his business anymore, anyway. Somehow, some way, she would get out of here with her pride intact. She'd fall apart further down the road, if she had to. Alone.

But Jeff wasn't finished, it seemed. ''Come back

sometime when you can stay longer," he suggested across the yards...the years...separating them. "Flying Rock is proud of you. If you give us some notice, we'll throw a parade. Make it an official 'Mickey York Day.' What do you think?"

Lashed by the sarcasm, Mickey stopped dead. As long as she'd known him, Jeff had never been deliberately cruel—though given the history between them, she figured he deserved the opportunity when it arose.

But she couldn't just ignore the implied insult. "I think that's a cheap shot," she informed him as she swung around. "Why don't you just let me leave—"

She'd forgotten her foot. The pain exploded like a bull out of the chute, slamming her heart against the wall of her chest with the force of a well-placed hoof.

And then the world went completely dark.

BRIGHT LIGHTS, an antiseptic smell and a cold, hard surface under her back...obviously she wasn't at the diner anymore. Struggling, she lifted heavy eyelids and focused her gaze on a scene of destruction.

"What the devil do you think you're doing?" Mickey demanded.

The man bending over her feet didn't seem to hear as he proceeded, calmly, to use a huge pair of deformed scissors on the seam of her two-hundred-and-fifty-five-dollar boot. Mickey would have jerked her foot away, if she could. But the throbbing had intensified to the point that she wasn't sure she remembered how to move that leg, so she had to settle for yelling at him.

"Jeff, stop it! These are my best boots—I won't let you ruin them! Stop!"

He looked up at last, his eyebrows a surprised arch over an analytical gaze. "You don't have a choice that

I can see. And if you don't quiet down, I'll find some Pentothal and put you back under. Wouldn't you like to know whether this foot is broken or not?''

Mickey dropped her head back and stared at the ceiling. "Actually, no. Not until after I've finished at Sheridan. Could you please—'' The whisper of splitting leather sounded loud in the silence. "Damn you, Jeff Buchanan.''

He shook his head, but didn't stop cutting. Resigned to the inevitable, Mickey turned her head to take stock of her surroundings and realized with a shock that he'd brought her to his office. Shelves filled with medical supplies lined two walls, with posters of cats and dogs, horses and cattle papering another. The hard, cold surface underneath her must be an examining table.

"I feel like a German shepherd that's been run over by a truck," she admitted pensively to the overhead light.

"More like a sheepdog stepped on by a steer, I'd say. How did this happen?'' He'd almost finished wrecking her boot.

"I'm not sure.'' Mickey lifted her arms and put the backs of her hands over her eyes. She'd enjoyed being unconscious, nothing hurt then. Now, in addition to the pain in her ankle, she had a headache the size of Texas. "I stayed on, had a good ride, but had some trouble getting off. The pickup man couldn't seem to get me, and I think I did some kind of somersault coming down, and landed wrong when I hit...or something.''

"Something bad. I've cut all I can cut, Mickey. No matter what, taking this off is going to hurt. Ready?''

She bit her bottom lip and nodded. One thing you could count on with Jeff—he never lied. The next few seconds almost sent her back into dreamland.

The real problem was that it hurt worse to have the boot off than on. "This was not a good idea," she said, panting, eyes still closed. "I felt better before. And you owe me five hundred dollars for a new pair of boots!"

"The boot gave you support and kept the swelling down." He sounded preoccupied. "I'll get you something in a minute for the pain." After a pause, he said quietly, "You can bill me for the boots."

Before she was prepared for it, Mickey felt his hand working up under the tight leg of her jeans, a sensation she'd have given all the money in her wallet to avoid. And not because it hurt. The pads of his fingers reached the skin above her sock; she felt their warmth in the pit of her stomach.

It wasn't a caress. It was *not*.

"Dog aspirin?" she asked breathlessly, grabbing for some way to pin down her thoughts.

"I imagine you'd need at least an equine dose." Knowing Jeff, it should have been a joke. But when she opened her eyes to look, he wasn't smiling. He glanced up briefly. "I'm going to take your sock off. Ready?"

She nodded. Gently, he drew the sock down over her calf and out from underneath her pants, then widened his fingers to put as little pressure as possible on her ankle. Another second, and she felt cool air on her foot.

He muttered a rude word. "That's quite a bruise you've got there. I think I'll give you something before I do any more fooling around here."

As his long strides took him out of the room, Mickey lifted herself onto her elbows to look at the offending ankle. Her foot had turned a lovely purplish maroon, from just below her toes to somewhere above the hem of her jeans. It looked, in a word, awful. It felt worse, but at least it kept her mind off the way she still reacted to Jeff Buchanan's slightest touch.

Experimentally, she wiggled her toes. When Jeff came back, she was lying flat again, trying to recover from that stupid maneuver.

"Here," he said, sliding a hand beneath her shoulders to help her sit up.

She gazed at the three pills lying in the square, callused palm of his hand, and then up into his face. "Can I really take animal medicine?"

He rolled his eyes. "Give me a break, Mickey. It's against the law to practice medicine without a license. This is over-the-counter, people pain reliever."

His rebuke barely registered as Mickey confronted her real dilemma. She didn't want to touch him. Didn't want the texture of his palm against her fingertips, brief as the contact might be, because it would remind her of more intimate pleasures. As hard as she tried, though, she couldn't keep from grazing his skin as she picked up the tablets. While she was still staring at the little white discs, trying to get her breathing under control, Jeff snapped his fingers and pulled away.

"I forgot—you need water, don't you? Be right back."

Mickey waited the few seconds for Jeff's return and swallowed the pills with a big gulp from the glass he brought, then kept her mind deliberately blank as she leaned back on her elbows and watched him stare at her abused ankle.

With his attention diverted, she took the chance to study him closely. He wore his hair longer now than ten years ago, but it was the same tawny, unruly blond, with bangs that fell over his forehead and brushed against his straight, level eyebrows. His worn chambray shirt and faded jeans looked as if he might have been wearing them for ten years, though the shirt fit differently over a chest and shoulders that were wider than she remembered.

But most of all it was the air of assurance and maturity he carried that was new. Jeff had grown up while she'd been gone. And, she had to admit, the man he had become was even more compelling than the boy she'd once known.

"You've been walking on it some, so it's probably not broken," he mused, touching a fingertip lightly to her instep. The pain brought Mickey up sharp, her breath whistling through her clenched teeth. "I'd expect a broken ankle to be unstable, even in a boot. We could take an X ray, but..." He looked up and surprised her with a grin, the first she'd received. "...that's illegal, too. Tomorrow morning I'll drive you into Sheridan to the hos—"

"No!" Panicked, she pushed up into a sitting position. "I'm not hanging around here all night. I'm signed on for the afternoon show tomorrow, and I can't spend the morning in the hospital. As soon as you're finished, I'm out of here."

The grin vanished. Arms crossed over his chest, impatience sparking in his eyes, Jeff looked her up and down. "Oh, really? Just going to hop right off that table, are you? Going to dance back over to your truck, slam the door and roar off into the night? These last ten years have scrambled your brain, Mickey. You didn't used to be that dumb!"

She clenched her fists in her lap. In that same ten years, she hadn't had anybody argue with her like this. She'd made sure of that. "I *have* to make this ride. If I don't show, I give up any chance at the championship.

It's a tight race this year, and there are three other women so close on my tail I can feel them breathing on me. I have to be there to win.''

His hands slipped into his pockets, just as they always did when he was trying not to lose his temper. ''That's still all that matters in your life, isn't it? Winning. Another championship, another prize, another title. Don't you ever think about anything else?''

They were teetering on the brink, Mickey realized, one step away from having it all out, right now. The appropriate comment—maybe a single, relevant word—would force them to confront the past. What had happened and why, how they'd felt, how they'd overcome the pain. Then it would really, finally, be over. At long last, they would both be free.

Mickey felt a shiver snake down her spine. There was no way she could handle a showdown with Jeff. Not here, not now. She would have to fight him off. Stoking her anger, she met his glare with one of her own. ''I am not going to argue about this with you. If you want to look at my foot, get it done. I'm leaving in five minutes.''

He took her at her word. The examination he put her through ranked right up there with having her fingernails pulled out. After one minute, she was sorry she'd invited him to inspect her foot. After three, she tasted blood on her lip. At the end, she was wiping tears off her chin with her shirt cuff.

Reassured that the damage wasn't as bad as it looked, Jeff finally straightened up away from Mickey's mangled foot. He glanced at her face, then stepped to the counter and pulled a paper towel off the roll. ''Here,'' he said tersely, extending his arm to hand it over.

He watched as she wiped her eyes, fighting his im-

pulse to offer comfort. She wouldn't take it, anyway.
"You won't believe I wasn't deliberately torturing you,
but I had to make sure it wasn't broken. As near as I
can tell, you've just ripped the hell out of the ligaments,
without actually breaking a bone. An X ray and an examination by an orthopedist would be a good idea. You
ought to stay off it until the swelling goes down. Aspirin
or other anti-inflammatory drugs will help with the
pain."

As he paused, Mickey broke the silence by blowing
her nose. Before she could look up from the paper
towel, Jeff turned away to fidget with the bandage scissors. "Of course, I know the chances of your doing any
of that are about zero. What you're going to do is drive
to Sheridan, ride tomorrow and Sunday, then *maybe*
think about seeing a doctor, decide it's not worth it and
just wrap a bandage around your ankle as you drive to
the next show."

"Probably."

He shook his head. "Then again, some things never
change. Stubborn doesn't even begin to cover it."

Jeff knew from experience he was fighting a losing
battle. Headstrong by nature, encouraged in her independence by her dad who'd hoped for a son and brought
up three girls, Mickey had never taken well to opposition. As likely as not, if you pushed her one direction,
she'd go the other.

But it wasn't his problem anymore. He'd already
risked too much, bringing her over here to make sure
she would be all right. Letting her any further into his
life would invite disaster. One chink, one crack in the
defensive wall he'd built around his memories of
Mickey, and the whole dam might crumble, flooding
him with pain, robbing him of the ability to control his

emotions and his life. He'd worked too hard putting things together to see it all fall apart now.

So he began to clean up the mess he'd made, throwing away her mascara-streaked paper towel, dropping the scissors into a jar of disinfectant...removing every trace of her from the room.

"If I let you go," he said, still without looking at her, "will you promise that you'll see a doctor? By Monday at the latest?"

Whatever else she'd done, Mickey had never lied to him, so he believed her when she said, "I promise, Jeff. I'll see somebody first thing Monday morning." He turned and met her honest, open gaze. She held up a hand. "If not sooner."

It was the most he could expect. "Good. Let me wrap this up for you."

He doubted that the support from the bandage did much to ease the pain, but Mickey got her foot to the floor and limped unassisted outside, carrying her ruined boot. She climbed into the seat of the Suburban by herself, with a lot of effort and a string of muffled curses, and tossed him a defiant look when she made it.

"I'm fine," she insisted.

"Sure you are." He stifled a skeptical snort and started the engine.

They didn't talk during the three-minute ride back to the center of town. Her beat-up old truck, draped in silver moonlight, still stood sentry outside the dark diner; Delia had closed up when he carried Mickey out. Jeff pulled over to the driver's side of the truck and cut the engine. Night sounds filtered through the open windows—the rustle of brush, the squeak of crickets, the far-off bark of a dog.

"Nice night," Mickey murmured. Her head dropped back to rest against the seat. "Peaceful."

"Mmm."

He saw her smile at his response. For an instant the present faded, the past came alive. In a second or two, just like always, he would put his arm around her, draw her close under his shoulder and set a kiss on her hair. And in another minute she would lift her face, touch his jaw with her lips, and he would drop his chin on the next breath, to catch her mouth with his...

No. Damn it, no.

This was not the past. This was the future *she* had created, a future they would spend separately because Mickey wanted it that way.

And now he wanted it that way, too. Jeff stirred in his seat. "I guess you'd better get going." He opened the door and got out. The crunch of his boots in the gravel sounded loud in the late-night quiet as he walked around the truck. A few more minutes, and it would all be over. For good.

Fumbling quickly, Mickey got her door open and her foot on the ground before Jeff arrived to offer help she didn't want. A quirk of his eyebrow told her the effort hadn't gone unnoticed. But he only asked, "Where do you head to after Sheridan?"

She fished through her pockets for the keys, taking the chance to organize her brain, control her runaway feelings. "Oh...back to work. I'm due back Monday morning."

"Where are you working nowadays?"

Where she worked was not something she wanted Jeff to know. Not that he'd try to see her, after she walked out on him, but still...

She found the key and fitted it into the truck door,

keeping her eyes away from his. "I'm a horseback-riding instructor at a summer camp."

"Sounds like fun." Mickey sighed with relief as he didn't push for specifics. And then tensed again as his strong hands clasped her waist and turned her slightly before lifting her onto the seat of the truck. He let go quickly and stepped back before she could protest.

"Is that how you pay the bills?" he said.

She took a deep breath over the pounding of her heart. "You know how it goes, I cover my entry fees with my winnings and sort of play patchwork with the rest. If I have to, I've got the money Dad left to fall back on." It wasn't exactly the truth, but it wasn't a lie, either.

Jeff's gaze dropped to his fingers as they toyed with the rubber padding around the truck door. "Champion bareback rider, woman of independent means. Sounds like you got everything you ever wanted, Mickey. A real success story."

The night noises seemed to stop with a gasp. Stunned, Mickey stared through the darkness, trying to read his face. Surely, after all they'd been through together, Jeff knew her better than that.

But then again, maybe not. She wondered what he would think of the real answer. She wondered what he would say if he knew the truth.

I don't have everything, she should tell him.

I don't have you.

And I don't have our child.

CHAPTER TWO

SHE WANTED to say it aloud. *I lost our baby, Jeff. Can you forgive me for that?*

Will you believe I didn't know? Not until too late, anyway. Not until after I took a ride and took the fall. The doctor thought getting thrown probably wouldn't have hurt, so early in the pregnancy. She said I shouldn't blame myself.

But when he lifted his face and met her stare with that dark, penetrating gaze, the words died in her throat. *Probably* had been the doctor's word. But ever since that night lying under the harsh light of a Denver emergency room, Mickey had known the truth.

The miscarriage *was* her fault. She had sacrificed a baby—*Jeff's* baby—to her own stubborn pride, her drive to succeed.

In the ten years since, she'd never found the courage to admit what she'd done. Not to her family, or the friends who knew her then, and particularly not the one man who had a right to know. To face his anger, his grief, his blame…

She didn't have that kind of courage.

Instead of explanations, she settled for gratitude. "Thanks for your help, Jeff. I appreciate—"

He nodded and cut her off. "Take care of yourself, Mickey. Good luck tomorrow." With a two-fingered salute, he got back into his truck and disappeared in the direction from which they'd just come.

Mickey didn't follow right away. She needed a break, a chance to get her bearings after this last, difficult hour. Leaving the key in the ignition, she sat for a minute, appreciating the peace. Little more than a wide spot on a back road winding through the Powder River basin, Flying Rock was just as quiet in the middle of the day as now, in the middle of the night. Only the darkness, and the yodel of a coyote out in the hills, marked the difference between midnight and high noon.

A deep breath drew in the fragrance of sage, with a tickle of dust. She could almost hear the stars twinkle, could almost see the moon move. Wyoming nights had a magic in them, a kind of enchantment she never forgot, no matter where she was. A spell that called out to her, begging her to come home.

But this wasn't her home anymore. Ten years ago she'd walked out, in the cruelest possible way, on everything and everyone here. All the pain she'd endured didn't begin to make up for the damage she'd done to her friends and family.

And to Jeff.

Oh, he'd recovered, made a success of himself and his life as she'd always known he would. He'd never needed her for that.

But the distance in his attitude, the wariness in his eyes—she was responsible for those. The losses he'd suffered on her account reached so far, cut so deep, she knew she could never make amends. Even trying would only hurt him more.

Mickey reached for the key, cranked the engine and drove out of town without a backward glance.

There was just one way to repay the debt she owed

Jeff—by staying completely and permanently out of his life.

FROM HIS DRIVEWAY a block off Main Street, Jeff heard the backfire on Mickey's engine. She needed a new muffler. Hell, she needed a new truck.

He shook his head. Not his business anymore.

Then he heard a footstep on the gravel behind him, and a voice broke the stillness. "This place is starting to sound like the L.A. freeway. What's with all this traffic in the middle of the night?"

"Hey, Ed." Jeff nodded to Ed Riley, Flying Rock's sheriff, as he came around the front of the Suburban. "What brings you out so late?"

"Had my windows open, heard you drive through and stop at the diner. Twenty minutes later, you leave. An hour after that, you're back, and the next thing I know it sounds like a gunfight out here." In the moonlight, the sheriff's grin shone white, though his gaze glinted like steel. "Thought it was my job to investigate."

The fatigue Jeff had kept at bay for the last two hours suddenly slammed him between the shoulder blades. He couldn't stand up much longer. "Want a beer?"

"Sure."

"Come on in."

Riley followed him into the kitchen. They both winced as he flicked on the light. Jeff pulled out the beers and set them on the table, then dropped into the closest chair. "Have a seat."

"Thanks." There was a moment of silence as they opened the bottles and drank. Then, without looking over, Riley said, "It was Mickey, wasn't it?"

Jeff sighed. "Yeah."

"I thought so. Just passing through?"

"What else?"

"She hasn't even done that, for ten years," the sheriff said. "Maybe something's changed."

"It didn't sound like it to me," Jeff told him. "She's riding tomorrow with an ankle the size of a fence post and the color of raw steak."

"Typical."

"Yeah."

"Still…she stopped," Ed said. "Here."

Jeff opened his eyes—he hadn't realized he'd closed them—and looked across the table. "What's your point?"

The sheriff got to his feet and crossed to stare out the window over the sink. Though he joked about how his forehead got a little higher every day, Ed's long, wiry frame didn't carry an ounce of fat and Jeff wouldn't have bet on beating him in a fight, even if the man was ten years older. Fortunately, their friendship meant the issue had never come up.

"She's held the reins for a decade," Ed said finally. "Maybe she's realizing now that she needs something more."

"In Flying Rock? Her dad's gone, her mom's moved. What's left here for Mickey?"

Ed turned around, crossed his arms over his chest and leaned back against the sink. His face wore the usual give-nothing-away expression. But his gaze was as sharp as blue steel. "Do I have to answer that?"

Jeff took a long gulp of beer. "Nothing." He believed it. "The answer is nothing."

"There's me. I watched that girl grow up. I'd like to see her settled and happy." Riley straightened up and set his bottle down on the counter with a thunk. "Which means tying up ten years of unfinished business with you."

"Forget it."

"Sure, Buchanan." He stepped to the back door, took the key off the nearby hook and unlocked it. Their eyes met as he replaced the key.

"I'll forget it...just as soon as you do. 'Night."

The sheriff closed the door behind him, which was a good thing, because the sound of a bottle bouncing off a screen door just doesn't provide the same satisfaction as the brittle crash of glass against solid oak.

And Jeff figured he deserved at least that much.

RILEY'S COMMENTS ASIDE, he knew the phone call he placed the next afternoon could not be considered one of his more intelligent decisions. His pride, his peace of mind and his self-respect looked likely to take a severe beating if he pursued this foolishness. A smart man would accept his reprieve and be grateful.

Smart or not, in the almost twenty years he'd known her, he had never been able to walk away from Mickey York. Maybe if he hadn't touched her last night, he could have let it go. Those few seconds by the truck—when he'd lifted her and held her weight between his hands—had awakened something he thought he'd laid to rest years ago. Something that had disturbed his sleep and buzzed in his head when he woke up.

He couldn't wonder anymore. He had to know. A simple answer to a simple question, that's all he wanted. And there was only one way to get it. So the sooner he got in touch, the sooner the worst would be over...

"Hello?"

"Hi, Kayla, it's Jeff Buchanan. How are you?"

Her answer evolved into an extended account of domestic bliss. Jeff let it flow over him, amazed once again at how much alike two of the York girls sounded. He had a hard time telling Kayla and Barbara apart, especially over the telephone.

But not Mickey. Mickey's voice held a huskiness, a sexy richness he didn't hear with her sisters. He'd stayed in touch with the family enough to keep that particular memory fresh; last night had proved just how accurate his recollection was.

As if he'd needed reminding.

Aggravated by the direction of his thoughts, he shook his head and brought his attention back to Kayla. "I ran into Mickey last night, as a matter of fact," he replied in answer to her query. "She seems fine. Is your mom around?"

He stared sightlessly out the window at his personal view of the Big Horn Mountains until Ruth York came to the phone. "Jeff? How are you, son? It's been too long!"

She was the only mother he'd ever known. Jeff felt the tension leave his shoulders at the sound of her voice. "Hi, Ruth. Yeah, I'm sorry about that. It's been kinda hectic lately."

As he'd expected, she skipped the chitchat and went directly to the heart of the situation. "Kayla says you saw Mickey last night. What happened?"

He gave her the gist of the encounter. "If she has any sense at all, she'll stay off that ankle, but I don't think it's serious enough to worry about."

"How did she look?" A mother's question.

Or a lover's. "Tired. Thin. But full of energy and enthusiasm. She's aiming for the championship again this year."

Ruth sighed. "Isn't she always?" A moment of silence acknowledged that truth. "What can I do for you, Jeff?"

His turn to take a deep breath. "Well...from the things Mickey didn't say, I got the impression she's not living in Denver anymore. I thought you might tell me if she's moved. And where." Ruth's hesitation telegraphed reluctance, causing him to backtrack. "It's okay, though. If she made you promise not to tell me, you don't have to. I—"

"No, Mickey didn't make me promise. It's just..." Another uncertain pause added to his bewilderment.

Maybe this was an even worse idea than he'd realized. Mickey could be living with some guy, and Ruth wouldn't want to tell him that. Hell, he didn't *want* her to tell him that, though after ten years he couldn't explain even to himself what difference it would make.

Before he could say anything, she hurried on. "It's just that I'm worried about *you*, Jeff. I don't want to see you hurt."

Her concern was a balm for the ache he hadn't deigned to recognize. "It's not like that, Ruth," he assured her, relaxing again. "I'm not interested in reliving the past. I just thought I could look her up occasionally, if she's back in the area. We were pretty good friends once." That, of course, was only the beginning.

And Mickey's mother knew it. "If you're sure..."

"I am. And I'd rather be prepared, if I'm going to run into her now and then, than have it be a complete surprise. You know?" Like last night, like having the part of his life he'd managed to amputate dumped back into his lap when he wasn't ready for it.

"Well, then," Ruth said, still sounding dubious, "yes, she moved about a month ago, at the beginning of May. She's got an apartment in Sheridan now."

"Do you know why? She's been settled in Denver ever since..."

He didn't finish, but Ruth understood. "You know she's never very informative, except about her rodeo work. But I gathered it had something to do with wanting to be closer to the summer camp where she works."

"Do you know the name of the camp? Where it's located?"

"Hold on and I'll get my address book."

Ten minutes later he had the information he'd asked for, as well as a comforting conversation to smile over. "Now that Mickey's got a place around here, maybe you'll come up for a visit sometime," he suggested as they said goodbye.

"I just might do that. If," Ruth added, "you promise me a night on the town. I haven't had a date with a good-looking cowboy in a long, long time!"

Laughing, Jeff promised and put down the phone.

The laughter died as he stared at the paper on which he'd scribbled Mickey's whereabouts. Now he could find her anytime he wanted. If she wasn't at some rodeo or another, she'd be at one of these two places. Compared to searching the whole damned country, this would be a piece of cake.

Once upon a time it had been even simpler. In the old days he'd known all her hideouts, all the places on the ranch she might go to escape if things got rough. When nobody else could find her, when an argument between sisters had heated up too much or Mickey's wild spirits had gotten the best of even her tolerant dad, Jeff had always tracked her down.

He remembered the fallout from one of her stunts, that spring when she'd turned sixteen. She'd been forbidden a weekend trip to a nearby rodeo because she'd flunked her last algebra exam. Being Mickey, she sneaked through her window into the night, hitchhiked to the show and came back with a belt buckle and two hundred dollars, sure that everyone would be just as pleased as Punch that she'd won.

But Bob York was a man who stood by his word. He'd made Mickey sit in the kitchen while he placed the calls that turned her out of every rodeo she'd entered for the next month. When he let her go, she fled the house.

Jeff had found her in the most distant of her refuges, between mighty red rocks on a hilltop at the very edge of the York spread. She lay so still, tucked into the crevice of the big boulders, that if he hadn't been looking so carefully, he wouldn't have seen her there.

He swung down from the saddle with a warning jingle of harness, but she didn't move. After tying his horse to the nearby fence, he came up behind her and leaned against the rock to stare out over the golden plains below them and wait for Mickey to talk.

"I'll go crazy, Jeff," she said finally. "You know I will. I can't just hang around here for a whole month doing nothing. How can he do this to me?"

"You blew it, Mickey," he said. "You caused your mom and dad some serious worry, sneaking out like that. You deserve what you got."

"Why, you—"

Before he knew what she had in mind, she came at him like a grizzly protecting her young. Her momentum sent him sprawling onto his back.

"Take it back!" She straddled his waist and drew back her fist for a punch. "You're supposed to be on my side. Take it back!"

He wanted to use his size and strength to repay her

for the attack. He wanted to laugh in her face, make her laugh with him and see the joke. But most of all, he remembered, what he'd wanted was to pull Mickey down beside him in the red dirt and take her mouth with his. Eighteen years old, and he'd been sure of his feelings, sure of the fire that consumed him when they got too close like this. Back then, she'd filled his dreams with wicked fantasies, made his days a roller coaster of desire and exasperation.

So far, he'd kept his feelings under control. But that afternoon, with her knees on either side of his hips and her breasts heaving in indignation and fury, her face flushed and her eyes sparking, she was the most gorgeous, exciting thing he'd ever known. It had taken every ounce of his will to rein in the force of passion. She was too young, he knew, too innocent, and he'd scare the hell out of her if he let go now.

He used a quick, dirty trick he'd learned on the wrestling team instead, and got her into a hold she couldn't escape, but which was as far from sexual as he could make it.

"I won't take it back," he muttered into her ear, and tightened his grip when she struggled. "What I *will* do is tutor you every day for the next month so that you come out of algebra with the grade you could make if you spent a little less time on horseback and a little more time with your books. And then your dad will let you ride again and we'll all be happy. Got it?"

She got it. She got an A for the semester in algebra, and the junior championship bareback title, despite her month of missed shows.

And Jeff remembered how good he got at tolerating cold showers and long, solitary rides around the ranch, remedies he'd needed more than once in his relationship with Mickey York.

Sitting up, he carefully folded the paper in his hand and tucked it under the edge of the desk blotter. It might take him a week or two to track her down this time. But track her down he would. Ed was right. They had some unfinished business between them, he and Mickey York. Ten years of wondering, ten years of waiting, ten years of patience had ended.

Like it or not, she owed him.

And like it or not, the bill had just come due.

WITH THE IMPACT of a bullet on glass, a shrieking wail shattered the sun-dappled stillness of early afternoon.

"Mickeymickeymickeymickeymickeymickey... Miiickeeeeey!"

So much for lunch. Mickey tossed a rueful glance at the fathomless blue sky and folded the second half of her sandwich back into its wrappings. She managed to grab one more swig of her drink before a human missile hit her shoulder blades.

"Karenkarenkarenkarenkaren," Mickey mimicked, taking hold of the thin wrists crossed over her throat. "Why aren't you in your cabin resting?"

"I, uh, went to the barn," the child said breathlessly as Mickey drew her around to the picnic bench to sit down.

Mickey smiled. "Did you go in?" Karen was completely fascinated by the barn. During her first few days at camp she'd spent endless hours leaning against the doorway, watching Mickey work with the horses.

"Um..." The only problem was that the little girl was as passionately afraid of the animals as she was attracted to them.

"That's okay." Mickey gave her a hug. "What did you see?" Maybe just talking about it would make her more comfortable.

"It was real quiet," Karen confided. "The white one—"

"Thunder?"

"Yeah, Thunder, he was looking over the door. A fly landed on his nose and he shook his head and made this funny sound." She shook her head and snorted, in good imitation.

Mickey laughed. "I guess I'd make that noise, too, if a fly sat on my nose."

Karen thought for a minute. "Yeah, me, too!" The little girl seemed comforted by the idea that she had something in common with the horse. "Then the brown one stuck his head out, too. And then Laurie came up—" She clapped her hands over her mouth. "I almost forgot! Laurie said to come find you and tell you that somebody's here to see you."

"Well, that's just what you did, isn't it? Good job." Mickey tapped the visor of Karen's Camp Crazy Woman baseball cap down over her eyes. "But the rules say rest period from one to three. So git!"

She propped her hands on her hips and watched the eight-year-old lope off toward the cabins, marveling once again at how well children coped with disaster. No one who didn't know would be able to tell that Karen's left leg below the knee consisted of metal frame-work...and nothing else. After losing her lower leg to bone cancer, the little girl had learned to walk and run with an artificial leg as if nothing had changed.

She wanted to ride, as well. The longing was there in Karen's big gray eyes, a desire as fierce as Mickey's own at that age. But for Karen, fear warred with desire, and so far fear had won.

Still, they had plenty of summer left, and the girl's spirit was strong. Someone who had conquered life the way Karen had wouldn't let herself be defeated by a couple of horses.

Meanwhile, though, this visitor was probably the vet in Buffalo Mickey had left a message for this morning. Clementine, the "brown one," had suddenly gone lame.

"And he's waiting to be told what happened," Mickey chastised herself, "while you stand here daydreaming!"

Clicking her tongue, she regretfully dropped her sandwich bag and drink into the trash can as she strode by. The way afternoons went, between riding lessons and cleaning up and playing with the kids, she wouldn't get another chance to eat until dinner.

The short uphill walk to the barn drew protests from her injured ankle. Even after two weeks, the swelling had yet to disappear, though the bruises had faded. At least the air brace the doctor had given her allowed her to walk almost normally. His prescription had been much the same as Jeff's—stay off it, take it easy, don't ride. Fortunately, she wouldn't see either one of them again and be forced to confess how poorly she'd followed their advice.

She glanced into the windows of the dark green Suburban she passed in the driveway and saw the expected tackle boxes of veterinary equipment stowed in the back. The passenger seat held a half-finished bologna sandwich and an open can of soda. It looked as though the vet was going hungry, too. At least he would get to finish!

The contrast between hot summer sunshine and the

cool darkness of the barn made Mickey's eyes tear up. As she stepped blindly through the doorway, she collided with Laurie Johnson, the camp director, who greeted her in typically breathless fashion.

"Sorry to break up your lunch hour, but he's asking questions I can't answer." A shake of her head tossed short mahogany curls back from her forehead. "And I've got to return a call to the insurance people in Denver."

She disappeared, faster than someone so short should be able to move, leaving Mickey grinning behind her. Without Laurie's compulsive efficiency, Camp Crazy Woman would never have existed and couldn't continue to function. As it was, they just managed to wobble along on the edge of financial disaster. But watching the boss hold it all together was enough to wear a body out.

A slow stroll through the barn allowed Mickey's eyes to adjust to the interior dimness. She touched a velvet nose here, stopped to caress a pair of twitching ears there, visiting her best friends. They'd had a good crew of horses donated this year, gentle in temperament but fun-loving enough to give the kids a good time. And heaven knew, some of these kids needed all the good times they could get. They were engaged in a fight for their lives—a fight no one could be sure they'd win.

When she reached Clementine's box, she found it empty. The vet must have led the horse out into the corral to observe her gait. Stepping up to the doorway, but staying in the shade, she saw the big bay first, with only a pair of booted, jean-covered legs visible under Clementine's belly to indicate the vet's presence. Mickey opened her mouth to draw attention to her arrival.

Before she could get a word out, man and horse shifted places. Suddenly the world tilted out of position, as it did when a ride went bad, and her stomach tilted with it.

Not again!

Jeff lifted his head and saw her across the corral. His eyes narrowed in the shadow of his hat, but he didn't say anything and Mickey couldn't begin to. The silence seemed to stretch out forever, although it probably lasted less than thirty seconds. A crow cawed in the trees nearby, the horse's bit jingled as Clementine shifted her weight, and in the distance a screen door slammed. Mickey heard it all, felt the heat of the day baking through the top of her hat, smelled dust and horse and hay.

And yet her mind remained absolutely blank, as empty as the desert at high noon, her attention centered on the man who stood not thirty feet away, waiting.

For what? What did he want?

Taking a deep breath, she summoned a voice she thought sounded almost normal. "This is a surprise. What…what are you doing here?"

"I came to see you. How's the ankle?"

"I…" She had to think hard to concoct an answer. "I'm walking and riding, which is all I can ask." Surely he hadn't come all the way up here to ask about her ankle. She took a couple of steps into the corral and propped her hands on her hips. "How'd you find out where I was?"

He dropped his gaze to watch Clementine ease her weight off her bad foot. "I called your mom."

"She told you?"

At that, he jerked his head up. His jaw was set, his

mouth a thin, hard line. "You didn't tell her not to this time, Mickey. She didn't have to feel guilty."

The pointed comment left her speechless. Last time...

Last time she hadn't told even her parents where she lived for over a year. Not that she'd spent much time in the apartment in Denver, anyway. Establishing a reputation on the rodeo circuit meant driving between Texas and Montana, from California to as far east as Kansas. Phone calls worked better for staying in touch, and kept your location a secret. Which was exactly what she'd wanted.

And if she'd had the slightest idea that Jeff would come after her now, ten years later, she would have demanded another promise from her mother. Damn, but she wished she had.

"Mickey?"

She focused on him again. Nobody would claim he was looking his best. He wore old blue jeans, a little dusty around the knees, and a red shirt, a little frayed at the cuffs. The shine on his boots had disappeared under a layer of dirt and his shirt was stained dark under the arms from the heat.

But he held himself with the lazy confidence of a man at peace with the world and his place in it. Jeff had coped with a lonely childhood by developing a strong sense of independence. And years spent taking care of his dad had fostered an attitude of caring and concern. His levelheaded perspective had steadied her in the past, supported her through some of her darkest times.

Until, that is, she cut him out of her life. And if he'd come up here to ask about that...

"Laurie mentioned you had a call in about Clementine." He pushed his hat back a bit and began rolling up his sleeves. "Since I'm here, I figured I'd take a look. What happened?"

The change in topic threw her. They were going to talk business? He wanted her to deal with this sensibly, as if she saw him every other day, instead of once—now twice!—every ten years?

Still, if she kept her head and watched her words, she should be able to get off without too much damage. "I can't tell you what happened," she admitted. "I don't know of an injury or an accident that could have caused her to go lame. I noticed it first last Thursday, and hoped a weekend of rest would help. But, as you see…"

"Yeah." His eyebrows drew together in concern as he knelt to run his hands along the horse's leg. Strong, square, workman's hands, they touched with a gentleness that had Mickey swallowing hard.

After a silent, concentrated moment, he straightened again. "Lead her around the corral for me, let me see her gait." He held out the rope.

That meant she had to move, had to get close to him. She forced down the lump in her throat, took the necessary steps forward and grabbed at the halter without meeting his eyes. At least now she could keep the horse between them.

Twenty businesslike minutes later, Jeff explained his diagnosis as Mickey settled Clementine back in her stall. "It looks like a popped knee—carpitis. In addition to the lameness, there's some swelling and point tenderness. But those could also be symptoms of a bone fracture. I need X rays to be sure."

With a final stroke over the horse's neck, Mickey backed out of the box, shut the gate, then leaned back against it. "Either way, though, it takes her out of action, right?"

"Definitely." He propped his elbow on top of the stall door, pulled off his hat and ruffled his sweat-damp hair with the other hand. "Some people think you should blister the joint, but that probably helps just because it requires the horse to rest. I'd rather see you keep her off her foot and bring her down for some films. Then, if there are no bone changes, we can inject some steroids to relieve the pain."

Ah, an escape. "We usually deal with the vet in Buffalo," Mickey explained, trying not to let relief creep into her voice. "He carries us on account."

Jeff nodded, his eyes on the rafters. "Yeah, I know. But this week, *I'm* the vet in Buffalo. I'm covering his practice to give him some vacation time, then he'll do the same for me later in the summer. I was out all morning on calls—"

"Wait a minute." It was too easy. Suspiciously so. "If you did this every summer, you'd have been up here before now. This isn't just coincidence, is it?"

His gaze dropped to meet hers. "What do you think?"

Mickey knew what to think. "You arranged this—this replacement excuse. *After* you called my mom."

He cocked his thumb and pointed his trigger finger at her. "Bull's-eye."

She looked at him, speechless. This meant he would want to know…she would have to say…

"So, anyway," he carried on as if this wasn't the most bizarre occurrence she could imagine, "you can bring Clementine to the office in Buffalo and I'll put her on your account there. Simple."

Yeah, right. The contented sound of Clementine crunching hay drifted into the silence as Mickey absorbed the implications of Jeff's plan. However she looked at it, what he had suggested meant seeing him *again*. How could she handle another meeting, when her nerves still stung from the last time? When she couldn't even begin to figure out how to cope with today's encounter?

But the needs of the horse came first, and she wouldn't consider shirking her duty. "Okay, well, I can probably get her down late Friday afternoon. The kids leave for the afternoon after lunch, and once camp is clear I can load her up. Will that be soon enough, do you think?"

She turned to Jeff, anxious to be sure she was doing the right thing. He was staring over the gate at Clementine, giving Mickey the freedom to watch him undetected. The light breeze blowing through the stable ruffled the layers of his hair, showing off the angle of his jaw and the sensitive curve of his ear. Laugh lines mapped the corners of his eyes. It took every bit of self-control she could muster not to lift her hand and smooth them with her finger.

Once upon a time, she wouldn't have hesitated. But the fairy tale had ended and Jeff was trying to conduct a reasonably intelligent conversation. "Oh, sure," he said easily in response to her question. "Three days isn't very long at all, is it?"

No, she thought miserably. *But ten years is.* Was that his point? Had he been trying to remind her? As if she could ever forget.

He glanced at her expectantly, obviously waiting for a rational answer. Mickey wasn't sure she had one. "Well...well, then, I'll see you on Friday."

Flustered beyond her ability to hide it, she pulled herself away from the support of the gate and started walking, too fast, she knew, toward the other end of the barn and his car. She headed directly into the sunlight, squinting at the brightness, glad for the camouflage it would provide as she turned around to look at Jeff.

He settled his hat on his head as he stepped out. "This is a great setting, that's for sure. I haven't had time to come this far into the mountains for several years. Do you tell the campers the legends about Crazy Woman Creek?"

Mickey grinned, not willing or able to stifle her pride. "Of course! We have a nightly reenactment around the campfire. Some nights the Indians are the bad guys and scalp all the settlers, some nights the white guys massacre the Indian village. And it's always a competition to see who gets to be the lone woman left wandering insane by the creek. They love it!"

Jeff tucked his thumbs into his belt and leaned back against the bumper of the Suburban, an answering smile in his eyes. "I'll bet. How many kids do you have?"

"We take about twenty for two weeks at a time. And some of the kids come for several sessions."

His eyebrows arched in surprise. "That's all? I thought most summer camps could handle more than that."

She tried not to sound defensive. "Most can. But most don't have kids with special needs."

"Special needs? I don't—"

"Mickeymickeymickeymickeymickey!" Karen's familiar war cry splintered the quiet. Hands on her hips, Mickey braced herself for the assault. She got hit from behind again, and when she swept her arm back to catch Karen around the shoulders, the girl's Camp Crazy Woman cap fell off.

It wasn't the way Mickey would have chosen to explain about these kids, but Jeff got the message right away. One look at Karen's softly fuzzed head, with hair just starting to come back in after another round of chemotherapy, completed the picture. His eyes widened as they lifted to Mickey's.

"I see," he murmured softly.

Mickey nodded, and gave Karen a hug. "Guess that's it for rest time, hmm?"

"I couldn't sleep."

"So what now, a swim?"

Karen shrugged and glanced at the barn longingly. "I don't know…maybe."

Mickey understood how her young friend felt, wanting something, yet afraid to try. Mickey cleared her throat. "Why don't you go peek in and see what Thunder is up to? I'll be there in just a minute."

"Okay!"

Jeff watched the child as she jogged up the rise to the door of the barn. "She looks at those horses like she's starving for them. Does she ride?"

Mickey shook her head. "Not yet. She wants to but she's scared. I was hoping to get her up on Clementine by the end of the week."

Pulling his keys from his pocket, he straightened up. "If anybody knows how to get her to enjoy riding, it's you. I never saw anybody so at home on a horse—" He stopped as if reluctant to finish the thought.

"She has to learn to trust me." Mickey traced a pattern in the soft dirt with the toe of her boot while following her own train of thought. "And herself."

A brittle silence followed her comment. She looked up to find Jeff staring at her. For the first time they faced each other head-on, neither trying to avoid the other.

"That's a hard lesson," he said softly. The intensity of his focus increased until she wondered if she would ever be able to break away. "It takes a lot of experience to know when your confidence is justified and when it's not."

He paused and Mickey heard the drumming of blood in her ears. "Especially since the people you trust the most," Jeff continued, his dark eyes holding hers, "are the ones who can hurt you the worst."

There could be no mistaking his meaning. Once, together, they had been the center of the universe, the point around which the stars revolved. They'd trusted each other with their lives, their love. Now ten years stood between them, a rift as wide and as steep and as dangerous as the gorge cut by Crazy Woman Creek.

As always, Mickey had the feeling Jeff sensed exactly what she was thinking, could tell exactly how unsettled he'd made her. He held her gaze for a long, silent moment, then turned briskly away. Yanking open the door to the Suburban, he eased himself in and started the engine. "See you Friday."

The sound of the engine faded as she stared at the billowing dust left in the truck's wake. For the first time in an hour she felt as if she could breathe, as if a weight had lifted off her chest. She had never expected to see Jeff Buchanan again.

But now he'd found her. And she could tell from his comments that Jeff hadn't let go of what had happened. Now he was going to force the issue. She should have known, only a fool would abandon a man at the altar and expect to avoid an explanation forever.

And he didn't even know *everything*.

He didn't know about the baby.

But if he pushed hard enough, Mickey knew she'd tell him the whole truth. She didn't lie well, and never to Jeff. Sometime, somewhere, he would catch up with her and the showdown she'd dodged all these years would finally take place.

Unless she left. Again. Unless she found a new place to live and a new life. She'd done it before, she had more money now. Why not pick up and move somewhere he could never, ever find her?

That would mean giving up the camp, of course. For five years, she'd worn herself ragged driving between Denver and this secluded spot in the Big Horn Mountains, with weekend marathons to the rodeos. This year she'd decided to ease up by moving closer, so she could grab a night or two in her own bed occasionally during the summer. Taking a place in Sheridan had, she thought, represented a chance to relax.

Relax, with Jeff around? Take it easy, knowing that any corner she turned could bring her face-to-face with him, with the past, with what she'd done? A decade hadn't made it any easier to explain. Hell, a century wasn't long enough to prepare for telling that particular truth.

So now she had a choice. She could stay put, with her kids and the camp she loved. Or she could turn tail and run, like the coward she was. The latter tempted her mightily.

Rubbing a hand over the back of her neck, she turned toward the barn. She had three days to decide. By the time she saw Jeff on Friday, she needed to have a plan of action, needed to know what to say, what approach to take. Ten years' worth of thinking to do in seventy-two hours. No problem.

In the meantime, she had a job to do. The afternoon sped by as she talked to Karen, still hovering at the door, while some of the other kids rode around the corral. A late-day swim with all the campers successfully kept Mickey's mind off everything except the pleasure of being with children who lived each moment to the fullest, because it might be all they ever had.

Walking back to her cabin, she caught sight of Laurie's profile through the window of the office, and detoured to share a joke one of the kids had told her. "Hey, Laurie, listen to this! There's this guy..."

Mickey let her words die as she caught sight of the camp director's tear-streaked face. Laurie sniffed, dabbed at her freckled nose with a tissue and sniffed again.

"What in the world? Laurie, what's wrong?"

"We're ruined."

The words stopped Mickey in her tracks. She let the door to the camp office swing shut softly behind her, but didn't come farther in. "What do you mean, ruined?"

Laurie threw a sheaf of papers across the desk. "Every single one of our insurers has notified us of a premium increase. They heard about what happened with Bobby Ingram, and even though nobody blames us, they're 'providing for possible future indemnities.' What a crock! They're covering their own—"

"Calm down, Laurie." Mickey didn't pick up the papers. She eased down into a desk chair instead, propped her elbow on a stack of files and rested her head on her hand. Bobby Ingram had developed serious problems during his time with them last summer and had nearly died before they could get him to the hospital. Camp Crazy Woman could not logically be blamed for what had happened, but insurance companies didn't reason like the rest of the world. "So why don't we just pay the premiums?"

Laurie groaned. "Because we can't! Because we

bought the bus for field trips and put electricity into the dining hall with most of last year's surplus! Because we held the camp fees at last year's level to be sure enough kids could afford to come, although medical costs and food costs and electricity have gone up! Because—''

Mickey held up her free hand. ''Okay, okay. We don't have a positive cash flow. Can we ask for an extension?''

Behind her round-rimmed glasses, Laurie's usually warm brown eyes telegraphed contempt. ''Those papers,'' she said with a gesture at the floor, ''are the responses to my requests. Denied. Without exception.'' Her voice sputtered out in a series of despairing sniffs.

Closing her eyes, Mickey took a second to give in to her own despair. This camp had filled her life for five years. If it folded she would have nothing left. Absolutely nothing.

But after a moment, she straightened her back and squared her shoulders. That would not happen. They had worked too hard, done too much, to let everything fall apart. ''Well, then, we're gonna have to come up with a way to raise some money. Can we ask for a donation from the parents?''

Horror distorted Laurie's face. ''How can we? Most of these kids are not even paying their own hospital bills. You know how much cancer treatment can cost. And a lot of them are in the reduced-fee bracket, as it is. No, if we ask for more money, I think their parents would take them out of the program. Which would leave us in even worse shape!''

''Right.'' What else? ''How about a fund-raiser, then? Can we get some donations from local businesses?''

''Mickey, I don't mean to keep shooting down your

ideas, but what local businesses? We're up in the mountains of Wyoming, sweetie, not downtown Denver. And the local grocery store already carries us on account without saying a word when we take months to pay.''

"Casper? Sheridan? We draw kids from all over the state. Why couldn't we put out an appeal at least that far?''

With a weary sigh, Laurie bent over to scrape up her paperwork. "Because raising money takes money. You need flyers, pamphlets, an expense account to take executives to lunch. The kind of money we want doesn't come in by nickels and dimes. We need rich people. Fast.''

Mickey laughed. "Well, let's mail out a letter calling all rich people to contribute. We might get something out of it.''

"Very funny.'' As she stacked the papers, Laurie seemed to gather her resources, recovering her usual controlled demeanor. "Anyway, I'm sorry I fell apart on you like that. It was just that I'd opened the last of those insurance rejections as you came in, and I simply couldn't stand it. We'll figure something out, we always do, don't we?''

With a push, Mickey got herself out of the chair. "Yeah, I guess we do. I'll keep thinking, Laurie.''

"Do that. And if you could come up with a filthy-rich uncle somewhere, I'd be most grateful. I might even give you a raise.''

Relieved to see the boss's sense of humor reassert itself, Mickey flashed a grin. "I'll believe that when I see it!''

As soon as she left the office, though, the seriousness of the situation overwhelmed her. She hadn't asked Laurie for an exact figure to define the problem—all it took was one look at the camp director's distraught face to know it had to be huge. What was left of her inheritance, Mickey figured, wouldn't make a dent. She'd put most of it into the camp already.

So where...how could they come up with the kind of money they needed, in a short time frame?

Too bad, she caught herself thinking as she cleaned up for dinner, they couldn't ask Jeff for his opinion. He tended to be a good organizer—too good, sometimes, at telling other people what to do—and he'd probably have some great ideas about raising money. His help might come in handy.

Braiding her hair, she shook her head. Yeah, and it might come with a price, too, one she didn't want to pay. After a decade of running away, did she really think she could invite him back into her life without consequences?

No. Somehow she and Laurie would come up with the solution on their own. She hadn't asked for Jeff's help ten years ago. She wasn't about to start now.

CHAPTER THREE

WHEN, for the hundredth time, Jeff caught himself checking the time, he dropped his pen, yanked the stupid watch off his wrist and hurled it at the door. "I don't want to know what time it is!" he muttered, looking down once again at the report he kept trying to write.

Finally he gave up all effort. Leaning back in his colleague's comfortable chair, he laced his fingers behind his head and stared out the window at the shimmering afternoon.

If she left at two, she ought to be here by now, he reflected. *Maybe she didn't get away as soon as she thought she would.*

"And maybe you'd like to explain exactly what difference it makes," he said aloud. Disgusted with himself, Jeff got to his feet and strode through the office to the back door, plucked his hat off the hook on the wall and slammed out into the heat. A fierce weather front gripped the countryside. The moderate temperatures of the usual Wyoming summer had surrendered to sizzling highs that did nothing to improve his temper.

Of course, the weather was only partially to blame. He hadn't realized how dealing with Mickey again would wear on his nerves. It had taken only a few calls to colleagues in the area to discover which vet Camp Crazy Woman went used, and only five minutes' worth of persuasion to have his friend in Buffalo plan a June escape to the mountains. A week covering that office, Jeff had figured, would give him plenty of time to pin Mickey down.

But plotting the strategy was easy compared to playing the game, because the stakes were so much higher than he wanted to admit. He'd started this with the intention of simply finding out what happened ten years ago. Purely as a matter of information, he'd told himself. It was a shock to discover that the "information" mattered just as much as it ever had. Maybe more.

The knowledge rubbed at him like a burr under a saddle. Why should he care? What difference would it make to know why she left? He'd conquered the self-doubt that had tortured him in the months afterward, made peace with the prospect of a future different than the one he'd always believed they would share. So how would it change things to confront Mickey now?

The answer to that question still escaped him.

He was just finishing his rounds in the barn when he heard the rumble of truck tires on gravel. Jeff forced himself to be calm, to finish wrapping a bandaged hock carefully and completely. He stood up slowly so as not to startle the horse, gathered his supplies and shut the gate to the box with exaggerated care. Only after the gauze and medications had been stored in the correct containers, precisely aligned on the bench, did he let himself glance out the doorway at the truck and trailer parked in the driveway. And the woman waiting beside them.

She stood in the slightly bowlegged stance he would recognize anywhere, looking assertive without losing an ounce of femininity. Years on horseback had kept her hips slim and her stomach flat. A white T-shirt with the green camp logo across the front revealed strong, tanned arms, small, round breasts, and emphasized her long, slender neck. Even across thirty feet he could see the pulse beating at the base of her throat—a never-fail indicator of her emotional state.

But little of that emotion showed on her face. Under the shadow of her hat brim, her eyes had narrowed and her mouth looked tight, creating an expression of wariness, or maybe just watchfulness. She was studying him intently, the way she would a rattlesnake in the middle of her path. Wondering, no doubt, which way she should jump.

Well, he wasn't going to give her a hint. Deliberately loosening his shoulders, he stepped out of the barn. "Hey, Mickey, how's it going? Did you get Clementine down okay?"

She relaxed a little as he walked toward her. Her mouth even tilted into a smile. "Without a hitch, so to speak. I'm a little later than I wanted to be because one of the kids lost his wallet and swore somebody had taken it."

"And had they?"

Mickey shook her head. "Of course not. Those kids don't steal. After an hour's search, it turned up under his pillow. 'Oh,' he said. 'I forgot.'" She laughed. "Anyway, I hope it's not a problem that I'm late."

The problem had nothing to do with the time and everything to do with seeing her again. But Jeff wouldn't say so. "Not a bit. Let's get her out and look at that leg."

Not for the first time, he was grateful for professional distractions. Four intense years at vet school had gotten him past the worst day of his life and taught him how to submerge himself in work whenever the need arose.

He called on those lessons now to help him concentrate on Clementine. After ten years, any questions he had for Mickey could wait a few more minutes.

The horse's condition turned out to be as good as they could have hoped for. "I don't see any bone damage," he concluded, squinting at the film on the light box in the office. "Looks like we might get good results with steroids and rest."

"Fantastic!" Mickey stepped up to peer over his shoulder at the X ray, making Jeff all too aware of her closeness, of the crisp, clean scent that had always been hers. His whole body tightened as the slight brush of her chin against his arm stirred memories.

Memories he didn't want to face.

He pivoted away to flip on the light. "Let me get a new vial of bute. Then we'll go out and make Clementine more comfortable."

Mickey started to follow as he moved into the pharmacy, but stopped in the doorway and bent over to look at the floor. When she straightened, she was holding his watch. "Is this yours, Jeff? What happened?"

He stepped close enough to take it from her, careful not to touch her fingers. "Must have...fallen off sometime today," he improvised, feeling his cheeks heat up.

"Looks like you need a new one," she said thoughtfully, letting the band slip through her long, sturdy fingers. "The crystal is cracked."

She lifted her face to his as she spoke, and Jeff found his purpose deserting him when confronted by having her so close. The ninth of April had marked her thirty-first birthday, but he was damned if she didn't look just as she had at twenty, with maybe a few more lines in the corners of her eyes and a leanness in her cheeks that spoke of hard work. The years had treated

Mickey with kindness. The only conclusion he could draw was that the decision she'd made had been the right one.

For her, anyway.

A nagging pain dragged him back to the present. Looking down, he saw that he'd clenched his palm around the watch and the tongue of the buckle had pierced his skin.

"Yeah, well," he managed to say, clearing his throat and loosening his grip, "it was a cheap watch, anyway. I'll pick up another one next time I'm at the drugstore."

By the time they got Clementine treated and settled, the sun had started its slide toward the west and the shadows of the Big Horn Mountains were cooling off the day.

"What's her name?" Mickey's voice seemed a natural part of the place, as familiar as the smells of hay and horse and feed. Jeff glanced up from the record he was writing to where she stood communing with the horse whose hock he'd bandaged earlier.

"That's Yip," he told her.

"As in Yippie Ti Yi Yay?"

"What else? She and her rider had a bad encounter with a barrel. Cut her leg up good."

Mickey nodded, placing another soft stroke on the palomino's nose. The scratch of Jeff's pen barely disturbed the quiet. Something about the soothing animal sounds, the familiar, earthy smells, eased her soul and cleared her head. The peace in the barn had always helped her to relax. If her parents had allowed it, she would probably have grown up sleeping there instead of in her bedroom.

Of course, years ago, with Jeff around, the barn also became a place for play and roughhousing, for furious arguments and stilted apologies. And a place for passion.

She had discovered desire in the barn on her dad's ranch, during her sixteenth summer, on a hot afternoon much like this one. A full day of work rebuilding fences had left her layered with dirt and sweat. Mickey remembered riding back off the range exhausted, knowing that as soon as she rubbed down her horse she would get herself into a cool bath and soak away her fatigue.

What she got, instead, was the freezing plop of a wet sponge on the back of her neck. "Hey!"

She'd turned around, expecting one of her sisters, but the sponge seemed to have materialized out of thin air. Not even the animals moved in the sultry stillness, no shadow stirred the shade of the barn. And that's when she knew...it had to be Jeff.

Moving carefully, she'd sidled toward the ladder leading to the hayloft, keeping an eye out for other missiles. With each rung she got a better view of the barn, until she was high enough to look down into every stall.

As she suspected, he was crouched in the empty box, gloating over a full bucket of water in which she could see ice cubes and other sponges floating. The wretch had been plotting this all afternoon. Well, turnabout was fair play.

She got up into the loft, slipping so silently through the rustling hay that he didn't even look up. Perched just above him, she waited patiently until he grew curious about the lack of noise and stood up to peer over the gate.

Then, with a banshee cry, she let herself fall out of the sky and onto Jeff's shoulders.

She took him down and backward, upending the icy bucket over them both. They fell into the straw, rolling over and over again, fighting, laughing, breathless, hands slipping over wet, dirty skin, legs straining for purchase, ducking blows and swallowing curses. They were having a wonderful time.

His superior strength and size won out eventually as she'd expected. They came to rest in a corner of the stall, with Jeff on top, pinning her arms out from her sides and her legs with his, still breathing in pants. She remembered staring up at him, grinning at the straw spiking out of his wet hair, the dust smearing his cheeks.

"You're a mess," she whispered hoarsely. "Totally disgusting!"

His eyes raked over her. "Well, you're not looking so great yourself, Miss Hell-raiser. Straw in your ears and dirt on your face, your shirt torn…"

The words died away. She followed the direction of his gaze, saw that the top two buttons had been ripped off her shirt. The way he held her had pulled the front apart, down to her ribs, revealing the gentle swell of one small breast.

Hunger was there, suddenly, beating in the air around them, and inside her head. Jeff didn't raise his eyes, seemed not to be able to move. Mickey could feel the rigid length of his body on top of hers, the tension in his hands on her wrists, as if he held himself still through sheer force of will.

But her body seemed to soften and melt, like wax left out in the sun. She wanted to fold herself around him, to relax into the heat flowing through her. She was sixteen, she barely understood the complexity of the union between a man and a woman, but she knew she loved Jeff, and wanted him. Now. In that instant. She couldn't wait a single minute more.

Looking back, she could appreciate the control he had

exercised, the painless way he'd steered them out of an explosive situation. One instant she was stretched out under him, filled with desire, the next she had curled in a ball as he found the ticklish spot along her ribs and exploited it. Leave it to Jeff to make frustration seem like another game.

The palomino shifted her weight and Mickey came back to the present, all too aware that the feelings of that long ago afternoon still burned in her blood. She took a deep breath, hoping to ease the tightness in her muscles, then turned toward the door without looking directly at Jeff.

"Well, I really should be going..."

He put a hand on her arm. "I thought maybe you'd like to stay for some supper. I've got a steak in the fridge."

The warmth of his palm on her skin and the vibration of his low voice along her nerves, coupled with the memories she'd just relived, blended past and present to set her adrift somewhere in time.

It would feel so good, Mickey thought. *I could say yes, we could share a meal, and then—*

The full implication of that situation struck like lightning from a clear sky. She'd never come up with a plan for today. Between her usual chores and the new concerns about money for the camp, she hadn't had a chance to decide what she could tell Jeff, or not tell him. If she stayed, if he asked...

Mickey shook her head, thankful for an easy excuse. "I appreciate the offer, Jeff, but I've got a ride tonight in Gillette. One go-round, three hundred dollars added money. If I leave now, I'll just make it."

She avoided his eyes as she walked out into the open

air, but she heard exasperation in his tone as he said, "Aren't you taking Clementine with you?"

Petty revenge wasn't Jeff's style. Or hadn't been, once. Surprised, she turned to face him and saw the stiffness in his stance. She hadn't meant to hurt him, but she had. Best just to get through it and get out before she made everything worse. "I can if I need to. But I thought I'd ask if I could leave her here for a few days. One of us could come down next week and pick her up. If that's okay."

He shrugged. "Why not?" Walking past her, he unhooked the trailer, then stood to the side as she opened the door to the truck.

When she was inside, she gave him a grateful grin through the open window. "Thanks, Jeff. I know Clementine's in good hands, couldn't ask for better."

He had no answering smile. His face remained solemn, his eyes looked sad. "I'm glad I could help, Mickey. Good luck with your ride. Hold tight!"

"You bet. So long." Tearing her gaze from his face, she started the engine and rumbled down the road.

AN HOUR LATER, she checked with the rodeo secretary to sign in for her ride.

"You want a guest pass?" Popping her gum, the woman glanced up as Mickey hesitated. "Guest pass?"

"Oh...no. No, I don't need one." She rarely did.

Taking her number, she walked slowly out of the office into the bustling, noisy night. Cowboys and cowgirls passed by in clumps, jostling her and each other. The whine of a steel guitar pierced her temples and started a headache. Maybe she did need something to eat.

The smell of food hung in the still air, taking away

her appetite, but she waited in line for a hot dog and a soda, then stood there looking down at the food in her hands, thinking of Jeff's steak. He'd probably have fixed baked potatoes and a salad, maybe pie for dessert. Jeff had always liked to cook, and been good at it. Then after dinner they could've sat and watched the stars come out, and talked...

Shaking her head, she took a defiant bite of the hot dog. What in the world could they talk about— old times? What they'd been doing for the last ten years? What they were doing before that? Why the hell she'd betrayed him the way she did...and what it had cost them both?

Retrieving her rigging from the truck, she walked over to the pens and surveyed the horses, trying to locate Flyboy, her ride for the night. A bad-tempered black, he could give her a high score if she handled him right. Mickey had concluded long ago that horses were just about the only creatures she really handled right. Horses and her kids up at the camp.

Her number came up, and she climbed into the chute. Crouched above Flyboy's back, she could feel his fury seething in the air around them, sensed the menace in his laid-back ears and sharp, jerking moves. She tightened her hold and set her spurs, praying his attitude would improve once he got out there kicking.

Wrong. He took a vicious twist away from her grip as they came out of the gate, threw her back so hard her head hit his tailbone, then he twisted again and jerked her forward and down. One second later, she swallowed dirt.

Tonight, even horses seemed to be beyond her.

ORDINARILY, WILD HORSES couldn't have dragged Jeff to a Saturday-night rodeo. He'd seen all he ever wanted of thrashing animals and adrenaline-addicted cowboys. On the spur of the moment, he could come up with about a thousand better uses for his time.

But the price for covering the practice in Buffalo was to step in as on-site veterinarian for the Johnson County Hole-in-the-Wall Rodeo. Which was why Jeff stood here now, explaining to stock contractor Jim Beacham that the man's featured bareback bronc, Terminator, would not be performing today.

"He looks fine to me," Beacham insisted through gritted teeth. "He always stands with his left fore pointed."

"Then," Jeff replied, keeping his voice level, "you should have had him looked at before now. It's a clear sign of lameness and I don't think he's fit to ride."

Hitching his pants up over his ample gut, the contractor took a menacing step closer. "That horse has a shot at the national finals and I want him in this rodeo!"

Jeff plowed his hands into his front pockets and stood his ground. "You can talk to the director if you want. His is the final say."

"I'll just do that," Beacham said tightly. "And I'll see about getting you kicked out of this arena while I'm at it. No tree-hugging animals'-righter is going to cheat my horse of a chance at the finals!" The big man stomped toward the rodeo office, mumbling to himself.

With a weary shake of his head Jeff turned back to the pen and the twenty or so restless animals it contained. A big Appaloosa with temper flaring in his eyes, Terminator roamed constantly, never settling for more than a minute or so in one place. He made the other horses nervous; they jumped and shied with every toss of his arrogant head.

If he hadn't been studying the animals as a way to avoid thinking about last night's encounter with Mickey, Jeff doubted he would have caught the pointed foreleg at all. But now that he watched closely, he could see a halt in the horse's gait which confirmed his suspicion of lameness. If forced into it, Terminator's nasty personality would drive him to give his rider a high score, at the cost of pain and, possibly, a crippling injury for the animal.

Though he didn't consider himself a "tree-hugger," Jeff figured rodeo didn't need any more bad press about ill-treated animals. Not while he could stop it, anyway. Old Terminator would get a checkup, maybe a vacation. There was always next year for the finals.

Hal Freeman, the rodeo director, agreed wholeheartedly with his vet. Terminator was scratched from the draw, his rider reassigned and Jim Beacham walked off with murder in his face.

Freeman sighed. "That's one ornery fella. Can't get through a rodeo without him makin' some complaint."

Jeff shrugged. "Sorry to be the cause of this one. Anything else you need me to look at?"

"Naw. You need to get yourself into the stands so you can watch the show. Ladies' bareback is comin' up next."

Great. "I, uh—"

"Go on now! You got one of the best seats in the house. Better use it."

Sighing, Jeff slouched down into the seat Freeman showed him to and took a bite of the hot dog he hadn't wanted. He didn't even have a program to tell him who he'd be watching. Not that it mattered.

He'd heard the radio announcements this week. Mickey was here, somewhere, waiting to get on a devil who would do his best to get her off again. If he left right away, he wouldn't have to watch, wouldn't have to feel the familiar, never-to-be-forgotten clutch in his gut as he waited to make sure she was okay.

Aw, hell, Jeff groaned silently. *Why do I have to go over this again?*

He didn't, he decided. He could take himself out of the arena, tell the rodeo secretary he'd be outside in his truck and listening to a ball game on the radio until he could escape. He had taken the first step toward the exit when the announcer's voice drew his attention.

"That's right, ladies and gents, as a special treat, tonight's performance of the Johnson County Hole-in-the-Wall Rodeo features the top four women in the rough stock events, riding some of the contenders for national champion bull and bronc. These girls..."

The hype faded from Jeff's awareness as he sank back into his seat. The first time he met Mickey, she'd been riding hurt. He'd come across her as she crouched in an empty stall, huddled over her left arm and crying.

She'd looked up as his shadow darkened the straw. "What do you want?"

He'd seen enough of hurt cowboys to recognize the signs. "You need a doctor?"

Biting her lips, she shook her head. "I've got one more ride."

Kneeling beside her, he'd eased her good hand away. "Is it broken?" She couldn't shrug, it hurt so much. He'd probed gently at her wrist and forearm. "What's your name?"

She gasped as he found the tender spot. "Mickey."

"I'm Jeff. You're riding in the junior bareback?" This time she couldn't even speak, but she managed a nod. "My dad's George Buchanan." He knew he didn't have to say anything else. Everybody in rodeo knew George Buchanan, national champion bull rider.

Easing back on his heels, he let go of her arm. "Well, I think it's probably cracked, Mickey. You at least need to get it wrapped up."

"My mom will make me go home," she wailed. "I want to win!"

He'd been fourteen years old, and already filled with a weary sort of amusement at that drive toward conquest. "Yeah, I know. Let me get a bandage and I'll take care of it for you."

Nobody had ever known about that particular save except for the two of them. She'd gotten her junior championship with a great bareback ride, and nobody had even noticed the bandage on her arm until after she claimed her prize. For Mickey, winning had always come first.

An increase in the volume of the announcements drew Jeff back to the present. "Riding first tonight is three-time national champion bareback rider Mickey York on last year's champion bucking horse, Lady-killer!"

Who thinks up these stupid names, anyway? Jeff scooted to the edge of his seat and grabbed the grandstand railing with both hands.

Ladykiller proved to be just that. Two seconds out of the gate he had both of Mickey's legs on the same side of the saddle, and her arms twisted to the side, trying to hang on.

Jeff winced—Mickey was being tossed about like a rag doll. He could imagine the strain on her wrists, her shoulders, the bone-rattling jar of four hooves pounding the ground. Two more seconds passed like a century.

He realized he'd stopped breathing, wondered if Mickey still was.

At five seconds—one precious instant short of the six she needed—the battling couple came apart. Ladykiller sent his rear quarters up into the air, lifted his front, gave a twist, and Mickey went flying.

Jeff was out of his seat before she hit the ground.

CHAPTER FOUR

THE COMPLICATED PROCESS of picking herself up was made possible by a helping hand at her elbow and an arm around her waist. Mickey didn't even realize it was Jeff until he propped her against a wall behind the pens.

He didn't say a word, which made it easier to open her eyes. "Thanks," she wheezed, still trying to get her breath.

"Look at me."

As he peered into her face, she distinctly felt the press of five separate fingertips on her skin, like small bursts of energy. He was being clinical, and she was being...

"Your pupils look fine. Are you okay?" He studied her through narrowed eyes as he mopped her face with a bandanna.

Get a grip. She shrugged, in answer and in exploration. "I think so. Nothing new hurts, anyway."

Jeff dangled the bandanna for her to catch, then stepped back. "How's the ankle?"

"You don't want to know," she said frankly, pressing the wet blue cloth into her eyes. "What are you doing here?"

"You keep asking me that. The guy I'm working for signed on for the rodeo here and I'm taking his place."

"Lucky you."

"Yeah. Are you riding again tomorrow?"

She nodded.

"And then what?"

The tension in Jeff's voice caused her to lower the cloth. Focusing her eyes on his face, Mickey registered the anxiety he was trying to control. But she remembered his expression from way back, from the afternoon they first met, when his dad had ended up in the hospital.

She had just come out of the cast room with a nice, heavy plaster sheath on her arm as an added prize for winning the junior championship. Jeff had been sitting by himself in the waiting area for the emergency room, looking serious and worried and mad, all at the same time. While her mom and dad took care of the bill, she stepped over to the boy who had helped her win.

"Thanks," she'd said then, too. "I couldn't have won if you hadn't wrapped me up." He grinned, but only for a second. She sat down in the chair next to his. "I'm sorry about your dad. How's he doing?"

"I haven't heard."

"Is your mom in there with him?"

"She died when I was two."

"Oh." Mickey's twelve-year-old pride had still been struggling to recover from making such a stupid comment when her parents joined them.

"You're George Buchanan's boy, aren't you?" Her dad knew just about everyone on the rodeo circuit by sight, and most of them considerably better than that. It had to do with the prize bulls he raised and supplied for the riders, and the years he'd spent on the circuit himself, roping calves. "Have they told you what's going on?"

Jeff got to his feet and dug his hands into the pockets of his worn, faded jeans. "No, sir."

Bob York dropped a hand to one thin shoulder and

gave the boy a reassuring squeeze. "Let me see what I can find out."

Fifteen minutes later, they knew it was terrible, but could have been worse. Two gores, a busted leg and a shattered career...not bad for one day's work. No thanks to a bull with the instincts and aim of a rhinoceros, George Buchanan would be around to tell the tale of his days as a champion bull rider. What he wouldn't be able to do was ride again.

By the time Jeff had spoken to his dad and to the doctors, Mickey's parents had made the inevitable decision. Regardless of his protests, Jeff Buchanan came home with them that night, to eat dinner at the table with the three York girls, to help with washing up the dishes and bedding down the animals afterward, to sit drowsing by the fire as they took turns reading aloud from a Louis L'Amour western. As they stumbled off to bed, Mickey had noticed with relief that the anxious expression had eased off Jeff's face. Temporarily, at least.

"Mickey? Did I lose you? Come in, Mickey!"

Fingers snapped in front of her nose and Mickey jerked back to the present. Her vision sharpened, showing her a face twenty years older than the one she'd been remembering, but not so very different. There might be a few more lines in the tanned and weathered skin, his shoulders might be broader and his chest wider, but otherwise Jeff hadn't changed much. He had kept himself lean, his hips narrow, his belly hard. She still thought he was the sexiest, best-looking man she'd ever met. Anywhere.

Not that it mattered anymore. A quick shake of her head cleared the cobwebs. She stood up away from the wall, ignoring the way her head swam, her shoulder throbbed and her ankle screamed. "Sorry. I was just thinking. What do you say we get out of here and get something to eat?"

But exhaustion hit her like a raging bull as they made the short walk to the concession stand, and her accumulated aches and pains started pounding with the thud of a cattle stampede. She stopped and swayed a little. "I don't think I'm so hungry, after all. I just need to sit down."

Jeff found a bench, and brought her a drink. Mickey sipped it with her eyes closed, waiting for the dizziness to subside. "Whew," she murmured finally. "That was quite a ride."

She turned her head and looked at Jeff, who returned her gaze with a lift of his eyebrows. He still seemed worried. She'd have thought he would have outgrown that by now.

He lifted her chin with his knuckle and stared at her eyes again. "How many falls have you taken this week?"

"Two rides. Two falls. No money. That's the way it goes sometimes." She tried a grin, hoping to get one back. "There's always tomorrow!"

"Right." No return smile. His hand dropped away. "Is it worth it?"

Mickey let her gaze drift toward the distance, watching the crowd as she tried to frame an answer. "As long as I'm still winning more than I lose, then, yeah, I think it's worth it."

Especially after all she'd cost them both to get this far.

The bench shuddered as Jeff dropped back against it. "Well, then, I guess that's all that counts." She heard doubt in his voice, but she was too tired to try to deal with it.

Instead, she straightened up. "I also think I'm going to call it a day, Jeff. Thanks for coming to the rescue...*again*." Getting to her feet took more effort than she was prepared for, and staying on them seemed almost impossible. She tilted her head, trying to keep the world level, and would have fallen if Jeff hadn't pulled her back down.

"You're in no shape to go anywhere by yourself," he growled. "So I guess you can just sit here, or in the stands, until the show is over and I can leave. Then I'll drive you to your motel, make sure you get there in one piece."

Mickey took a deep breath. "You don't have to—"

He stood up and looked down at her, his face unusually grim. "Damn it, I know I don't. Just accept it for once, okay? No arguing. I'll be back as soon as I can." Without waiting for her to agree, he strode off into the crowd.

Leave it to Jeff, she thought as she watched him go. *Always taking care of somebody...* For a while after he'd come to live with them, the York girls had thought they'd acquired their own personal servant. Every chore Mickey or her sisters left undone, every task that might conceivably need doing, Jeff was willing and able, until Bob York had tried to put a stop to it.

"You leave those girls' work alone!" The twinkle in her father's blue eyes always took the sting out of the words. "I want to know when they're slacking—what good will they be if you do their jobs?"

Jeff had tried, really tried, to back off. But it was in his nature—and in his upbringing—to rescue people. At whatever cost to himself. That was why—

"Are you planning to sleep here all night?"

She gazed up hazily into a familiar face, aware that time had passed, but not how much. "Am I asleep?"

He gave her a grin and held out a hand. "Close enough. Come on, let's get you some food and rest."

Mickey let him pull her to her feet and then hesitated, thinking of all the reasons this was not a good idea, going for the least important. "What about my truck?"

A casual arm slipped around her shoulders and turned her toward the exit. "We'll lock it up tight and leave it just where it is. I'll bring you back tomorrow to get it. No more arguments." The support felt too good to give up, so she gave in.

All the bruises had stiffened while she sat, and climbing into Jeff's Suburban felt like climbing Everest. "Aaahh," she sighed, sliding down into the soft, molded seat.

He looked over as he turned the key in the ignition. "I take it that means you're not interested in stopping for dinner somewhere."

"I don't think I could do it," she mumbled. "Just drop me off at the nearest motel and go on. I'll live without dinner."

His rich chuckle rippled across the cab. "No, you won't. That's what they make fast-food places for, and Buffalo has its share. I don't like eating alone."

She knew that. He'd done so much of it, growing up, following his dad around the circuit for twelve years, staying alone at night while George Buchanan went out with his rodeo cronies. Life at the Triple A Ranch with the Yorks had been a revelation for the shy, quiet boy they'd practically adopted. It took him a month to stop standing up every time Mickey's mother came into a room, and two weeks before he would ask for seconds at the dinner table. After a few days, Mickey had started serving them without even asking him.

"What are you doing?" he'd hissed at her, when her mother and father weren't looking.

"You're skinnier than a snake in winter," she hissed back. "You need to eat!"

His cheeks had taken on a dull red color, Mickey remembered, and his eyes had dropped. But he finished every last morsel of food on the plate.

He still had a healthy appetite. They picnicked in her motel room and he finished up the last of the chicken as they watched a newscast on TV, hoping for a report on the rodeo. When the film clip of her ride came on, Mickey grinned as she watched Ladykiller jerk her around.

"I guess the crowd got their money's worth tonight." She wiped her hands and sank back against the pillows. "Judging by that, I should be in the hospital."

"You probably should." Jeff was packing up the trash. "And I should be held on criminal charges for aiding and abetting you. Again."

Glancing over, she saw him wince as her television image hit the ground. "Oh, come on. You know it's never as bad as it looks."

His mouth thinned, and he shook his head. "I know how many times I've had to scrape you out of the dirt."

"But the best rides come when you're out on that edge where things could break either way. A fall is just the price you pay to win."

"Maybe not everybody wants to live on the edge." He smashed the trash hard into the wastebasket. "Did you ever think of that?"

What was his problem? "Give me a break, Jeff. How many times did I hear you yelling at me to hang on tight? You can't pretend you didn't push me as far as I could go!"

It only took a second to realize her mistake. As she watched, his eyes changed, darkened, and she got the feeling that his recollections had gone beyond adolescent pranks and college rodeos, had moved somewhere she didn't want to follow. There were ways they had found of driving each other to the very brink of sanity...

Scooting to the edge of the bed, Mickey tried to break up the uneasy silence with a joke. "If you stick around here much longer, I'm going to make you scrub my back while I take a bath."

But that was another fumble, because it had happened just like that, all those nights after her competitions for the college team. She would come back tired and sore and slip into the big tub in their tiny apartment, and Jeff would join her there, to scrub her back and massage her shoulders, and then love her out of her mind.

Which was exactly what she didn't want to remember.

And neither, she recognized with relief, did he. After a breathless instant, he shook his head and walked toward the door. "Sorry, you'll have to live with a dirty back. I think I'm going to turn in instead. See you tomorrow."

Before she could say another word, he'd closed her in by herself.

Mickey didn't want to think about what she'd said, or what it meant about the way she was feeling. And, as ten years had taught her, the only way to avoid pain was to ignore it. On a deep breath, she got herself off the bed and into the bathroom, where she filled a glass with water and took two of the pills the doctor had given her for her ankle. Then she sat down on the side of the tub and turned on the tap. The splashing rushed through the silence like a spring torrent, filling her thoughts to the exclusion of everything else.

She slipped the buttons on her shirt and shrugged it off, broke the snap on the jeans she'd worn for two days now and eased the stiff denim over her hips, then bent over to work the legs off. A bruised shoulder and a barely healed ankle didn't enhance the experience.

But the hot, hot water was a more-than-adequate reward. She sank gratefully into the steam, feeling the tightness in her muscles loosen with each second. Even her ankle stopped throbbing, or maybe the sting of the water took over all the other aches. Her eyes drifted shut, her brain closed down, and she floated into unconsciousness on a tide of warmth.

JEFF DIDN'T EVEN get across town before he realized that the last thing he could do at this point was go into a strange house and fall sleep. He turned around instead, and started driving up and down the streets of Buffalo. One trip didn't take too long, so he did it again. And again.

The chill of the night should have worn off his energy. It had been a hell of a day—he should be tired enough to drop in his tracks. But his brain was feverish with long-ago memories of Mickey, the slickness of her skin as he soaped it, the way the tendrils of her hair curled in the steam, the little gasp she always made when he—

Damn it all, what was he thinking?

And what exactly was he doing now, pulling back into the motel parking lot, getting out of the truck, standing here staring at her door, lifting his hand to knock? What was he going to say to the woman who had, no doubt, been asleep for an hour or more while he roamed around town like a rutting stag?

Jeff had no idea. But he knocked anyway. And again, louder, when she didn't answer. "Mickey? Wake up, Mickey!" He paused, listening intently. "Are you okay?"

An echo from the past caught up with him. He saw himself standing in a narrow hallway, knocking on a plain white door marked Ladies. "Mickey? Mickey, are you in there?" he'd called.

Kayla ducked under his arm. "Let me go in, Jeff. I'll talk to her."

It doesn't take long to search a bathroom. Kayla came out in less than a minute, her face pinched, her eyes scared. "She's…she's not there."

Then his memory showed him Ruth York, hours later, still neat and trim in her best church dress, and Bob, Mickey's dad, with his tie crooked and his starched shirt creased. As if it were yesterday, Jeff could see their shocked white faces as he forced himself to admit that he and Ed had torn Flying Rock apart…and their daughter wasn't anywhere to be found.

Shaking off the past, Jeff gritted his teeth and pounded on the motel-room door again. "Mickey, damn it, let me in!"

Still no answer. She could be asleep, but he didn't buy it. She'd always been a light sleeper, no matter how tired. He'd always been able to wake her up to make love…

The night manager gave him a hassle about getting her key. Twenty bucks solved that problem. Jeff's hand shook a little as he turned it in the lock, and he cursed himself for it. What did it matter if she'd run out on him? Surely he was getting used to that by now.

But her duffel bag still sat on the table in front of the window, and her lace-up riding boots still flopped by the bed. A dim light drew him toward the tiny bathroom. "Mickey? Mickey, are you in there?" He peeked inside the open doorway.

For a bloodless second he thought she was dead. She floated in the water, totally relaxed, totally at peace. And lobster pink, from chin to toes.

Would a dead person be pink?

"Damn you, Michelle Elizabeth York! Don't you know better than to fall asleep in the bathtub?"

He swooped down on her, dragging her up by the arms, holding her around the waist until he could grab one of the flimsy towels to wrap around her. By then she had started to stir. Her head flopped against his shoulder, and she put a hand to her hair.

"Jeff? Wha…" A huge yawn shuddered through her. "What's going on?"

Jerking her roughly off her feet, he grabbed the other two towels and swept her into the bedroom, sat her down on the side of the bed and began to dry her off.

He muttered at her as he worked. "Of all the stupid stunts, this has to be the worst. I'll bet you swallowed a couple of those codeine pills on the sink in there and decided to take a bath afterward. You idiot—I remember, if you don't, how hard those things hit you. You should never take them until you're ready to collapse. Damn it, you might have drowned!"

With another yawn, she flopped back to lie on the bed. "No great loss."

Jeff jerked his head up at the soft, clear comment. Dropping the towel he held, he lifted himself to sit beside her. "That's the medication talking, Mickey.

You're important to many people, in a lot of different ways. You've got fans all over the country.''

She had one arm flung over her face. ''They'd get over it.''

''The kids at the camp wouldn't.''

A weary sigh lifted her shoulders.

''And I...'' Jeff closed his eyes in a desperate, hopeless bid for control. How had he ever thought he could avoid this? ''I never did.''

Opening his eyes, he watched as Mickey lowered her arm. He held her incredulous blue stare for a minute, then let his eyes sweep the rest of her barely covered body.

''No,'' he murmured, knowing it for the absolute truth. ''I never did.''

She didn't protest as he bent over her, didn't do anything except part her lips slightly, waiting for him. He hesitated at the instant of contact, breathing in her scent, her taste. Ten years. Ten years since he had kissed Mickey York. And he'd wanted to every day since.

There didn't seem to be any way to take it slow. They seized each other's mouths with a decade of hunger inside them, a decade of emptiness and loneliness and wanting. Before he knew it, Mickey's towel had vanished and his shirt was gone, and the tips of her breasts, hard, aroused, rubbed against him, driving him wild. He eventually managed to drag his lips from hers, but only so that he could scatter kisses down her throat and across her chest, could cherish the pucker of her nipple with his tongue and feel the familiar arch of her body as the sensation shot through her.

Ten years vanished into thin air.

Raking her fingers across the smooth, sculpted planes of Jeff's back, Mickey ignored the warning bells in her brain. For the first time in ten years she was home, in Jeff's arms, where she'd belonged since she was twelve years old. No man on earth could make her feel the way he did, could set the wind to rushing through her veins and the sky to spinning around her head. She hadn't planned this, hadn't expected it, and not for anything in the world would she stop it.

As if she could have stopped it, even if she wanted to. The passion between them had broken through every barrier they'd built, every wall they'd erected. She wasn't on top of it, able to control the direction, but inside, caught in the middle of a violent cascade of feeling, drowned in the current.

Only the habits of the past helped her respond. Her body remembered, before her mind, all the ways she had once found to pleasure Jeff Buchanan and she revisited them all—the sensitive spot joining his neck and shoulder, where a slow stroke of her tongue could drive him crazy, the soft down under his arms, the flat button of his nipple, where a quick twist of her fingers could make him groan.

He retaliated by dragging his teeth across her breast, a strategy that left her gasping. Jeff lifted his head. "You still like that, do you?" His voice was a husky whisper. "You always did."

"Always." Mickey let her hands drift to the waist of his jeans. "Among other things."

His chin lifted slightly, and his eyebrows rose. "Oh, yeah?"

She shifted her legs underneath him and saw his eyes widen as he settled into the cradle of her thighs. "Yeah."

He rocked his hips, and she softened against him, feeling his arousal strengthen at her eagerness. He lowered his mouth to hers again, kissed her gently. "Ten years, Mickey." Another kiss, glazing her lower lip with his tongue. A quick press of his loins into hers. "We could have been together like this every night for ten damned years."

Through the haze of desire, Mickey heard anger thread into his voice. And then his kiss turned hard, and all softness disappeared. This harshness, this punishment, was not the Jeff she'd known, and she didn't like it. She stiffened, tried to move, but he had her pinned. When she jerked her face away from his, he drew back and propped his weight on his elbows, without releasing her. Her hands came to his biceps and pushed, but couldn't budge him. She waited, wariness and despair filling the space in her chest she needed for air.

Jeff held her eyes with his. "I would have scoured the entire country looking for you," he said informatively, as if she'd asked a question. "But I waited. I figured you would come back to me on your own, when you were ready. We had so much…it was so good… It only took a couple of months to shoot down that idea."

He shrugged, without letting her go. "So I got mad. For over a year I cursed and muttered, when I wasn't studying, and sometimes, you know, I really hoped to hear that you'd died, just so it wouldn't be possible to see you again."

Mickey closed her eyes to stop the tears. They crept out from underneath her lashes anyway, trickling in hot trails across her temples and into her hair.

"Then," he went on, and she looked at him again, "well, I figured it was just simply too late." He shook his head slightly. "I gave up and got on with life. Over the years I tried to catch up with you a time or two, but you were always too good at getting away. I could have kept track of your performances, I guess, and cornered you in an arena somewhere. But I didn't think the national finals would be the best place for a showdown. And after a while, it didn't matter so much. I kept busy, I found other women—''

He saw the reaction she couldn't stifle. The corner of his mouth twitched. "Did you think I'd be a monk for you, Mickey? Think again.''

A silence developed as she dealt with the pain. This...*this*...was what she'd run away from for ten years. And it was every bit as bad as she'd expected. If not worse.

At last, his voice penetrated the cocoon of hurt. "Still, I thought one day I might have a chance to find out what went wrong. It didn't consume my days, mind you. Just hung there in the back of my mind, as a possibility for the future.''

One side of his mouth tilted, but it wasn't his usual smile. "It looks like the chance I was expecting has finally arrived. We're here, together, and neither of us is going to run away this time.''

Mickey turned her head to the side, trying to avoid that rock-hard gaze. He wouldn't do this, he couldn't make her... Jeff wasn't like that. Or hadn't been, once.

Hard fingers closed around her chin and slowly pulled her head around. She couldn't help but open her eyes as he positioned them once again face-to-face.

"So, Mickey.'' His tone was conversational, almost casual. His face was a mask of stone. "Why don't you take this opportunity and explain to me exactly what was in your mind the day you walked out on our wedding?''

Jeff watched Mickey's eyes widen; she shook her

head once. He tightened his grip a fraction. "Oh, yes, Mickey. Now."

She closed her eyes and he noticed the blue veins on her lids, the purple shadows underneath that spoke of too little rest. This was all wrong, of course. He'd never meant to do it this way. But now that he had...

He could count on Mickey to defend herself. The tension in her body telegraphed a determination that continued to build as he waited. After a minute, her dark, spiky lashes fluttered up and she met his gaze, pride and dignity in her own.

"I will not answer any questions like this." The hiss of her whisper sent a chill up his spine. "If you expect to talk to me, you'd better let me up."

Jeff had no doubt she spoke the truth. He'd never been able to force an answer if she didn't want to give it to him. Moving away from their angry embrace, he gave a quick thought to how much he should despise himself for what he'd done. Later. Right now, what mattered most was to hear the truth.

He picked up his shirt and stood with his back to the bed as he put it on, fumbling with the buttons. Behind him he heard Mickey stumble and curse, heard the zip as she opened her duffel bag.

"Okay."

At the sound of her level voice, he turned to find her in sweatpants and a long-sleeved T-shirt. And socks. Despite the situation, her outfit struck him as funny and he surrendered to a grin. "Are you sure you're protected enough? Would you like a trench coat, while you're at it? Maybe a chastity belt with a combination lock?"

A joke wouldn't buy him out of this one. Her stern face didn't change. "You had something you wanted to know?"

Pulling in a deep breath, he dropped into the only chair and braced himself by staring up at the ceiling as he answered her question.

"Call me dense, Mickey..." Another ration of air forced the rest of it out. "But after ten years I'm still wondering what the hell could have been so wrong that you walked away from marrying me without even saying goodbye."

The bed squeaked as she sat on it. "What difference does it make now?"

He jerked his gaze down to glare at her. "The same difference it made then, damn it! I loved you and I want to know what went wrong!" She flinched at his shout but he ignored the impulse to apologize, waiting in silence for her to say something. Anything.

But she didn't speak right away. Instead, fidgeting, she lifted her hands to the tail of her braid and slipped off the band. Her fingers combed through her hair, pulling it out into a soft fall around her face. The dim light had made reading her expression difficult. Now the shadow from her hair rendered it impossible.

"I loved you, too," Mickey said in a low voice, at last. "And I wanted to marry you. But..."

Jeff sat up, propped his elbows on his thighs and clasped his hands between his spread knees. That way they wouldn't shake. "But...?"

"It was going all wrong, Jeff. You were thinking one thing and I was thinking something else. And—and I got scared."

"I don't understand. What was I thinking that you weren't? You're not being clear, Mickey."

He caught an impatient flash of blue from her eyes as she glanced up. "You were thinking about vet school. About...babies...and settling down. And I—"

"That's what people logically do when they get married."

She nodded, and he heard her swallow. "I know. And I couldn't. That's why I left."

Putting a hand up to rub his weary eyes, Jeff cautioned himself to be patient. Mickey had always taken the long way around with any explanation. He looked back at her, spoke carefully. "You couldn't do what?"

Without anything else to do, her fingers were twisting in her lap. "I was lost, Jeff. Everybody was so proud of you, so impressed with your degree and your plans. And they all thought I was just going to slip right into the groove, fit into the pattern. What I wanted, what I planned didn't seem to matter anymore."

"What was it you wanted? I thought—" He stopped as she shook her head. Obviously, what he'd thought had been part of the problem.

"I wanted what I've had. A chance to make my own way, and my own name. I wanted to be Mickey York."

"Mickey—"

"Not..." She cleared her throat, but her voice still came out softly. "Not just Mrs. Jeff Buchanan."

CHAPTER FIVE

JUST Mrs. Jeff Buchanan.

If he'd known it would hurt this much, Jeff might not have asked the question to begin with. Too late now.

He took a deep breath against the pain. "So, in other words, you felt trapped. Felt that marrying me would force you away from what you wanted to do." Lifting his head, he tried to catch her gaze. "But, *why*, Mickey, didn't we talk about it? Why didn't you tell me what you were thinking?"

She shook her head, avoiding his eyes, and her hair floated around her shoulders. "I—I wanted to. But there were always people around those last few weeks. My mom and sisters, the women at church, all telling me how lucky I was and what beautiful babies we would have. Babies! I was only twenty-one, and they wanted me to get pregnant!"

A shaft of remorse reminded Jeff how long it had taken that particular dream to die. He swallowed hard to stifle his reaction at hearing it resurrected. "Okay. But it wasn't me putting the pressure on, Mickey. You should have talked to me. I would have—"

She looked up sharply. "That's just it, Jeff—I 'should' have talked to you. You were always saying things like that to me. 'We should wait until we finish college to get married,' never mind what I wanted, or the fact that my parents didn't like us just living together. 'You should take that job at the newspaper so we'll have some money,' even though it meant weekend work that would make it hard for me to compete. 'You should this or that' until I felt like I had nothing to say about what was happening in my own life!''

He couldn't help wincing at the picture she drew. "Mickey, I—"

"We weren't even making…having—" her voice faltered as she searched for the word "—being together anymore. Remember? Four weeks before the wedding, you decreed that this would be the last time until our wedding night." A huge sigh stirred her hair. "We always talked best afterward, you know."

Jeff knew. Before he could answer, she went on. "And then, that afternoon before the rehearsal, we met with the minister, remember?"

He nodded, summoning up a vague memory of an impatient hour in a dim office. He hadn't, he thought, needed any counseling to be sure. He'd wanted to marry Mickey York since he was fifteen years old.

Mickey, clearly, had felt differently. "He talked to us about commitment, about staying true to each other, and to ourselves, and not going any further if we weren't absolutely sure."

Her voice dropped as she spoke, until he was straining forward to hear what she said, then moved onto the end of the bed because he couldn't. "And when we went out into the church, there was Kayla, her stomach big with a baby—that was Jeremy, I think. I could hear Aunt Helen joking with Dad about being a granddad again within the year.

"Ricky Sanders came in—you know, the one who didn't make it into vet school—and started teasing you about being the rich vet, and how nice it would be to have someone waiting at home for you on those cold winter nights when you'd been out on a call.''

Her hands, still writhing in her lap, were wet, and her voice was thick with tears. "And you said, 'Yeah, if she's not out on the road heading toward some show halfway across the country.' Then you looked over at me, Jeff, and you said, 'You should think about cutting back on your riding, Mickey, or we'll never see each other.'''

After a paralyzed minute, Jeff relaxed, stretched himself slowly onto the bed. Now he understood exactly what had happened. He had the answers he'd wanted. Mickey had finally explained.

But what he was hearing was the last thing he'd expected. For ten years he'd held one person completely accountable. She ran away, she should take the blame. Tonight, in this quiet room, echoes of his foolish, thoughtless, *arrogant* words bounced off the walls. And each time they came back to him, the realization of his part in the wreck grew stronger, until it felt like a vise gripping his throat.

The damning voice resumed in a near whisper. "I almost started screaming. I went to the bathroom to try to calm down. But all I could see was this narrow path stretching in front of me, leading me somewhere I didn't want to go. And it suddenly seemed like I had to escape or I would lose myself forever. So...so I left."

A long silence, saturated with their broken past, pressed down on the room. After a while, Mickey looked up. Jeff had stretched out on his back at the foot of the bed, was lying there with his hands clasped behind his head. She might have thought what she'd said didn't matter at all, except for the rigid line of his jaw, the pulse beating double time at his temple.

His eyes were open, but he spoke without looking her way. "I can see how that must have sounded. I...I guess I understand how you felt." He rolled to his side and faced her then, confronting her with what she'd done. "But you walked out without telling a single soul where you were going, Mickey. We didn't know what had happened to you for almost a week. Everybody in town was worried sick. Ed didn't sleep for days. Your mother was beside herself, your dad was broken. And I...I—" His hand lifted off the bed and then dropped back. He didn't finish the thought.

He didn't have to. She knew just how cruel she'd been, how unpardonable her abrupt exit was. And she'd suffered over it, along with all the rest, for ten years. But at least she'd had a reason. "I needed to get far enough away. If I'd called from anywhere nearby, somebody would have found me. I—I wasn't ready to be found."

"I guess not."

The drip of the faucet in the bathroom ticked away silent seconds. Jeff didn't move, had closed his eyes. Mickey wiped her cheeks and nose on the sleeve of her T-shirt, wondering if he'd fallen asleep. She wondered if he had any more questions to ask. She wondered if she would have to tell him *everything*.

At last he stood with a single fluid motion and walked to the door, tucking his shirttail into the waist of his jeans as he went. He put a finger on the doorknob, traced its contours clockwise and counterclockwise, then gripped tightly and gave a vicious twist. The door swung free.

She thought he would leave without another word, but then his voice—tense, tortured—reached her. "I'm sorry about tonight, Mickey. You might not believe it, but I didn't come in here to seduce you into this. I...I...it just happened. Thanks for telling me what I needed to know."

He sounded like an old man. Mickey started to slide off the bed. "Jeff—"

But he was gone before she could get her injured foot to the floor.

Two BLASTS on the horn summoned her out to Jeff's truck late the next morning. He looked worse than Mickey felt. Something about his bleary eyes and the gray color under his skin told her he'd spent at least part of the sleepless night drinking. She hadn't dared try alcohol on top of the strong painkiller, so she'd just lain awake in the dark, thinking.

Thinking about the pain in his eyes, about the damage she'd done him. It had been so unfair to keep him from getting on with his life. She knew that now, if she hadn't before. Even a letter would have released him to start over.

But instead she'd avoided him, run away from seeing him, and never, ever thought about writing that letter. Why?

Partly, Mickey thought, because it hurt too much to do anything else. The year after she left had been filled with guilt, loss, and a desolation she hated to remember. She'd lived in a fog of remorse, prevented by cowardice from admitting her mistake and going home.

If it had been just the wedding on her conscience, she might have gone back eventually, or at least written. Maybe she would have let him catch up with her sometime, somewhere. Being without him, those first days, had been like losing half of herself. She'd walked around bleeding.

Or at least feeling as if she was.

And maybe Jeff would have forgiven her running out on him. They might have gotten past the ruined wedding, the week of silence. Heaven knows, he'd been through enough with her to understand her fears, her temper, her doubts.

But not even Jeff could forgive her for killing their baby.

Ten years, and she still shook if she thought about it too long, still fought back tears. Her first ride after leaving. A small show in Colorado. A fall...no big deal, since she'd held on long enough and won anyway.

Then, two days later, she'd started bleeding for real. It had taken a doctor to explain why.

Rebuilding her life on top of such pain had been an exercise in determination. She'd done it, though, had pulled herself up and gone after what she'd decided she wanted, putting the past out of her mind. To look back, to think about what could have been, would have threatened the rigid control she maintained over her thoughts and her life. As time passed, it became easier. Almost anything could be borne, if you gave it enough time.

But she'd always known that she couldn't see Jeff—couldn't *be* with Jeff—and not tell him. And she couldn't bear the thought of telling him, of hurting him that way, of letting him hurt her.

So now it should be simple to let him go. He knew why she'd left, and when he'd thought about it for a while he would realize they could never have worked out well together. His life plan and hers had always been different, but they'd been too blinded by love, by the physical beauty they could find together, to admit it. She had chosen to divide their paths a decade ago, and all that remained between them was an echo of the passion they'd never been able to tame. Maybe now that they'd set it free, the echo, too, would die.

But at least for the time being they could act like friends. She turned sideways in the seat and surveyed his ashen face with sympathy. "Have you had some coffee?"

He started to nod, but winced instead. "Two pots. I wouldn't feel this bad if I was still drunk."

Mickey grinned. "You always did go straight from riding-the-moon crazy to well-digger's boots hung-over." The ironic glance he threw as he turned onto the highway reminded her of how stupid it was to keep remembering the past. Every shared memory had turned into a two-edged sword that cut them both. If they didn't say goodbye soon, they'd bleed to death.

As it turned out, though, goodbye came quicker than she was ready for. "Another vet in town is working the show this afternoon," Jeff commented as they covered the last mile or so to the fairgrounds. "I need to get back and check out Clementine and the other animals I'm keeping. So I guess I'd better drop you off and get to work."

Stupid, irrational disappointment flooded through her, and Mickey turned her face toward the window so he wouldn't see it. She and Jeff had to separate, and the quicker the better, right?

"That's no problem, Jeff. I appreciate the ride and...and everything." Pulling in a deep breath, she felt blindly for the door handle. "Just let me off at the gate."

A few seconds later, still favoring her sore ankle, she slid out of the truck seat and turned around. "It's been great seeing you again," she told a point somewhere over his left shoulder, in a voice that sounded as if it belonged to someone else. "Thanks for all your help. See you around, okay?"

"Bye, Mickey." He nodded without a smile or the usual twinkle in his eyes. She lifted her hand, but the wave or salute or whatever it was fluttered into nothingness in the face of Jeff's somber stare. His knowing the truth—most of it, anyway—had not, she thought, made anything better. For either of them.

After a frozen second, he cut eye contact, swiveled in the seat and shifted gears. She took one step back, then another, to give him enough room to back away. And then, stupidly, she stood there and watched until even the plume of dust raised by his wheels had vanished into the clear Wyoming sky.

"Bye, Jeff," she whispered.

After a minute, Mickey squared her shoulders, pivoted on her toe and headed into the arena.

Hanging around behind the animal pens all day, she fought a losing battle with herself as she tried to put her thoughts and memories of Jeff back into the dark hole where she'd kept them hidden all these years.

But those moments on the bed last night refused to be banished. He was more muscular than she remembered, filled her arms more completely. His chest had more hair on it now than when he was twenty-three. But the excitement of his hips pressing into hers had been as familiar as his name on her lips, the anticipation was just the way she remembered in her dreams. Oh, Jeff...

Gathering her focus for the last ride took more effort than she could remember needing in years. It started out well, though, with Haymaker bucking high, kicking out, and giving her a good chance to use her spurs. Time expanded, as it always seemed to during a ride, and she registered the separate motions of the horse underneath her...the rise of his back and the thrust of powerful rear legs, the arch of a silken neck, the jolt as his front hooves bit the dirt. The woman riding in second place had fallen off—Ladykiller had been up to his old tricks. Mickey figured she had a chance to win this one.

She made it safely to the whistle and started thinking about getting off. But Haymaker had other plans. He jerked away from the pickup horse before she could get her hand free, dancing and strutting halfway across the arena. Mickey looked around, got the impression of herself alone in the middle of space. Then all hell broke loose, and the horse went into a frenzy she couldn't prepare for, couldn't control and couldn't possibly stop.

Mickey loosened her hand on the rigging; falling off had to be better than getting thrown. But Haymaker beat her to it. She knew a moment of weightlessness, a sensation of flying. And then a really ugly thud as the world went to pieces.

HE HAD PLAYED OUT this scene too many times and he didn't appreciate the rerun. Tense with frustration and anxiety, Jeff paced back and forth and wished, for once, that he smoked. Cigarettes would give him something to do, something to think about besides the silence, the time, and the fear. For years, hospital waiting rooms had been as familiar to him as his own bed. Bull riders like his dad spent a lot of time on a table being put back together. Bareback riders weren't far behind.

But his dad had died and Mickey had left him, and he'd figured he wouldn't have to go through this hell again. Her desertion had spared him years of restless, energy-draining worry. He should remember to thank her for that sometime.

After an hour of agony, a doctor appeared. "You're with Mickey York?"

Jeff nodded. "Yes. How is she?"

A shake of the gray head stabbed dread into his chest. The doctor flipped open a chart. "Concussion, abrasions. Dislocated shoulder. Cracked ribs. And an ankle," he said pointedly, "no one in their right mind should walk on, much less ride with."

Shoving his hands in his pockets, Jeff kept his temper. "I know. She never would listen. But she's going to be okay?"

"Sure. But she needs some real recuperation time. The shoulder dislocation was extensive, with soft-tissue damage. The ribs are going to give her problems for several weeks. I'd advise against any rodeo work at all for at least a month."

Right. "Did you tell her that?"

The doctor looked up and a smile flashed through his tired eyes. "Yes. Her answer is not one I intend to repeat."

"Thanks. When can she leave?"

Snapping the folder shut, he turned away. "Tomorrow—we like to observe concussions overnight. Pick her up about ten."

How in the world did I end up being responsible for Mickey York? Jeff asked himself as he made his way up to her room. Last night, influenced by more whiskey than he wanted to remember, he had resolved to walk away as soon as possible, never to see her or think of her again. Out of sight, out of mind. She had given him the answer to the riddle and he could stop wondering now, stop torturing himself. He was free to get on with his life.

But he stared down at the woman asleep in the hospital bed, her cheek scraped, her shoulder taped, an IV running into her blue-veined wrist, and knew that he hadn't seen the end of it yet. He and Mickey were tied together by history, by friendship, by a love that had taken up every square inch of his soul, once upon a time. Even if that was no longer the case, he couldn't turn his back on the bond between them.

She stirred as he watched, and her eyelids lifted. "Another hospital?" she murmured.

"The other half of rodeo life," he whispered back.

"Yeah…" Her eyes began to close, then fluttered open. "How'd you get here?"

He couldn't stop himself from reaching for her hand. She squeezed back weakly. "You came around for a few seconds and gave them my name. The rodeo tracked me down. Go to sleep."

"Okay."

For a while she seemed to have done it. Jeff eased one hip onto the bed, waiting until she was deep enough under not to miss him when he let go of her hand. If he did.

And then her lashes fluttered once again. "Jeff?"

"What is it, Mickey?"

"Did I win?"

A brief chuckle shook him. "Yeah, you won. They'll keep the check until you get out."

"Good." Her lids drifted shut. Another long pause. "Jeff?"

"What now?"

"I've got to ride next week in Cheyenne."

He lifted her fingers to his lips, laughing helplessly, silently, as she went back to sleep. "Sure you do, Mickey. Sure you do."

THE MORNING'S FIRST argument was the shortest.

"You can't even get out of a chair without wincing," Jeff said. "How do you expect to lift a kid onto a horse?"

Mickey opened her mouth to protest.

But he had more to say. "And how do you expect to make sure that kid is safe? If he gets into trouble and you hesitate because something hurts…"

He didn't have to finish the thought. She knew she couldn't risk her kids.

A quick call to Laurie at the camp got her a week off work. The preoccupied tone of the boss's voice said more clearly than words that the insurance crisis still loomed over them, getting bigger by the day. And Mickey still hadn't come up with a brilliant idea to raise money. She hung up the phone, feeling bad for deserting the kids—especially Karen, who wouldn't even go into the barn without her—bad for letting Laurie down, just bad in general. Her ribs hurt like hell.

And then, to make matters worse, the doctor refused to sign her release papers until she promised not to drive.

"What am I supposed to do?" she demanded, her voice squeaking with anger. "You want me to treat this like a hotel?"

A glance flashed between the two men. "No," Jeff said in a drawn-out tone. "That would be sort of expensive."

"You're damned right it would," Mickey agreed briskly. "So I'll just get my truck and head home. If you'll sign those papers—"

"Ms. York," the doctor interrupted, "I can't, in good conscience, let you walk out of here and resume your life as if nothing had happened yesterday. You suffered some significant injuries, on top of the ones you've already endured. Our tests indicate you are borderline anemic, underweight, and my personal observation is that you need some rest. I don't want to release you without a guarantee that you will take better care of yourself.''

Echoes of another room like this, another gentle voice explaining, comforting, excusing…

Violently, Mickey shook her head. "Fine. You have my word that I'll take it easy and eat everything I can get my hands on. Okay?''

"I don't think so.'' Jeff's tone had steel underneath the velvet cover. "I think your word is about as good on this issue as a three-dollar bill.'' The doctor faded discreetly out of the room.

Mickey let her feet slip to the floor. "Why, you—''

Jeff held up a hand. "No insult intended, but I know you, Mickey. If we let you go off on your own, you'll be back in the race, ruining your health, probably riding before you're ready and doing yourself some serious damage. I can't let that happen.''

"*You* can't let…''

"So, as I see it, you've got two options. You can stay here for a week, paying for hospital care. Maybe you have insurance that'll cover it. Or—'' he leaned back against the wall and crossed his arms over his chest, looking relaxed but far from easy "—you can come home with me.''

"You're doing it again!'' She took two angry steps toward him and stopped, hands clenched at her waist. "You're trying to run my life, Jeff. Didn't you hear anything I said the other night? Didn't it make any impression on you at all? I'm an adult, I'm reasonably intelligent and I can look out for myself. I've been hurt more times in the last ten years than anybody could count, and I've managed to survive every time, thanks to nobody but me. I don't need you to tell me what to do!''

Something flashed in his eyes that might have been anger, or even hurt. He drew a deep breath and blew it out again before he spoke. "I am not telling you what to do, Mickey. I am offering you an option. It's up to you to make the decision."

"Some option! Money I can't afford or incarceration in Flying Rock. Thanks, but no thanks, Jeff. I'll be just fine on my own." Ignoring the pain, she limped past him and reached for the door handle, planning to stalk into the hallway and leave an unbearable situation behind.

His voice, calm and quiet, stopped her cold. "What are you running from this time, Mickey?"

She pivoted on her good heel to stare at him. His eyes smiled and a corner of his mouth tilted, and she knew, because he'd done it so often in the past, that he was daring her to go against her inclination.

"Come on," he wheedled, his voice lowering persuasively. "Just a couple of days in a real bed, with decent food and a chance to relax. You look tired, Mickey, and beaten. It's got to be hard, doing this all by yourself. Why not kick back for a bit, in your own hometown? Nobody could fault you for that."

"Why?" The question came out before she'd realized what she was thinking.

Jeff lowered his eyebrows in bewilderment. "Why what?"

"Why do you want me to stay?"

She could feel her cheeks heat up while he considered her question. It was a stupid, adolescent thing to ask;

she wished she could take it back. And whatever his reason, he was having a hard time putting it into words.

"You were my best friend," Jeff said at last, slowly. "The only one I ever had. I knew you as well as I knew myself. Maybe better." He hesitated and she nodded, encouraging him to go on. "Things got complicated when we made it more than friendship, and both of us ended up hurt."

That was a kind way to put it. But then, there were things he didn't know. Mickey dropped her gaze to her bare feet.

"Now you've explained what went wrong," Jeff continued, "and I want to reclaim some of the past. Not," he said quickly as she lifted widened eyes to his face, "not all of it. But the friendship mattered to me, Mickey, and I never got used to losing it. So I'm asking you to stay with me as a friend, as someone I care about who looks like she could use a little coddling, a little vacation. That's all."

That's all. A chance—one she'd never thought she'd get—to come home again. To visit the people she grew up with, the places that had defined her childhood world. Once, Flying Rock had seemed like a prison, and all she'd wanted was to break free. Now the prison looked like a cradle, and all she could think of was how much she needed to be held.

It had been a long, lonely ten years.

She stared at him as she thought over his offer, let the warmth of the smile in his eyes soothe her doubts. What he was really asking, though he didn't know it, was for her to spend time with him and still keep her secret. Could she be that strong? And then walk away, after even one day, and go back to a life without Jeff?

Maybe. If he didn't ask questions—and why would

he, now that he knew the reasons she'd run away?—maybe she could. She managed to keep the baby out of her mind most of the time, hadn't thought about it for weeks before that night at the diner. Surely the memories would die down once she was over the shock of seeing him again. Being with Jeff didn't *have* to mean reliving the past. Did it?

You never knew how the ride would turn out until you got on the horse. Mickey shifted to slip her hands into her back pockets and realized she was still wearing the stupid hospital gown and robe. Not much chance of running off in this outfit, anyway—might as well give in.

She started to shrug but, at the protest from her shoulder, settled for a nod. "Okay, I'll come. I won't deny I could use a break. But I'm still going to the show in Cheyenne. You can make me relax, but you can't stop me from riding."

Jeff closed his eyes and groaned. "Mickey..."

AFTER ARRANGING to get her truck picked up and stowed with Clementine at the Buffalo vet's office, they debated the Cheyenne ride all the way back to Flying Rock. Mickey adamantly refused to consider cutting back on her schedule. "I'll be fine by Friday. I don't have to cancel those rides."

Jeff aimed the truck at the Flying Rock exit, his voice calm and reasonable, as it had been all morning. "Wouldn't you have a better chance at winning if you let yourself recover a bit before you rode again?" He'd made the same point five times in the last hour.

"It's not so bad," she assured him. Of course, that was before she couldn't even get the door of the truck open because it hurt too much to move. "It will be better tomorrow,'' she prophesied, sliding out. And then she banged her left foot on the running board, setting up waves of pain that rattled her teeth. "Well," she sighed, glancing up with a grin, "maybe the day *after* tomorrow."

Jeff just smiled and held the door until she was completely out. While he pulled their duffels from the back of the truck, Mickey stared at his house.

"I didn't realize…"

"What?"

She looked around. "You redid old Jones's house! Mom never told me—and your practice is here, too?" He nodded. "I guess I didn't notice, the other morning in the dark. It looks great, Jeff." More than great. Like a real home. The one he'd always wanted.

Because until he was fourteen, the only home Jeff had known was his dad's camper. They had lived the life of nomads, traveling from rodeo to rodeo, never in one place longer than a day or two. School had been hit-or-miss, and Jeff had taught himself, more often than not, which was why he was placed in Mickey's class when he came to live with them, although he was two years older.

Those two years made a big difference because most of the sixth-grade boys had yet to begin their real growth, and Jeff topped them by a foot, at least. Despite the size difference, he'd made a place for himself in the class, and found friends.

He made a place for himself at home, too. While his own dad quietly drank his sorrows away, Jeff became the son her parents had never had, the brother she and her sisters could torment and turn to for help.

Of course, Mickey remembered, the relationship between her and Jeff had always been closer than with

Kayla or Barb. They'd found a unique level of communication from that first day, a bond which had gripped the very core of who and what she was. She'd never really been a whole person since leaving him behind.

"Coming in, Mickey?"

With his question, all her second thoughts came crashing down around her ears. How, with everything that stood between them, could they go back to mere friendship, especially when just the set of his shoulders and the tilt of his head could turn her insides to mush?

Shaken, Mickey turned away to stare down the street at the familiar storefronts of Flying Rock while memories flickered through her mind like images from an old silent movie. She saw summer days spent in the practice ring and at the creek, swimming and reading and horsing around. Summer nights driving with Jeff to this rodeo or that, performing at some, just watching, learning at others. Autumn afternoons spent in Emmitt's diner at the table by the door, doing homework and reading rodeo magazines. Winter chores in the dead darkness before dawn, quizzing each other for the day's exams on the long ride to school.

And the night of her seventeenth birthday party...the first time they'd kissed.

Ten years ago, Jeff had meant everything in the world to her. If she'd foreseen how complete the break would be, she might have tried to stay. Maybe she would have tried harder to talk with someone, sharing her fears, getting advice. But, young and foolish, she hadn't given anyone a chance to help. Instead, she'd cut herself off—from her family, from Ed. And from Jeff.

Now, like the friend he'd always been, he was giving her a second chance, the opportunity to come back and spend a little time in the town she'd walked out on, with people from her childhood. Including Jeff. How could she refuse, when this was exactly what she needed?

He said he needed it, too. And if friendship was all he wanted from her anymore, how could she deny him?

So she squared her shoulders and turned back to him with a grin. "Sure, I'm coming in. Just promise me two things."

The tension in his stance only became apparent when he relaxed and pulled his hands from his pockets. "What's that?"

Walking slowly, Mickey took the steps up onto the porch and reached the front door. "One, that you'll let me know if I get in the way or cause you any trouble."

He motioned her to go inside. "I can't imagine that, but I promise anyway. What's number two?"

She turned in the cool dimness of the entryway as he shut the door behind them. "That you'll make me a huge pot of your chili while I'm here. I haven't had chili that hot, that thick, that delicious in—"

"Let me guess—ten years?"

"Oh, just about that long!"

CHAPTER SIX

IT CERTAINLY SEEMED like a reasonable enough plan. Jeff reviewed the arrangement as he worked through the afternoon—visiting with the new litter of retriever pups born last week, psychoanalyzing a cat who couldn't stop eating the wrong houseplant, catching up on the messages he'd received over the weekend. Having Mickey around for a short time would restore their friendship and settle the past once and for all. Then she would move on, and so would he.

But that was before he walked into the house about five o'clock and found her asleep in the living room. She'd taken him at his word on relaxing and lay stretched out on the couch, the red and blue pillows strewn all around her, a book—*The Count of Monte Cristo,* he saw as he picked it up—taken from the shelves beside the fireplace. Something about her total vulnerability, the pull of her light cotton shirt across her breasts and the curve of her legs in denim cutoffs, made her look young and innocent again, and stirred him in ways he recognized from a long, long way back.

The past was just that. Past. So what was she doing here?

He couldn't deny that he'd coerced her into coming home with him. But he'd done so for her own sake. She might be an adult, she might be perfectly competent, but Mickey had never let mere physical limitations get in the way of her goals. Time and again he'd watched her drive herself beyond the point where most people he knew would quit.

And no matter what had happened between them, despite what he'd said to her in that motel room, he needed to know she was still on the planet somewhere. It mattered that Mickey was, simply, alive.

More important, he owed her.

For ten mistaken years, he'd held Mickey responsible for ruining his plans, his dreams. He'd railed against her selfishness, hated her more than once for being stubborn and stupid. But with the clarity of hindsight, he saw now how he'd contributed to her leaving. Sure of himself and, to be completely honest, sure of her, he'd backed her into a corner so tight she'd had little choice but to run away. For a man who prided himself on his insight, he'd been remarkably blind.

That the damage was unintentional didn't change anything.

Every time he reviewed the situation, his part in it seemed more intolerable. His had been the first mistake, his the stubborn stupidity. He'd loved Mickey for her soaring spirit and yet had tried to rope her down, fence her in. Faced with such confinement, she'd reacted as a wild filly might when forced to wear a halter and saddle. Breaking away, she'd stayed homeless, rootless, for all the long years.

And so he would make amends. Ensuring her physical health was a first step. Giving her a chance to rest up and an opportunity to make her peace with her hometown was another. It was the least he could do. A responsibility he couldn't possibly ignore.

He left her alone under the soft breeze stirred by the ceiling fan until after seven. She was still asleep when he bent over and grazed her cheek with his knuckles. "Mickey? Want to wake up for some supper?"

She awoke instantly, completely, as always. "Sounds good. Chili?" A grimace as she tried to sit up betrayed the true state of her shoulder and ribs.

Jeff put a hand on her back to give her some help. "You know it takes two days to get my chili right." The ripple of lithe muscles under his palm provoked all the wrong responses. He made sure she was steady and then stepped away deliberately. "I started it about an hour ago. We might be able to taste for seasoning tomorrow night. In the meantime, I've got a couple of steaks."

"Mmm. I'm ready. Just give me a minute to get up."

But the couch was low and the pillows clutched like quicksand, denying her the leverage she needed. So he stepped in again, putting an arm around her waist to provide extra lift. In the second or two Mickey needed to get her balance, Jeff took most of her weight in his arms.

The sweet familiarity of holding her, the sense of total *rightness,* almost overwhelmed him. Her unbraided hair floated against his shoulder and chest...tempting, sensual, soft. He found himself lowering his chin to press a kiss to her temple, felt the muscles in his arm tighten to pull her closer, to turn her around to face him so that he could cover her mouth with his.

"Thanks," Mickey said casually, and Jeff dropped abruptly back into reality. Loosening his grip, he let her step away, then watched as she walked down the hallway to the bathroom. An active life had kept her rear end tight and her spine limber. Even injured, she managed to put a sexy sway into her walk.

Damn! He couldn't let her get to him this way. He

had no intention of becoming involved with Mickey beyond the boundaries of the friendship they'd enjoyed when they were young. It would be unfair to ask her here under those conditions then push the relationship into something else.

Besides, what kind of man still had romantic feelings for the woman who'd left him at the altar and never looked back?

Jeff caught sight of himself in the oak-framed mirror over the fireplace as he straightened up the sofa. Shaking his head, he refused to accept his reflection as the answer to that question.

He diverted his thoughts with practical matters instead. "Steak medium rare, right?" he called on his way down the hallway to the kitchen.

The bathroom door opened and a shocked face peeked out. "Don't tell me you forgot *that!* I've never eaten a steak less than well done in my…"

Her voice faded as she recognized the joke. Jeff winked and grinned. "Gotcha!"

MICKEY INSISTED on helping clean up after dinner. They'd made it through the meal fairly easily by sticking to current events for conversation. Interesting, she thought, that Jeff had turned out on the liberal side while she tended more toward conservative politics. They hadn't cared much one way or the other ten years ago, but now the prospect for a lively evening of arguments beckoned. Putting away the last of the pots, she grinned in anticipation as she predicted his opinions on the economy and got her ammunition ready to shoot them down.

Then the phone rang.

Five minutes later, the veterinarian had his hat and

boots on. "That was Dex Hightower. He's got a sick cow that sounds pretty bad. I don't know when I'll get back. Make yourself—"

"Can I come?"

He stopped dead on the way to the back door, then turned slowly around. "I didn't think you'd want to. I mean—"

She shrugged. "I'm here catching up with the past, right? So I should see what the old place looks like. Give me a second to get my shoes."

Slipping into the sneakers she rarely wore, Mickey didn't stop to question the wisdom of going back to the family spread as a visitor. Nothing she did now would change what had happened. All she could do was find a way to live with it. And move on.

Still, she could have driven the road out to the Triple A with her eyes closed. As the truck swayed and bounced over the crushed-clinker road, she found that ten years' absence hadn't erased a single curve or bump from her mind. The landmarks were old friends. "Remember the day it rained so hard and I ran the truck off this bridge into the gully?"

Jeff grinned. "Boy, do I! Your dad was spitting mad and wouldn't talk to either of us for a week. You because you were driving too fast and me because I wasn't driving in the first place."

"He never did figure out that I was really the better driver of the two, did he?"

"Right, Mickey." He threw her a sardonic look. "That's why *you* ran the truck off the road. And why *you* ran down that fence post over there one night, not looking where you were going."

"Well, if you hadn't been..." She saw the pitfall looming ahead of her and allowed the comeback to die away. What Jeff had been doing that night was driving her crazy with his wandering hands and hot, seeking mouth. They didn't need to remember that.

After a few silent minutes, she found a different direction for the conversation. "New fence," she commented with interest as they crossed onto Triple A land.

"Yeah. Dex is trying some different pasturage options, and brings his steers down here for part of the spring. It's a long ride from the main buildings, but he likes the forage."

"Sounds reasonable. I think I heard Dad mention that once, but he never got around to doing anything about it."

"He had plenty to do."

"That's true enough."

This silence felt better, less strained. She'd made her peace with her parents, had been sure that her dad knew she loved him before he died. If he hadn't understood why she ran away, well, he'd blustered a little and cried a little and hugged her close. And he'd kept a record of her career, of her wins and losses, her championships and the years she didn't do so well. She couldn't have asked for more.

Mickey recognized the last curve before the driveway and drew a deep breath, wondering what changes to expect. The marker for the Triple A was the same one she'd grown up with—an arch over the entrance with three connected A's burned into the weathered wood. The same scrub and trees framed the trail up to the house. Only the mailbox was different. The shiny black metal had received a paint job recently and had Hightower blazed across it in white.

Jeff took the turn into the ranch at his usual high speed. Mickey took a deep gulp of air.

They cleared the top of the hill and she saw it at last—the house she had grown up in. Built like a log cabin, but with modern comforts hidden behind the rustic walls, it nestled securely under the trees she had climbed, the yellow glow of lamps inside welcoming stranger and friend alike. The swing she had helped her dad hang still dangled in the space behind the kitchen door, and two rockers on the front porch waited for their occupants' evening chat, just as they had all the years she was growing up.

The truck slid to a stop in the dust, and she pushed the door open. Stepping out, Mickey couldn't decide whether she was thirty-one years old or nine. Everything, *everything* seemed exactly as she'd left it to go to the rehearsal for her wedding. How could so little have changed...and so much?

A deep voice hailed them from behind the house. "Jeff!"

She jerked her head around and took in a definite difference between the present and the past. The man striding across the open space between the big barn and the house looked as if he owned the place. But he wasn't her dad. Dark-haired and tanned, Dexter Hightower in no way resembled Bob York. He did fit the cowboy image, though. Wide shoulders and narrow hips told of hours on horseback, while the corded muscles in his forearms revealed long hours of hard labor. A man of the outdoors, indeed.

"Hey, Dex!" Jeff stretched out a hand and the bigger man took it; he topped the vet by several inches and at least thirty pounds. "Let me introduce someone. Mickey York, Dexter Hightower."

Mickey stepped up and got a bone-crushing shake in her turn. From Dex's vigorous walk, she expected a jovial, outgoing individual. Instead, his face was solemn, with lines around his mouth that a thick mustache didn't hide. She tried a smile. "Mr. Hightower."

"Miss York. It's good to meet you. Your dad always had something new to brag about when I met him for business in Denver. He was proud of you."

Mickey tried a smile. "Thanks."

He didn't smile back. And as soon as he released her hand he turned back to Jeff. "This looks real bad. Thanks for coming out tonight."

"No problem," Jeff assured him, matching his stride to Hightower's as they headed toward the barn. "What have you got?"

What they had, Mickey could see as she stood at the door to the stall, was a very sick cow. A beautiful red Brahman, not old, stood listless and uninterested, head down, her cheeks wet and dripping. Brown eyes that should have been deep and shiny were frosted with an ugly dark haze. In the quiet barn, her breath sounded loud and harsh.

Jeff dropped his equipment box outside the stall and pulled on a pair of sterile gloves. Easing past Mickey, he placed a hand under the cow's chin and pulled her face up. Angry sores covered her lips and muzzle.

"How long has she been sick?"

Hightower spoke tersely. "Two days. I've been away since Thursday night, but the hands tell me her nose started running Friday and got worse yesterday. When I got back this afternoon, I took one look and called you."

"Yeah." Jeff's sensitive hands had slipped around behind the cow's jaws, while his eyes roamed her face. "Fever?"

"No."

The examination took half an hour, and all the time the poor cow barely registered a protest. Finally, Jeff left the stall, pulled off his gloves and dropped them in the trash. When Dex closed the door behind him, the two men faced each other.

"Catarrhal fever?" Hightower's voice was light for such a big man.

Jeff nodded. "I'm afraid so. The dark mucous from her nose is a pretty good sign. Swollen lymph nodes, the ulcers on her muzzle and elsewhere—I don't have much doubt."

Hands braced in his pockets, Hightower tilted his head. "Any possibility she'll make it?"

Stepping to the side, Jeff knelt down by his box. "You know the chances aren't good. But I'll get her on antibiotics. And we'll give her fluids. That's about all we can do." He paused in filling his syringe and looked up. "This is the one you bought at market last month, isn't it?"

"Yes."

"How many others did you bring back at the same time?"

"Five."

"I'd better see them all."

Mickey watched in silence as Jeff worked with the sick cow. She'd seen him with animals for a good portion of her life, and knew the calming effect he could have. As he injected medication and fluids, he talked softly, soothingly, and a very occasional flick of a bovine ear signaled that his comments had been heard.

No visible improvement had occurred by the time he closed his box, but Jeff said none should be expected. "We'll just have to see how it goes. I'll come out tomorrow and take a look. Now, where are the rest?"

"The south corral."

Mickey could have led them there blindfolded. It was her practice ring, the place she'd spent most of her childhood, learning how to fall off a horse, how to get back on and stay there. At first she rode a barrel suspended on ropes, pretending for hours every afternoon that she had a bucking bronc under her, then graduated to the unbroken horses her dad bought to train. Even before Jeff came into her life, she'd eaten the dust inside that fence more often than she cared to remember.

Now it contained five head of young cattle, one with an obvious problem. While the others huddled into a clump of ears and backs and twitching tails, a smallish brown steer roamed restlessly, butting and raking the fence with his horns, making strange sounds of distress and discomfort. As she drew closer, she saw that this one's cheeks were wet, too, and when he flung his head, a dark fluid streamed from his nose.

"Oh, hell." The rancher's hands tightened on the top rail of the paddock.

"We need to isolate him." Jeff climbed the fence and sat on top. "Can you get him roped?"

Dex disappeared. Prevented by her aching shoulder and ribs from joining Jeff on his perch, Mickey irritably kept her feet on the ground. "Is it the same illness?"

Jeff kept his eyes on the wandering animal. "Yeah, I'm afraid so. It's a viral disease that can show up in a number of ways. This is the nervous-system variety. That calf could get really mean." He glanced down with a grin. "Too bad you're in no shape tonight for bulldogging!"

She shook her head at him. "I'll leave that to you, Doc."

He grimaced. "Thanks. If you remember, I gave up rodeo stunts in my youth."

"Well, that's a long time ago, but it'll come back to you."

He proved her right, but only with great effort. With a leg anchored on either side of the top fence rail, Dex threw the rope with practiced ease, but the noose around his head drove the already excited steer crazy. He bounded around the paddock, assaulting the other animals and inciting them to run. Mickey held her breath as Jeff dodged the stampeding crowd, aiming for his patient. One slip and he'd be underneath their hooves.

Dex kept the rope taut, limiting the range of the sick steer. Coming close, Jeff grabbed the brawny neck once, but the struggling animal kicked his way free of the hold and planted a hoof on his captor's knee for extra effect. It took two more tries and a lot of swearing and sweat to drag the brute to the ground.

"Somebody bring my case in!"

Mickey did some swearing of her own as she dodged panicked animals to get the heavy box close to the fallen steer. As she came up, Jeff tied up the animal's rear legs and stepped back with the flare of a rodeo competitor. "Hope that holds him—it's been a long time since I did any roping." He cocked an eyebrow in her direction. "I didn't mean for *you* to carry the gear in, and you know it. Think first, why don't you, Mickey?"

She started a shrug, and just managed not to groan. "No problem. Get to work."

With the instigator quiet, the other animals gathered into a clump as far away from the action as they could get. After a glance to make sure they'd settled down,

Mickey knelt by Jeff in the dirt. "I wish I were in better shape. I'd be more use."

He had pulled on another set of gloves and was filling a new syringe. "You're doing fine. Dex will be back in a minute with some hands to move the others and then you'll have backup. Hold tight."

"If these two animals die, will he have to destroy them all?"

Slowly compressing the plunger to drive antibiotic into the twitching flank, Jeff shook his head. "It's not very contagious. We wouldn't be working this hard over these two, except that Dex had hoped to set up a breeding program with them. They're pretty valuable, all told."

By the time the hands came running back, Jeff had almost finished with the struggling, writhing steer. As soon as the rest of the animals had been taken away, he closed his box and handed it to Mickey. "Get outside the fence. He'll be dangerous when he's loose."

"What about you?"

He bent over and grabbed the rope. "I'll be okay."

Famous last words. Muzzle down, horns in position for maximum contact, the sick steer exploded to his feet as soon as the rope loosened. Jeff covered the width of the corral in five long, hurried strides and took the fence at a leap, pursued by the sound of an enraged bellow and ripping cloth. A series of dull thuds reached him as the animal continued to butt his head against the barrier, but he dropped down on the safe side, breathing fast and wiping beads of sweat from his eyes. "That was close," he said, panting.

Mickey walked behind him and looked at the rip in his jeans. "More than close, cowboy. He almost...Jeff, you're bleeding!"

Suddenly aware of a searing sensation on the back of his leg, Jeff propped a hand against the rail and probed the torn denim with his fingers. When he held his hand up, his fingertips shone black and wet in the dim light. "You know, I thought I felt a scrape." He flexed his knee experimentally. "It's not too bad. I'll survive, I do believe."

He wasn't going to mention that there seemed to be a razor slashing at his leg every time he took a step. No sense causing a fuss.

But Mickey saw through the camouflage. "Yeah, sure, it's not too bad," she agreed heartily. "Your jeans are just soaking wet from the seat down with your blood. Want to put your arm around my shoulders while we walk back to the house?"

"No, I don't." Jeff took a couple of rapid steps in that direction, then slowed considerably as a wave of dizziness crashed over him.

"Okay. I'll put my arm around you." He felt her hand at his waist, then she drew a quick breath. He'd picked the wrong shoulder. "The *other* arm, I think."

"What a couple of gimps!"

By the time they got back to the ranch house, he was glad of the support. As Dex held the back door open, Mickey ushered Jeff into a brightly lit kitchen that hadn't noticeably changed in almost twenty years, and dragged him straight through to the hallway.

"I'll get some first-aid stuff," he heard Dex promise as he brushed past them.

"Unbuckle your belt and lower your zipper as we go," Mickey ordered in a cool voice. "I want to get your pants down as quick as possible."

"I haven't heard you say that in a long time." Jeff

knew he had to be out of his head even to think such a thing, let alone say it. But it just seemed so damned—

"Very funny. I don't seduce bleeding men."

A light flared in front of him, and he recognized the downstairs bedroom. The one he'd slept in for six years. Where he'd dreamed about Mickey…

"Come on, Jeff, cooperate." Her hands tugged at the waist of his jeans, air rushed cool around his hips and thighs. And then, without realizing exactly how it happened, he started to fall, landing backside up on the narrow single bed.

The room went quiet for a while because he had his face buried in a pillow, and Mickey, he guessed, was too busy to talk. He could measure the length of the rip in his leg by the places she touched, the progress of the fire. All in all, he was glad he couldn't see what she was doing.

But he could feel. He sensed the balancing pressure of her fingertips on his other thigh, the slight brush against the back of his knee as she worked on the bottom of the cut, the indentation of her knuckles against his rear as she reached the top. Against his will, against his good intentions, his body reacted with excitement, with desire. Damn it all, he was lying on a bed, half-naked, with Mickey York touching him and he was, but wasn't supposed to be, getting turned on!

The bandaging process was appropriately painful. Jeff welcomed something to concentrate on besides a heart-pounding silence that only emphasized her nearness, her touch. When he felt the last tape stretch into place, he barely suppressed a sigh of relief.

But he heard one from Mickey. "That's an ugly graze," she informed him sternly. "You used to move faster than that."

Jeff propped his chin on his fists; he wasn't about to roll over yet, not with only a pair of Jockey shorts to disguise what he'd been thinking. "I used to be sixteen. Thanks for the help."

He turned his head to watch her, but she didn't meet his eyes. She gathered up the bloody towels on the bed and dithered with the wrappers for the gauze. "No problem. I owe you. Do you want me to wash out your jeans?"

Jeff gave it some thought. "Eventually, somebody will have to. But I'm not riding home in my skivvies, so I'd better just pull them back up. After," he said emphatically as she showed every sign of helping him dress, "you leave."

"Well, excuse me!" With a brisk about-face, she was across the room. "I'll get out of your way."

The door slammed behind her and Jeff rolled over. He didn't quite feel up to a sitting position, so he crossed his arms over his eyes to block out the light and let himself drift for a few minutes.

Where he drifted, of course, was right back into the past, back to the time when Mickey would have fixed up a cut and then kissed it...him...to make it better. They'd been children when they met, best friends as they matured. His love had sprouted from liking, flowered early into passion, but he'd bided his time, knowing he couldn't push her, not wanting her to grow up too soon. Just seeing her every day had been enough. For a while.

But that night, after her seventeenth birthday party, they'd walked out to the barn as they usually did, just to say good-night to the horses, and he'd known the time had finally come.

She was all girl for once, no jeans, no T-shirt, no

deep-brimmed Stetson shading her face. Not that he minded her that way; that was the Mickey he knew best. But this one was nice, too, in a rose-colored dress short enough to show off her legs, and stockings and nice shoes. She'd left her hair down, and kept tucking the sides back behind her ears to keep it out of her face. A touch of blush kissed her cheeks and a hint of shadow deepened her eyes. He'd never seen her more beautiful. Or more grown-up.

And of course, she was all business. "I'm thinking of trying out Splinter in the next few days," she'd said, passing the ornery stallion's stall and matching the horse stare for stare. "He and I need to get used to each other."

Jeff's mind had not been on horseplay. "Sure," he said softly, leaning against the post and picking up a lock of her silky sable hair between two fingers. "Sounds reasonable."

Mickey flashed him an unreadable look and moved to the next box. "Curly's been kinda down recently. Think he might be sick?"

"I doubt it." He stepped close enough to flick a golden hoop with his nail. "Nice earrings."

"Th-thanks," she stuttered, backing like a skittish colt.

Jeff followed. Bypassing the last horse, Mickey moved up against a closed and latched barn door. "You...you're different tonight, Jeff. What's wrong?"

Gently, he shook his head. "Nothing. Everything is just exactly right." And in the soft dimness of the night-time barn, he'd lifted her chin with his knuckle, looked deep into her eyes for just a second and then touched her lips with his.

He could still remember every nuance of that explosion, every thrill that had ripped through him. He could relive the instant of Mickey's surprise—that brief, funny squeak she made—and the moment of stillness afterward. And then the incredible rush of warmth when her lips softened for him, and she began to kiss back.

Lying on the bed in what was now Dex Hightower's house, Jeff felt every cell in his body awaken to the tenderness, the vitality of that moment. He'd been so surprised, so startled by the rush of sensation, it had taken a move from Mickey to deepen the embrace. She'd put her arms around his neck, twined her fingers in his hair, and suddenly he was holding her tight against him, experiencing the softness of her body in a way he never had before, and thinking that it might be okay if he just died right now because life couldn't possibly get any better than this. Little did he know...

"No!" With a groan at the flare of pain in his thigh, Jeff rolled himself up and off the bed. Grabbing his jeans, he pulled them over his legs, ignoring a painful rearrangement of the bandage, and struggled to get the zipper up. Then he walked to the window and stood staring out into the night, carefully emptying his mind of everything except the peace of a high plains moon. By the time he heard a knock at the door, the fit of denim across his hips wasn't quite so tight.

Dex poked his head in. "You okay?"

Jeff let the curtain fall and turned around. "Sure. Thanks for the first-aid supplies."

A wave of a big hand dismissed the gratitude. "Your rodeo rider must be really whipped. She's asleep on the couch."

Jeff came into the living room and grinned at the sight of Mickey, head back, mouth open, passed out from exhaustion. "She's had a hard time the last week or so. Guess I'll have to carry her out to the truck."

But she woke up with the first touch of his hand. "Jeff?"

He straightened up. "Sorry it took so long to get dressed. Are you ready to go?"

Brushing a hand back through her loosened hair, she nodded and stood up. At the door she extended a hand to Dex. "You're doing a good job here, Mr. Hightower. My dad would be pleased."

Jeff noted with amusement the blaze of red over the other man's cheekbones as they shook on it. "Thanks, Miss York. You didn't really get to see the place, though. Come back out sometime and prowl around. Oh, and call me Dex."

Mickey nodded, and stifled a yawn with her hand. "I'll do that, Dex. And call me Mickey. 'Night."

Shaking hands in his turn, Jeff issued final instructions about the sick cattle. "I'll come out tomorrow afternoon to check on them. Call me if you need me before that."

Dex followed him out. "Sure."

Getting into the truck was tricky. Jeff lowered himself carefully onto the seat beside Mickey, then waited a second or two for the worst of his body's protests to subside. He reached for the key, but hesitated. "You went to Denver this weekend?" he asked the rancher.

Bracing a hand on the window frame, Dex nodded. "I got four whole days."

"Good ones?"

A rare and gentle smile softened the solemn, weathered features. "Real good. Lots of time to talk, to play…it was great."

"I'm glad."

With another quick nod, Dex stepped back. Jeff gunned the engine, decided his thigh would last the trip and headed the truck down the gravel driveway into the black, black night.

He'd driven almost five miles in silence when Mickey spoke up. "Dex has a girlfriend in Denver?"

Jeff smiled. "In a manner of speaking. It's his daughter. She's six."

"Oh." Another two miles of quiet. "Not to be nosy, or anything…"

"Which you always have been."

"Is he divorced?"

An unwelcome thought crossed his mind, one he wouldn't begin to give voice to. "Yeah. About four years ago, not too long after he bought the ranch. His wife didn't like being out in the middle of nowhere, and Dex had no intention of returning to the big city. So she took his little girl and left."

Mickey shifted on the seat to face him. " 'Returning'?"

"His career up to that point was in finance. He made big bucks and decided he'd had enough of suits and ties and meetings, so he found himself a spread he liked and brought his family here. But she couldn't deal with it."

"So now he makes the trip into the big city to see his little girl. How sad."

"Yeah, it is. Especially since he doesn't have any control over how she's raised. He doesn't say much, but I gather there are some problems, and it drives him nuts. It's amazing how often divorced dads get no rights."

Mickey didn't respond, and in the quiet that followed his comment all the questions he wanted to ignore crowded in on him. Was she attracted to the big rancher? Would she consider getting to know him better?

Their speed jumped up ten miles an hour as he let the tension in his body affect the accelerator pedal. What difference did it make to him what Mickey did with her life? For reasons he now understood, their paths had split a long time ago. Jeff could hardly kid himself that she'd been alone all that time, any more than he had. Not that he'd ever raised any false hopes or made promises. Or ever found anybody who completed him the way Mickey did.

"Things sure have changed around here," Mickey commented after a glance at the speedometer. "Used to be the speed limit in town was a little less than sixty-five."

It was too dark to be sure, but she thought Jeff flushed. Then he shook his head and lifted his foot, slowing their speeding-bullet pace. "Medical emergencies get special priority."

She noticed how carefully he held himself, and drew the obvious conclusion. "You should take a couple of those pills when we get back. I imagine that cut hurts."

He shrugged. "I was thinking about the calf."

Another irritated shrug discouraged further conversation, so Mickey turned her face to the window and watched the houses and stores of Flying Rock roll past.

He only got this touchy when he didn't want his thoughts to be read. At thirteen, she would have teased him out of it. At seventeen, he'd taught her a new way to communicate and she'd learned how to touch him, kiss him, love him until the problem was solved.

Mickey stiffened her knees, trying to quell the responsive quake in her body as she remembered those days...and the minutes not long past, with Jeff lying still under her hands as she bandaged his cut and fought against the reawakening of a familiar desire, a desperate need to caress.

Some nurse I'd make, she thought. *No patient's virtue would be safe!*

That wasn't really the truth. She could imagine other men—Dex Hightower, for instance—whose cuts she could dress without a qualm. Whose skin she wouldn't ache to stroke. Whose tight, flat butt wouldn't draw her gaze from her work, inspire a tingling in her palms and a quiver in her belly.

Damn! It was still Jeff. Only Jeff. After all these years, after she'd stupidly thrown him away, he was the only man she'd ever wanted this way. Though she'd tried, a time or two, to replace him, he remained the only man she'd ever been close to, the only man she'd ever really loved.

And the only man she knew she couldn't have.

"Coming in?"

While she'd been dreaming, he'd stopped the truck and come around to open her door. Standing there in the moonlight, dusty and grimy, hips out of alignment because he was favoring his left leg, eyes shadowed and his usual grin missing, he still took her breath away. Just as he had the first time he'd kissed her.

And what Mickey wanted to do was fling herself at him, make him catch her in his arms and hold her, make him kiss her until neither of them could stand up and they fell to the ground so that hands were free for touching and stroking and exploring...

"Yeah," she said, easing herself off the high seat and making sure she kept as much space between them as possible. "I think it's time to call it a day."

CHAPTER SEVEN

"WELL, IF IT AIN'T Mickey York! What are you doin' here, young lady? Didn't I see your name on a poster down in..."

Everywhere she went in town that day, she got the same reaction. Floyd Tucker, in the feed store, nearly sent her back to the hospital with his hug. His daughter, Delia, towing a pair of redheaded twins behind her and looking as if she'd give birth to another set any minute, favored Mickey with a harried smile before dragging her boys out the door.

As she wandered through Tucker's familiar aisles, the dusty scent of animal chow and grain and medicine that permeated the dimness sent her diving once again into the past. She and Jeff had spent hours here together, mulling over catalogs and debating the advantages of different feeds, bridles, currying tools—whatever came to mind or hand. The first Christmas present he'd ever bought her came from Tucker's—a pair of spurs set with turquoise and silver, ordered by Floyd from a fancy place in New Mexico. She'd hung those spurs in the place of honor in her new apartment just a week or so ago.

"What brings you home, Mickey? After all this time?"

Startled back to the present, she looked up from the

comb she'd been fingering as Floyd eased his bulk and a big box past her in the narrow passage.

"I...um..." Stupid, to have come out this morning without thinking up an explanation.

Not that Floyd needed her input. "Martha heard you were stayin' with Jeff at his place. 'Not a chance,' I says to her. 'Those two split ten years ago. A man who took it that hard wouldn't let a woman come waltzin' back into his life at the drop of a hat.'"

He emptied nails into a bucket with a bone-rattling din. "Nearly worked himself to death, he did, that summer after you took off. Your daddy was down here every week, seemed like, tellin' me how the boy wouldn't eat and wouldn't come in to sleep."

Mickey closed her eyes, wondering how to stop the flow of words. With Floyd Tucker, there wasn't much chance.

"'Course, after you let them know where you were—Denver, was it? I had a cousin in Denver, died last year in a car wreck, those city drivers—Jeff eased up a bit, got himself together and went off to vet'rinary college up there in Idaho. And then came back here to work. I like that in a man, knowin' what he owes his town. And he's a damned fine doc, no doubt about it. So," Floyd inquired over his shoulder, his round face gleaming as he hoisted a sack of feed onto a high shelf, "what brings you back, Miss Rodeo?"

She pulled in a deep breath, summoned up a professional grin and backed toward the door. "Just passing through, Mr. Tucker. Just passing through."

Escaping from Floyd out onto the sidewalk, she immediately fell into much worse trouble as Roberta Fender grabbed her arm with a red-taloned hand and dragged her into the post office.

''Mickey York, as I live and breathe! Now you come right in here this minute! Your mother would never forgive me if you came to town and I didn't sit right down and find out how you are and what you're doing and where you've been.''

Easing away from the deadly grip, Mickey remembered her manners. ''How are you, Miss Fender?''

''Never mind about me, young lady. Why didn't you let us know you'd be visiting? Your mother was my best friend, still is, if it comes to that, though we don't talk every day like we used to, how could we, with phone rates so high? But we still write on a real regular basis and I know she had no idea you'd be back in town or she would have asked me to look after you. And you certainly look like you could use some rest, child. I haven't seen circles under anybody's eyes like that since I can't remember when!''

Roberta drew in a gasp of air, allowing Mickey to say, ''I'm just fine, Miss Fender. Really.''

''And what she'll say when I tell her you're staying with Jeff again is more than I can imagine.''

Mickey bit the inside of her cheek to stifle a groan.

''You know she never liked it that you two were living together all during college, down there in Laramie, always thought it looked bad to the minister, Jarrod Nelson it was then, you'll remember, though he's since retired and we have a new man, Tim Weaver, and he's real nice, though not the preacher Jarrod was. But I always told her, 'Ruth,' I said, 'Ruth, if there's anybody that understands kids and their wildness, it's Pastor Jarrod, he has five of his own, spitfires every one of them. And it's not like Mickey and Jeff are just kicking up their heels, when everybody in town knows they've been meant for each other from the very beginning and you'll be planning that wedding before you know it...'"

Amazingly, her voice died away for a moment of its own accord. When Mickey looked over, she found tears glistening in the little woman's faded blue eyes. "Miss Fender?"

"I never saw anything as sad as your wedding day," as she sniffed. "Your mother and daddy sitting in the kitchen at the table, pretending to drink the coffee I made, but mostly just staring at each other with that worried look I'll never forget as long as I live. And your sisters, creeping in from their bedroom every so often, then creeping back out again because nobody knew anything more. And Jeff...Jeff was wild. I don't know if he slept that night, I don't think so, because he kept driving around in that beat-up black truck he held together with baling wire, searching the hills, driving all the way to Buffalo and even to Sheridan, I think, and not finding you anywhere. I thought that crazy look would never leave his eyes."

Paralyzed, Mickey couldn't say a word. After a minute, Roberta sighed. "But it did, of course. When he came back from vet school and set up practice here, he was pretty much the same Jeff we all loved. I had hopes of him and Susannah Daley for a while there, three years ago that was. He seemed to be taking a real interest in her and that boy she's raising all by herself since her husband got frozen to death out there looking for some strays. But then Susannah and her boy moved to Cheyenne and last I heard she was engaged to some lawyer with kids of his own, so I expect she'll do just fine. A born mother, she was, always playing with baby dolls, pushing that carriage around town. And what are you doing with yourself these days anyway, Mickey?"

Words…forbidden, horrible words choked her throat, making speech impossible. For a few strangled seconds Mickey really thought she might pass out from the agony of it.

Just before the silence became rude, the door behind her opened, letting in a rush of hot wind and a shaft of late-morning light, along with a welcome interruption. "Now, now, Roberta, you get the letters put up and leave the poor girl in peace. She doesn't look strong enough to deal with you this morning."

Roberta sputtered like a wet hen. "Why, Ed Riley, what ever do you mean? All I did was ask a simple question, and if you think that's too hard for the child, well, all I can say is—"

With an arm around Mickey's waist, the sheriff guided her to the door. A finger on his free hand touched the brim of his hat. "'Morning, Roberta."

Outside, Mickey sagged against the wall. "Thanks, Ed. I was in way over my head there."

"Anytime." Leaning against the post holding up the porch roof, he looked her up and down. "I'd say you're looking just fine, for somebody who's had a little trouble staying in the saddle recently."

The tension in her chest eased a bit. "You're still keeping track?"

"Sure." Like a young uncle—he was twelve years older than Mickey—Ed had taken a real interest in her rodeo work, and his office had always been her first stop in town. Laconic, attractive but single, Ed had let her play with his sheriff's badge and wear his big hat. When she'd asked him why he wasn't married, he'd told her he was waiting until he found the time.

The memory made her smile. "Got yourself a wife yet, Ed?"

He followed her as she turned to walk up toward the north end of town and Jeff's house. "Nope. Too busy."

"Yeah, I guess being sheriff in a big place like Flying Rock keeps you up lots of nights."

"It has its moments. We had a cattle stampede through here couple years ago."

"Sounds like fun." She tended to fall in with Ed's brevity of expression when they talked.

"Mmm. Some fool down at Bustard's spread left a gate open, late one Sunday afternoon. Damned animals made it down the highway, over the bridge and to the filling station, where a motorcycle on the interstate backfired and spooked 'em. Now we got fifty steers heading toward us at top speed. Could have used a real rider in town that day."

His dry tone made her laugh. "You handled it, I bet."

"Yeah, me and Buchanan managed to throw saddles on a couple of horses in his barn and get out there before they spread too far."

A new voice took up the story. "You forgot to tell her we were well into our second six-pack, Riley." Jeff rounded the corner and stopped in front of them. "It gave our performance a certain *fluid* quality."

Ed barked a laugh. "You mean when you fell off into the creek bed?"

Jeff's eyes crinkled in response. "Well, I was thinking more about your loose cinch. Ever seen a cowboy round up cattle from the side of a horse, Mickey?"

She looked from one man to the other, envious of the comfortable rapport she could sense between them. They spoke as if they'd spent a lot of time together, in work and play. The thought bothered her, made her feel as if she was on the outside looking in. The knowledge

that she'd chosen to leave and lock the door behind her
only increased her discomfort.

One sure cure for that. "I think I'll head back for
some lunch," she told them, hoping she sounded easier
than she felt. "Can I fix something for you two?"

Ed shook his head. "Not me, thanks. Another time."

Mickey looked at Jeff, who said, "Sure. I'll be along
in a couple of minutes."

Watching her walk away, Jeff took a few seconds to
admire the tanned strength of her arms, left bare by a
white tank top, and the narrowness of her waist, cinched
by a belt worked in silver and turquoise. Though she
held herself carefully, the stiffness in her shoulders had
eased a little after a good night's rest. He wished he
could say the same for his leg, which still throbbed like
the devil.

Ed noticed his uneasy shift of weight. "What happened to you?"

"Got caught by a horn up at Hightower's last night.
Don't move as fast as I used to, I guess."

"Or maybe your mind was somewhere else?"

He met the other man's level gaze. "Could be. This
is just about the last thing I expected to happen."

"I know what you mean. She's doing okay?"

Jeff shrugged. "You know she won't admit it when
she's not."

"What happens now?"

If anybody had a right to ask, Ed did. In the same
way that the Yorks had become his adopted parents, Ed
Riley was the big brother Jeff had always wanted—a
man to admire, to imitate. And as Jeff got older, a friend
to depend on. They'd searched for Mickey together, that
week after the wedding fiasco, when nobody had known

where she was. Then, once she'd called, they got drunk together too. In celebration and in mourning.

Now Ed evidently believed there was an opportunity for Jeff to get her back. Fat chance. "What happens now is that I try to keep her from killing herself for a week or two, and then she's gone. End of story."

"That's what you thought last time."

"Yeah, and I was right. I'm not trying to resurrect anything here, Riley. Mickey needs some rest and I'm giving her a place to get it, that's all."

The sheriff levered himself away from the wall. "I didn't say you were trying anything, Jeff. You don't have to—it'll happen all by itself. Have a good day."

For several seconds Jeff fought the urge to call Ed back and challenge him on that comment. Nothing...*nothing*...was going to happen with Mickey, he insisted to himself as he headed toward the house and the lunch she had promised. The past would stay where it belonged, and they could both move into the future. Separately. Because he wanted it that way.

But the assumptions being made in town about why she was here and what would happen had already driven him crazy this morning. He'd come out for a breath of air to regain his perspective, only to run straight into the problem he was trying to avoid.

First it had been Lucy Tyler, wanting him to look at her limping German shepherd and tell her how long Mickey planned to stay. And then Roberta Fender had bustled in, with absolutely no excuse except nosiness. That woman...she'd given him enough trouble three years ago when he'd tried to date Susannah Daley.

In all fairness, though, he couldn't blame that failure on Roberta. He and Susannah just hadn't worked, some-how. Jeff thought he'd gone in with his eyes open, intending to set up a relationship based on liking that would end in marriage and kids. He'd always wanted kids. And Susannah had a son already, a boy he'd enjoyed being with and showing off for.

He'd enjoyed Susannah, too, though her interests began to seem limited, after a while. Maybe a little dull. One thing you could say about Mickey—she had never, ever been dull.

Surely, he reasoned as he mounted the porch steps, there was a halfway place between monotony and reckless craziness?

On the thought, he walked into the kitchen. Mickey was there, presiding over the jumble of sandwich fixings she'd spread over the counter, slapping mayonnaise onto a slice of bread with what appeared to be violent intent. Temper energized every move she made, stiffened every line of her usually lithe form.

Jeff leaned against the doorjamb and crossed his arms over his chest. "You planning to eat that sandwich or just beat it to death?"

She sent him a withering glance. "I haven't decided yet."

Feeling unsettled himself, he couldn't resist the urge to prod. "What put you in such a great mood?"

A shake of her head answered him as she picked up a package of bologna and wrestled with the seal. Her obvious aggravation sparked an answering flare in Jeff. He'd spent a lot of time recently tiptoeing around Mickey's feelings. Today, for some reason, he pushed. "Did you have a good morning?"

One vicious tug ripped open the bologna; juice splattered the cabinets as slices of meat fell with a splat onto the counter and floor.

Staring at the mess, Mickey muttered a string of rude words.

Jeff bent and peeled bologna off the Mexican tile to hide the grin he couldn't smother, even with anger. When he turned around from the trash can, though, Mickey hadn't moved. And she wasn't laughing.

"Come on, Mickey, lighten up. What's the problem?"

She lifted desperate blue eyes to his face. "I spent the morning," she said, her voice soft but intense, "being told in so many words exactly how selfish, ungrateful and cruel I was to leave. Everybody I talked to made damned sure I knew just how much it hurt my mom and dad—not to mention you—that I left the way I did."

Try as he might, Jeff found it hard to empathize. "What did you expect? No questions, no complaints, just 'Welcome home, Mickey'? It made quite an impression, your walking out like that. You should expect that they'd want an explanation."

"Why don't they stop and think about what it was like for me? What about the way I felt?"

Slipping his hands into his pockets, Jeff deliberately relaxed his jaw. "What about it? Are they supposed to be sympathetic? Here's a girl who's had her whole life handed to her on a platter—loving parents, a stable home, good friends, plus the freedom and support to pursue a career she loves."

"Jeff—"

He felt his hold over his temper slip. "But this girl, she decides that what she's got isn't good enough. That she just might, God forbid, have to make a sacrifice here and there for what she wants."

She lifted a hand in protest. "I don't think—"

"She just might," he plowed over her interruption, "have to realize that she can't have it all. So what does she give up? Not the career, no. Not the rodeo which, when all's said and done, will give her maybe ten more years of success before she's too old and too injured to compete.

"No, she gives up the people. The family who cared for her, the man who loves her, the friends who've stood by her all her life." Bitterness rose like bile in his throat. "Just throws them away, reaching for the glory without any hindrances, any regrets."

Mickey's desperate gaze had grown savage and cold. "I do not have to take this."

"And how does she do it? Not with an explanation of her feelings. Not with gentle persuasion, or violent argument or—"

She took a step forward, her hands clenched. "I'm warning you, Jeff!"

He shrugged. "Or even with a damned note. She just walks out of the church, leaving them all wondering and worrying at the wedding rehearsal, expecting to find her body at the bottom of a canyon, raped and murdered by some lunatic on the night before her wedding. And you wonder why people are a little miffed?"

Mickey spun on her heel and stalked across the kitchen. "That's it. I'm out of here. I don't have to take this, not from you, not from anybody."

"At least I'm getting a goodbye this time. Are you sure you don't have to go to the bathroom first?"

His sarcastic question braked her headlong rush to the door. She halted, her good arm holding to the door frame, her head bent to expose the vulnerable nape of her neck under her braid.

Heartbeats measured the silence; Jeff felt her struggle

with the instinct to run. He hoped that, for once, good sense would win.

And then the door slammed behind her and Mickey was gone, leaving only the echoes of anger to keep him company.

RUNNING AWAY in a town the size of Flying Rock required special talents. Particularly when you didn't have a truck or a car or a horse. As she paced around Jeff's barn, Mickey struggled with her temper, fighting the urge to get far away, as fast as possible. If he hadn't convinced her to leave her truck in Buffalo, she'd be gone.

Nobody talked to her like that. Nobody. Never in her adult life had she allowed anyone to criticize her behavior that way. And Jeff, of all people! He was the one person she'd always depended on to take her side. No matter what the issue.

Well…maybe not always. They'd had their share of fights, and she'd lost more than her share of those. Usually, reliably, though, it was the two of them against the world.

The truth came to her so suddenly that she stumbled. The unity, the confidence she'd placed in him…that was ten years ago. *Before* she made her decision, before she took the step that severed the bond between them. Jeff wasn't on her side anymore because she'd pushed him away. He owed her nothing, not even loyalty, after what she'd done. And he didn't even know the whole story. If he ever found out…

She hid in the barn for over an hour, expecting him to come out and find her, shocked to the core when he didn't. She thought about taking his horse, but didn't really feel up to putting on a saddle by herself. And that made her mad all over again—he'd been so sure she shouldn't go back to work because she wouldn't be able to keep the kids safe.

Damn it, did he always have to be right?

Finally, when he didn't come to get her, she slipped out the rear door of the barn and around the far side of the house from the kitchen windows, heading into town. Instead of taking Main Street, though, Mickey ducked into the narrow alley running behind the buildings. The last thing she wanted was to run into any more of her mom's friends—or Jeff's.

She grinned when she found the back door to the sheriff's office unlocked. Some things never changed. Inside, she went down the narrow hallway, past the door on the left that led upstairs to Ed's apartment and the one on the right opening into the mostly unused holding cells. Flying Rock had never seen major criminal activity, didn't even get its share of rowdy drunks on Saturday nights. For a town in the Wild, Wild West, this place was almost too quiet.

The door to the hallway from the office had been propped open. Ed looked up as she stepped through. "Trouble?" he asked.

Was she that easy to read? Mickey shook her head and eased into the chair across the desk from his, just as she would have ten years ago. "I guess I missed a few details in the story of the prodigal son. Or maybe—" she grabbed the tail of her braid and brushed it over her chin "—maybe it's different for prodigal daughters."

As he used to, Ed leaned back in his chair, fingers laced over his belt buckle, to give her the benefit of his opinion. "Facing the past takes guts."

He didn't know the half of it. "I don't think I have enough."

"Most people don't." Something in his voice made her look at him more closely. Ed's focus wasn't her, or the office, or even Flying Rock. He seemed to be staring into the distance, though she couldn't imagine at what.

Ten years ago she wouldn't have hesitated to ask. Now, though… She remembered Jeff's words. *Ed didn't sleep for days.* She'd run out on this man, too.

Just another victim of Mickey's folly.

Which made it safer to say simply, "I guess everybody has regrets."

His blue eyes, sharp, perceptive, came back to the present, back to her face. "Damned right they do. But sometimes mistakes can be mended."

Which let her know more or less what he was thinking. She cleared her throat. "Sometimes they can't."

Again, she got the feeling his attention had wandered. But only for a second. Then he blew out a deep breath and sat up straight again. "You're right, sometimes they can't. How will you know, though, until you try?"

Mickey closed her eyes. The answer to that question required all the courage she didn't have.

I killed a baby, she should say. *How can I mend that?*

If he knew, Ed might be horrified…sad…sympathetic…comforting. It happens to lots of couples, he would say. They get over it. They try again.

But Jeff would be devastated.

And Mickey believed, from the bottom of her soul, that together they would never, ever get to try again.

So there wasn't any point in making amends. She'd known that for ten long years. "Call it intuition," she said flippantly, getting to her feet. "Or water under the bridge. Can I borrow your truck?" she said abruptly.

Ed stretched to stand behind the desk, his gaze never unlocking from hers. "Jeff deserves more than that, Mickey. So do you." But his hand went to his pocket and brought out a jangle of keys on a leather thong.

She managed a grin against the reproof in his eyes. "Thanks! I'll have it back tonight."

He lifted a hand as she ducked back down the hall. Ed had always let her have her way. Unlike some people she could name.

With a pair of wheels underneath her, Mickey headed out of town, back up the road they'd taken the night before to the Triple A. Long before she reached the main gate, though, she turned off onto a track barely visible through the brush and dust of years, heading into the back acres of her dad's spread with hardly a thought for what she'd say to Dex Hightower if she met up with him. She'd worry about that later.

The shack showed up before she expected it—the distance had seemed longer back then. Slowing to a stop, she relaxed against the seat and stared, bemused. Built long ago to provide shelter for men working the range in bad weather, the old lean-to, crouched underneath a ridge, looked about the same as it had when she'd played there as a child. Or when she'd come here with Jeff, the last week before they started college.

They'd been caught in a sudden summer storm that afternoon, and drenched in seconds. When the hail started, she'd headed for the only nearby shelter. Pulling the horses close under the overhanging roof, they'd tumbled into the shed, laughing, panting, teasing about who should've noticed the change in the clouds.

The wind whistling through the cracks in the boards soon chilled them both, but in midsummer no one had stocked the woodpile; the rusty old stove was as clean as an empty bucket. Jeff went back outside to pull the saddle blanket off his horse, then stepped up behind her to wrap it around her shoulders. She still felt damp. And in just a few minutes, she began to shake.

"Damn," he had muttered, rubbing his hands up and down over her blanket-covered arms. "You're not supposed to get colder, Mickey!"

"I—I—I'm s-s-sorry," she'd stuttered.

He'd kept rubbing her arms for a few more minutes, but she got more and more miserable. Finally, with a wary expression on his face, he backed away.

"You need to get out of those damp clothes. This storm could last a while, and you'll just get more chilled. So take them off, then wrap back up. That'll make you warmer." Turning, he walked to the door and stared out into the rain-doused twilight. "I promise not to look."

But Mickey remembered wanting something different. The chill was real, of course, but so was the desire that licked along her veins as she felt him standing behind her. They'd been playing with fire for over a year, sharing deep, searching kisses that left them shaking, finding dark corners and odd moments for a trembling exploration of the contours underneath their clothes. She'd lain in bed night after aching night, picturing Jeff's spartan room directly underneath hers, imagining him there on the bed—or with her, in hers. Living together the way they did, with her family all around, made any real intimacy impossible.

But now here they were. Alone. Miles from anyone, with all the time in the world. And the moment had come. Mickey let the blanket fall to her feet, put her fingers to the first button on her shirt. She nearly crowed with triumph when she couldn't get it loose.

"Jeff?" she croaked.

He didn't turn. "Yeah?" His voice held a world of tension.

"I...I can't get the buttons. My fingers won't work."

His comment was profane. But he stalked across the floor, eyes down, and pushed her hands away. "Let me." A few seething minutes later, he reached the last button. For good measure, he released the snap on her jeans, too. "There."

He meant to walk away. She knew that. And before he could, she caught his hand—lifted it, cradled it in hers, and then, breathless with her own daring, placed his warm, callused palm inside the loose flap of her shirt. Over her breast.

Time stopped. Silence roared around them. Jeff lifted a startled brown gaze to her face and Mickey let him see every bit of the longing she'd kept dammed up inside. His serious, troubled eyes widened...and then ignited. He didn't ask why, or if she was sure, or any of the questions she'd thought he might.

He simply made her his.

Shifting her weight on the front seat of Ed's truck, Mickey decided not to get out and look inside the shack. She could see it clearly in her mind's eye, the tin roof and rough boards, could smell the must and dirt and damp, could feel the blanket harsh against her back and Jeff's smooth skin sliding over her own. She heard again his smothered laughter when he asked about birth control and she confessed she'd been on the Pill for months, waiting for him.

And her breath stopped, just as it had then, when she thought of that perfect moment, the first time their bodies became one.

"This," she told herself as she backed up into a cloud of dust, "was a big, big mistake!"

Running from the past, Mickey kept herself diverted for the rest of the day. She drove to Buffalo and went to a movie, then ate dinner at a fast-food place before browsing the mall to pick up a couple of shirts and another pair of jeans. Most of her clothes were still up at the camp, and she wouldn't get back there until at least the weekend.

Thinking about the camp brought her mind around to the dilemma facing them. She stayed well under the speed limit as she made the trip to Flying Rock, pondering the camp's money problem all the way. Two weeks had passed since Laurie's announcement, two weeks in which they hadn't made any progress toward a solution. For the last day or so she'd practically forgotten the whole issue; something about the crash at the rodeo and waking up in a hospital and, yes, being with Jeff again, had driven the only really important consideration out of her head.

But the facts hadn't changed. If they didn't get the money, the camp wouldn't last another year, and might not even survive the summer. That would leave a lot of needy kids with no place special to go.

And Mickey would be left without the anchor she'd depended on for so long. Camp Crazy Woman gave her the chance to see herself as more than just a machine programmed to sit on a bucking horse without falling off too soon. She even hoped, sometimes, that her work there made amends for some of her past mistakes. Maybe, just maybe, by bringing hope and pleasure to other desperately fragile children, she could compensate for that one lost life.

Either way, her small part in improving life for these

kids gave her the strength to keep going. If she lost that incentive, she would suffer as much as the campers themselves.

It was after 10:00 p.m. by the time she drove into town. Leaving Ed's truck behind the sheriff's office, she walked slowly back to Jeff's house, her mind still chasing after fund-raising ideas that seemed as useless as they were far-fetched.

"Good evening." She looked up quickly to see Jeff reclining on the front steps, ankles crossed and elbows propped behind him, a half-empty bottle of beer within easy reach.

Mickey swallowed hard. "Hi."

"Missed you at dinner." His voice was almost too level.

"I, um, had some shopping to do." She held up her parcel as feeble proof.

He nodded, then cleared his throat. "I didn't mean to drive you off this afternoon. I'm sorry about that."

On a sigh, she dropped down beside him. Not close—this afternoon's memories were too fresh for that. But not too far away, either. "I'm sorry, too, Jeff. I didn't mean to lose my temper. I just never—"

He held up a hand in the moonlight. "Let's not go into it. Tell me instead what's got you so worried."

She didn't even question how he knew. And she didn't bother trying to put him off. All at once, Jeff's help, his insight and creativity, looked like the only life-line she had.

So she told him about the camp's financial troubles, about the insurance and the shortage of funds. She even explained about their shaky first year and how her dad's bequest had allowed her to get Camp Crazy Woman firmly established.

"That's a side of you I never knew, Mickey," Jeff reflected as he brought her a beer and another for himself. "I never realized you had such a concern for kids."

She stated the obvious. "A lot can change in ten years."

"I guess so." His tone held a question he didn't have to ask.

Sheer force of will kept her voice casual as she shaped an explanation. "I've got a lot of friends on the circuit who have kids. One of my best friends has a little boy who developed leukemia. And I met up with Laurie five years ago, just about the time Stevie was going through chemo and having a hard time being a regular little guy because nobody wanted to play with a kid who had cancer. Laurie was a nurse in pediatrics, looking for a way to use her skills and spend more time outside. Somehow the pieces just all seemed to fall into place."

And if Jeff didn't know about one of those pieces, what could it hurt?

He stretched out again beside her. "So, what you need to do is come up with a plan to make some big bucks fast."

"Yeah, but killing off a rich uncle has already been suggested, and I don't have one."

His white grin flashed through the dark. "I know. How about a raffle, or a prize drawing?"

"For what?"

"Hell, I don't know! But you could get a prize donated, and sell tickets—"

"For a dollar or two apiece. The population of Wyoming is decreasing, Jeff. There aren't enough people left in the state to make the money we need at that rate."

"Okay, okay. It was just an idea."

They tossed the problem back and forth until the moon dropped behind the mountains and the black night hid the pointed peaks. Mickey had reached a pleasant state of unconcern, when Jeff sat up suddenly beside her.

"We're stupid, Mickey."

"Yeah?"

"We're ignoring a great moneymaker, right under our—or rather your—nose."

"What are you talking about? What have you come up with?" She sat up, as well, and stared at him suspiciously. "Jeff? Are you thinking what I think you're thinking?"

His eyes caught a flash of light from the stars. "Why not?"

"Could we really?"

"I think so."

"Would it work?"

"If you...hell, if *we* worked hard enough."

They looked at each other in the darkness, broke into a simultaneous grin and then announced their decision together.

"It's a rodeo!"

CHAPTER EIGHT

THEY TALKED into the wee hours of the morning, brainstorming and laying out strategy and logistics. They were so excited about their plan, they called Laurie, who came awake instantly and took barely a minute to match their level of enthusiasm. Mickey doubted any of them would be able to sleep after such a miraculous inspiration. She drifted into Jeff's comfortable guest room around dawn, thinking no further than a change of clothes.

It came as a surprise to wake up at ten o'clock and realize that she had, after all, slept. Maybe the relaxation of having a possible solution for the problem had been enough to let her rest. Leave it to Jeff to see a simple way around a big mountain; his mind had always worked on a straight-line path, clearing away obstacles as he moved ahead. That kind of thinking had, she was sure, made him a good vet, a great businessman and an all-around handy guy to have along.

The handy guy obviously hadn't snatched much sleep for himself, though. By the time she wandered into his big, bright kitchen, the only trace of Jeff was a note on the table.

Have some eggs and bacon. I'll be in and out all day. Leave the chili alone. I mean it!

She had to grin. His spiky handwriting hadn't improved in ten years, and he hadn't discovered a facility with words. Letter-writing had never been his specialty; one summer away at camp had taught her not to look for more than a line or two. Of course, after that one summer, she'd refused to go off and leave him that long again. Until...

With an irritated curse, Mickey limped to the counter and poured warm coffee into the mug Jeff had left waiting. Leaning her hips back against the cabinet, she let her gaze wander over the room, considering the golden oak woodwork, with brass knobs on doors and drawers, the wooden drying rack beside the double porcelain sink which spoke of a man who didn't often use too many dishes, and the state-of-the-art dishwasher which said sometimes he did.

Well, he'd gotten his home, the way he'd wanted it, the way he'd dreamed it with her in college. Only...not *with* her. Mickey contrasted the life she'd lived with what Jeff had built for himself. Could he have done this if she'd stayed around? Would they be this settled now, together? Or would he have sacrificed the comfort, the organization he'd always prized to her crazy, unsettled, nomadic career? Would entry fees and traveling expenses and—hell, yes—doctor's bills have eaten up the money it took to live like this?

Probably. She drifted through the house, savoring cool, quiet rooms where sunlight flickered over warm woods and brilliant colors—sage and gold and russet, the colors of the land, accented by the profound blue of the Wyoming sky.

Poking her head around doors, she discovered extra bedrooms, a couple of baths, and one big, empty space that hadn't yet been given a purpose. Knowing Jeff, he was thinking about a playroom, somewhere indestructible for kids to set up trains and games and toys and horse around. Children had always been part of his plan.

But then, Mickey reflected, *so was I.*

She ended up at the door to his bedroom. He'd left it open slightly. All she had to do was push. And step inside.

In college they'd slept on a water bed. Jeff had moved beyond those days, in more ways than one. Mission-style furniture, authentic for all Mickey could tell, filled the huge room with quiet elegance. A bedspread in his favorite slate blue covered the bed; the same color draped the wide window without covering it. Taking in the view, Mickey figured he could watch the sunrise as he came awake. He'd always been an early riser.

She turned to the chest of drawers. No pictures on the top, not his dad, or hers, even. Certainly not one of her. Just a small mirror on a stand, and a silver-backed, tortoiseshell comb. The silver weighed heavy in her fingers when she picked it up, cooled the warmth of her palm. She traced the intricate engraving with her eyes.

It had cost her a weekend's prize money, that comb. Hand-carved, handworked, she'd given it to him that last Christmas before the wedding. They'd laughed, because his hair was light, so stubborn that only heavy-duty goo would hold it down for long. A comb-through or two really didn't help much. He'd used the comb on her hair instead, smoothing over and over again in the firelight until it flowed like silk across her shoulders, and his, as their lips met.

"Mickey?"

She heard the front door slam, felt the thud of his boots on the hardwood floor. Given her distance from the bedroom doorway and the state of her health, the chances of getting out before he found her looked poor, so she didn't try. She was putting the comb down in its place when he arrived at the door to his room.

The shock of seeing her there held Jeff speechless for a measurable pause. Finally, he got his throat cleared. "Looking for something?"

Slowly, Mickey turned to face him, a ribbon of red riding her cheeks. "I'm sorry," she said in a low voice. "I didn't mean to intrude. I just…wondered…"

The situation felt unbalanced, poised on a knife-edge between catastrophe and chaos. Jeff lifted his eyebrows, trying for detachment. "About where I sleep? A penny for your thoughts, Mickey."

"No. I mean…" She swallowed hard. "I was looking around the house and just ended up here. It's a nice room."

"Thanks." He dug his hands into his pockets and leaned his shoulder against the door frame, easing his injured leg. The cut had felt a little better this morning, but after three hours of standing up, it pounded with the rhythm of a steam engine. So did his head, after a night without sleep. "We combined two of the bedrooms in the old house to make this one, and enlarged the window. I like being able to watch the sky."

"I know."

It was almost a whisper, but he heard it. Of course she knew. Mickey had always known the important things.

Like how much he'd wanted a home. How he'd hated the years in a trailer, how he'd thought the log house on the Triple A was the closest he'd ever come to heaven. To have a place in that house, a place in that family, had meant Christmas three hundred sixty-five days a year to the boy he had been. For the months it had taken George Buchanan to recover, Jeff had lived in fear that his dad would spoil the dream, would take him away and kill the joy. But the Yorks had found a space for George in the old bunkhouse, had let him settle there to work when he could and drink himself into the past when he couldn't. And Jeff had finally come home.

He'd shared that home with Mickey, his best friend. And when she became his lover, the woman he wanted for the rest of his life, they'd built a dream around a home of their own. Back in their cramped, dingy apartment in Laramie, with a kitchen the size of a postage stamp, they'd planned an enormous bedroom that let the sky in, a kitchen where their friends could share meals and chores and laughter. And a living room with a fireplace to warm them when they made love.

Even though Mickey had walked out on him, Jeff had held on to the dream and fulfilled it. He had created the house they should have shared together.

And now she was here.

She stood in the morning light that streamed through the window, her hair a fire-tipped halo around her head. The wide neck of a big, soft, black T-shirt slipped off her shoulder and her legs were bare, except for sloppy white socks.

Desire took him with the crash of an avalanche. He'd never been able to resist Mickey in the morning.

Without even being aware of moving, he found himself standing next to her. She looked up at him, her blue eyes wide. "Jeff, I—"

"Shh." He placed a hand on her elbow, slid it down her arm to take the mug she carried and put it on the windowsill, out of the way. Then he let both palms cup her shoulders, drawing her close.

Her hands came to rest against his chest. "Jeff, this isn't—"

"Shh," he said again, and lowered his mouth to hers.

Memory, strong as it was, couldn't begin to match the reality of her taste, her touch. Her lips welcomed him with softness; he drank it in with a breath of pure joy, slowly, gently, exploring the different ways their mouths could meet, could blend together in a fit as timeless as the mountains, as ageless as the sky. Her palms on his chest created a sweet warmth over his heart.

But sweeter still was the friction of her touch when she released the last of the buttons and smoothed his shirt away. She swept her hands over his heated skin, his tight nipples, measured the throb of his heart beating against her fingers. He heard the low moan of approval in her throat and echoed it with one of his own, but still couldn't let go of her mouth, not even to breathe. The air he took came from Mickey's lungs.

A familiar fire tore through him, burning away past, present, future, leaving only the searing need that this one woman could satisfy. Her arms slipped around his ribs. Her hands played wickedly over his shoulder blades, and the press of her breasts against his chest compelled him to loosen his grip in her hair. He dropped his hands to her waist, to the sweet curve of her hip, gathering the soft cotton he found there, pleat by pleat, slowly, tortuously, until the velvet of her skin grazed his knuckles.

At the touch of his palm against her back, she broke their kiss with a gasp. Jeff took advantage, tasting the delicate inner skin of her lower lip with his tongue while he sampled the curve of her thighs with his palms. A part of him smiled with satisfaction as he heard her shortened breaths and felt the tension in her legs, sure signs that she wanted this as much as he did.

And part of him could hardly bear the pleasure of touching her again, of exploring the line of her spine and the firm swell of her bottom, feeling the strong muscles there tighten as he caressed. Her tongue tangled with his, issuing an erotic invitation, and he accepted, commencing a dance of give-and-take that left them both breathing hard and quick. He'd forgotten just how far Mickey could take him. And how fast.

But it was the same for her. He knew it from her panting sighs, knew it from the clutch of her fingers against his back and the tremble in her belly as he stroked across to slip his fingers under a satin barrier into the silky curls beneath.

She broke free of their kiss with a strangled cry. "Jeff!"

He heard the plea; she didn't have to say more. His own body craved the same solution, the same release. He swept his arms around her, pulled her up against him and fell back onto the bed.

Mickey's shriek of anguish coincided with his groan of pain. "Damn it, Jeff, my ribs!"

He let her go at once and put a hand to his thigh. "Hell, Mickey, I'm sorry...I forgot. And I think I just broke open that cut on my leg."

She rolled to the side and clutched her middle. "You deserve it," she muttered from somewhere inside the huddled ball she had become. And then said nothing else for a long, long time.

Mickey measured the silence by the slowing of her heartbeats and the easing of the ache in her chest. She'd goofed again, allowing old habits to override common sense. Jeff had started it, sure, but she hadn't stopped him, hadn't even wanted to. He made life simple and fun and incredibly intense. Other than the time she spent on horseback, she hadn't felt so alive, so *aware*, in years.

But passion wasn't—couldn't be—a part of their lives today. Too much had happened, too many corners had been turned. What lay between them could never be undone, or even forgiven. They had to stop reliving their memories and forge some kind of new relationship out of the scraps of the old. Or she'd end up telling Jeff about the baby…and then there wouldn't be any kind of relationship between them at all.

Mickey didn't think she could face that possibility again.

"This isn't getting us anywhere," she said finally, pushing up to sit awkwardly on the edge of the bed, facing away from where Jeff still stretched out on his back.

"It depends," he said, his voice husky, "on where you want to be."

She couldn't move fast, but she turned to give him a surprised stare. "What's that supposed to mean?"

He shrugged. "Hell, I don't know. It's just—" Groaning, he sat up beside her on the bed. "I guess I'm not doing a very good job at separating the present from the past. The spirit is willing, as they say, but…" He grinned. "You know how it goes."

Yes, she knew. And she saw in his eyes that he read her response. Desire flared once more between them, and a single touch was all it would take to drive them together into the storm. Mickey started to weaken.

But she pulled herself together. After everything else she'd done to wreck his life, she couldn't allow Jeff to ruin his future with their past. He needed a chance to look forward, not back. Freedom was the only thing she could give him now.

Mickey pushed herself awkwardly to her feet. "Well, then, since neither of us seems to be particularly trustworthy, I guess I'd better clear out. It's time I got back to work, anyway."

He came up after her. "That's not necessary. I give you my word, I won't—"

Hard as it was, she stepped close enough to put a hand on his cheek and look directly into his mesmerizing dark eyes. "Give me a break, Jeff. You know the problem's not just you. This isn't a case of the poor defenseless virgin and the evil seducer. We both want it, because we both remember how good things were between us. And if I stay here, we'll end up in bed together, and then where will we be?"

His fingers caught a strand of her hair. His smile was wicked. "I can think of worse places."

"Mmm, yeah." She tweaked his cheek and stepped away, forcing him to release her hair. "So think about them. I'm going to get my stuff together and hit the road."

He followed her down the hallway to the guest room. "I don't suppose it will do any good to remind you about the doctor's orders."

"No, it won't."

"Or to suggest that you really could use more time to recover."

"No."

"How about the chili?"

That made her pause in the packing. "Oh, yeah. I haven't tasted the chili yet, have I?"

He leaned against the door frame with a Cheshire cat

grin. "Nope. How can you leave without sampling my chili?"

Her heart ached to see him there, so confident, so comfortable, so...so Jeff. It would be easy to stay, so fatally easy to love him all over again. "You're absolutely right, Dr. Buchanan. I can't!"

OVER A LUNCH of chili and corn bread, they made a deal.

"No more looking back," Mickey ordered as he settled into his chair. "We keep our distance, physical and emotional, and we treat each other like distant friends. That's all."

"Right." Jeff spooned up some chili and pretended to consider. "Strictly a business relationship—we'll need to keep in touch because of the rodeo, but otherwise, our lives go in different directions." A sound concept, he thought.

Impossible to enforce.

But Mickey seemed determined. "I think that's the best idea. If we focus on business, on setting up this show, then we shouldn't have any reason to, um—"

"Step over the line?" Wherever that was.

"Right!" Her vigorous nod conveyed certainty, but the way she avoided his eyes as she buttered a piece of bread told a different story. Mickey wasn't any surer about this plan than he was.

Jeff didn't push. He'd already done that, pushed her way beyond where she wanted to be with him. If he'd retained even the smallest hope that there was some future for their relationship, this morning had killed it. Mickey still didn't want to be tied down, had no intention of picking up any baggage. He'd been foolish to think that friendship would work between them—it really was an all-or-nothing situation.

Once he'd had everything; for the past ten years he'd had the nothing part. He thought he'd accepted it, had become comfortable with the void. So why, suddenly, did he feel as if he'd had his gut ripped out?

The situation would, he told himself through the afternoon, get easier again. She'd go back to the camp and they'd see each other only on rodeo business, which meant roughly two months of regular contact. After the show in August, they could take up their separate lives again. Which suited him fine. All he'd ever planned for this interlude was a chance to settle the past and move on.

If only he could figure out exactly where he was headed. These days with Mickey had him wondering what would be the point of going anywhere if he couldn't take her with him.

And that was a dangerous state of mind.

They spent the next two days, when he wasn't working, drawing up plans for the Camp Crazy Woman Charity Rodeo. Entry fees, spectator admissions, a percentage of the concessions—it would add up to a hell of a lot of cash. But they had to get the setup right. Mickey made lists of her contacts in the business—a stock master and crew to handle the animals, riders to perform, announcers and judges for the events, media people who could publicize the cause. Jeff contributed his own connections with the livestock industry—a list of ranchers who might be willing to donate steers and broncs for the rough-stock competitions, as well as calves for the roping events.

"Sponsors," Mickey muttered at one point late Thursday night. "We need big-name sponsors."

Jeff looked over from his chair by the window to where she'd perched at the far end of the sofa, all the way across the living room. Since Wednesday, they'd been excruciatingly careful to keep an insurmountable distance between them. He hated it.

But he had promised to play fair. "Who have you got in mind?"

"Well, I can probably get my people to stand behind me, but one boot company isn't enough. I wonder if we can get these corporate people moving on such short notice."

"Make a list. We can start calling tomorrow."

"Um, yeah." Her hesitation telegraphed clearly across the quiet room.

Jeff rested his journal on his knees. "You have a problem with that?"

Scribbling on her paper, she avoided his eyes. "It's just, well, you know, I've got to leave tomorrow."

His temper reared, but he beat it down. "No, you don't."

"I've got a ride this weekend in Cheyenne. Remember? Tomorrow night."

"You should call and turn out. You're not in any shape to ride."

Her chin lifted, her blue eyes flashed fire. "You can't tell me what I should and shouldn't do anymore. You don't run my life!"

He counted to ten in the silence. "I'm not running your life. I just think—"

"No." With a rustle of paper she struggled to her feet. "We're not doing this again. I'll try to make some calls tomorrow morning, set up some appointments. I'll be out of your way by noon. Good night."

She was as good as her word. When Jeff walked into

the kitchen at twelve-thirty on Friday, Mickey had her duffel packed, her papers in order and her goodbye speech memorized. She started before he could even take off his hat.

"I want to thank you for everything," she began, using all her willpower to meet and hold his startled gaze. "I did need a vacation, you're right—and I can't think of a nicer place to have spent it than here. I enjoyed the chance to see the town again, and talk to people, and I'm really glad we got everything settled between us. I should have done it a long time ago. If you're ever up in Sheridan—"

"Cut the crap, Mickey."

His voice, tight and tense, sounded strained, and there were lines around his eyes that told her he hadn't slept much. Well, neither had she. Her heart twisted in her chest, but she wouldn't let emotion sidetrack her. She couldn't afford to weaken now.

"I mean it, Jeff. You've been a real friend, and you came up with the idea for the rodeo, which is going to work out great. I'll be in touch about the stock arrangements, and—"

He cursed under his breath and tossed his hat at the kitchen table. And then he was across the room, in front of her, closer than he had been in days. His hands closed over her shoulders, tight on one side but gentle on the one she'd injured. The fact he could remember, in the midst of turmoil, brought her to the verge of tears.

"Don't turn this into a farce," he said through clenched teeth. "There's too much between us for that. If you're going to say goodbye, just do it." His gaze roamed her face for an endless, silent second; his fingers tightened a fraction. "And do it right."

Mickey hadn't anticipated a kiss. If she had, she

would have expected anger. But what she got, as his mouth moved softly over hers, was heartbreaking, soul-wrenching tenderness. The sheer pain of it, the ache in her chest at what was clearly farewell, showed her exactly why she hadn't said goodbye all those years ago.

As if he realized how much it hurt, Jeff ended the torture. Taking a shaky breath, he loosened his grip and stepped back.

"I won't apologize," he said as his hands dropped to his sides. "But I'll stick to the deal from now on. Okay?"

Her throat full of tears, Mickey couldn't speak. She nodded, and felt droplets shake onto her cheeks. Ducking her head, she bent to pick up her duffel just as a horn sounded from the front of the house. When she straightened, Jeff had one eyebrow cocked in question.

"That's Ed," she managed to say in a rough voice. "He's going to drive me to Buffalo to get my truck."

Jeff nodded. "Good idea." But his voice sounded cold.

Out on the front porch, with a hot wind blowing and Ed waiting, the potential for disaster diminished. Mickey summoned a grin. "Thanks again, Jeff. For everything."

"Anytime." His face solemn, he slipped his hands into his pockets.

"I'll call you."

"Sure."

"Bye."

Another nod was all she got on that one. And he didn't even wait to see her drive off. As she eased down off the last step, Mickey heard the screen door clatter, then the solid thud of the oak front door. She ignored the temptation to turn around. Walking straight ahead instead, she threw her bag into the back of Ed's truck and climbed in.

"Next stop, Buffalo!" she declared, blinking hard.

"HOLD YOUR HAND OUT flat, like this." Mickey uncurled Karen's fingers from around the carrot. "Then nothing will be in the way when Clementine goes for her snack."

Gray eyes wide in her white face, the little girl let Mickey pull her hand out, extending the carrot toward Clementine's interested nose. The tension in the thin arm telegraphed through a faint trembling, and Mickey bit her lip in sympathy. To be so fearful, and yet so determined to conquer that fear.

Clementine got a whiff of carrot. She stretched her neck and drew her lips back, showing big yellow teeth. With a squeak, Karen dropped the carrot and backed up against the opposite wall, her hands behind her. "It's going to bite me!"

"No, no, honey, she's going to bite the carrot." Mickey bent to pick up the vegetable, blaming the tears in her eyes on the ache in her ribs. After ten days, she expected not to hurt anymore. "Horses don't eat people," she explained, straightening slowly. "They eat veggies. Want to try again?"

For a long time Karen stood there motionless, staring across the aisle of the barn at the horse she wanted so desperately to ride, and Mickey waited quietly, hoping for the best. She understood the dilemma, wanting something and being afraid of it at the same time.

Finally, Karen swallowed hard and came away from the wall. "I-I'll try again."

"Good girl." This time, Mickey moved around behind her, and extended her own arm underneath

Karen's, with her palm cradling the back of the small, pale hand. With her other hand, she dropped the carrot into Karen's grasp. "Let's do it this way, okay? I'm right here. Now, straighten your fingers. That's right."

Slowly, so slowly, they eased up to stand just about an arm's length in front of Clementine. And that sweet old girl, as if sensing the importance of her reaction, waited without even a twitch as the two hands came within an inch of her nose.

Mickey clicked her tongue. "Have a carrot, Clem?" She edged Karen's hand underneath the soft muzzle.

Clementine blinked. And then, with the daintiness of a finicky cat, she lipped the carrot off Karen's hand and into her mouth. A second later came a distinctly satisfied crunch.

"I did it." Karen's voice was a shredded whisper. And then, louder, "I did it!" She whirled in Mickey's grasp. "Can I do it again?"

Mickey laughed. "Until Clementine gets sick of carrots or we run out, whichever comes first."

"Will you help me?"

"Sure."

But in two more carrots, Karen had gained the confidence to step forward by herself. Clementine, still on her best behavior, nuzzled the girl's palm as she took the treat. "That feels funny." Karen giggled. "Like a tickle. And sort of hairy."

"Pretty good description," Mickey agreed, thinking what a miracle this was. "Two more and they're gone."

"Can I go ask the kitchen for more?"

"Not today. We wouldn't want Clem to get spoiled, would we?" At the droop in Karen's smile, she nearly gave in. Then inspiration hit. "Would you like to groom her a little?" Or was she moving too fast?

But the girl nodded. "What do I do?"

Playing it safe, Mickey left Clementine in her stall, and showed Karen how to use a curry comb on the horse's neck. Since Clem loved being groomed, it wasn't a big risk; if she could have, she would have purred. Instead, she whickered off and on in contentment, while Karen's whole face glowed with the joy of achievement.

Mickey leaned against the door of the next stall, talking softly and watching, until footsteps behind her signaled an arrival. She turned to see three people come into the barn...Laurie, with a man and woman she'd talked with twice before.

Karen's parents.

Backing up, she met the group out of Karen's earshot. "Mr. and Mrs. Wheeler, how are you?" She extended a hand to each. "We're happy to see you up here."

But Linda Wheeler was looking beyond Mickey at her daughter. "Is it safe for her to be alone with that animal? What if it bites?"

Aha. "Clementine doesn't bite," Mickey assured her. "Karen's fed her a bushel of carrots this afternoon and they get along just fine."

"But it's so big."

Don Wheeler sighed. "Horses are designed big so they can carry a person, Linda. My wife," he said with a grin, "grew up in Chicago, never saw a real horse until our honeymoon. She's still not used to the critters."

"Well, Karen's so little, Don, and she's had so many problems..."

"All the more reason she should enjoy her time at the camp. It was her choice, remember."

"Yes, but she wouldn't have known about it if you hadn't brought home that brochure—"

At Mickey's panicked look, Laurie held up a hand. "Folks, you might not want to argue this out right now. Karen's fine, we're taking really good care of her, and she's having a ball. She's been begging Mickey to let her help with the horses, and Mickey won't take her any further than she's ready for. In the meantime—"

"Mommymommymommymommymommy!" Karen had heard the raised voices, and now streaked toward them. She crashed into her mother's embrace. "Did you see, did you?" She lifted a shining face. "I fed Clem carrots, and she didn't even bite me and then Mickey showed me how to brush her and she really liked it, she kept talking to me with this funny sound and then she would close her eyes just like Mittens does when I rub her tummy! It's really neat!"

"But you need to be careful, Karen—"

"That's fantastic, sweetheart!" Don Wheeler broke into his wife's warning without apology. "What else have you been doing? Can we see your cabin?"

"I swim every day," Karen said, taking him by the hand and dragging both parents behind her toward the door. "And we made clay pots in craft class and painted them, and I got to be the Indian woman in the play at campfire..." Her voice faded with distance, still detailing her adventures.

Grinning, Mickey glanced at Laurie and saw the same silly smile on her face. "What a pistol that kid is. But she's coming along."

Laurie's smile faded. "Her mom doesn't help. But I can't blame her. Nobody should have to face such a threat to their child's life. And kids shouldn't know anything but joy."

"That's why we're here, isn't it? To make sure they have the best possible time at this point in their lives, whatever comes in the future?" *And at least they've had a life,* she thought. Some children...

"You're right." Laurie took a deep breath and straightened her shoulders. "That's the job, and that's what will happen. This rodeo idea of yours should put us in a good position to keep going. How's the sponsorship angle?"

Mickey didn't mind leaving her train of thought. "I'll know more Monday. I've arranged a lunch meeting in Denver with a number of prospective sponsors. I'm hoping thick steaks and whiskey at lunch will make my case. And if they don't, I imagine the camp video will."

"Can we afford thick steaks and whiskey?"

"Don't worry, boss." She put an arm around Laurie's shoulders and walked her toward the door. "I won in Cheyenne last weekend. My prize money will cover lunch, with enough left over to pay for gas."

CHAPTER NINE

JEFF STROLLED past the long oak bar and Western memorabilia of one of Denver's fanciest restaurants to a private dining room, wondering what kind of afternoon he had ahead of him. Mickey had set up lunch with representatives from most of the sponsors she hoped to secure for the show. He'd been more than a little surprised when she called to ask him to come as backup.

But then, Mickey was nothing if not full of surprises. And this event did qualify as a business meeting.

Nothing personal, right?

He reached the dining room without getting a glimpse of the hostess. Glancing around, he saw only executive types, mostly men in dark suits with power ties. The women wore suits, too, one a somber gray, the other an eye-catching white with a short skirt that showed off excellent legs. While her back was turned to him, Jeff took the chance to enjoy the view.

He needed less than a second to recognize those ankles. He'd rarely seen them in high heels, which was a pity, because they looked fine. As did the slim hips in a narrow skirt, and, when she turned, the rest of her elegant, athletic figure. Above the purple blouse, Mickey's fine-boned face broke into a smile.

"Jeff!"

She crossed the room, and he saw heads swivel to

catch her walk. Yes indeed, Ms. York had made an impression already.

"Hey, Mickey. This looks good." *You look great.*

She took the hand he held out and shook it, laughter in her eyes. "I think we've got half of them hooked already. Come help me land the rest."

Not that she needed much help. When she put her mind to it, Mickey could perform miracles. He'd seen that determination in her single-minded conquest of a problem pony, and he could see it now in the production she'd arranged to showcase the camp. A video presentation, clearly set up by one of her friends in the professional media, captured the spirit of Camp Crazy Woman with heartrending accuracy. Food and spirits carefully calculated to mellow the sternest mood, and a brief but effective speech left Jeff very little to do but walk around cementing goodwill.

"Impressive," he commented as they watched the last guest leave.

"Exhausting." Mickey dropped into the nearest chair and kicked off her shoes. "I've got a friend in marketing who planned everything for me. She's the real brains behind this lunch."

"Sure." Jeff turned a nearby chair around and straddled it. "You had nothing to do but follow orders." His gaze dropped to the carpet, where her toes wiggled coyly in the deep pile. Something about the sight set off fireworks deep in his belly. He brought his eyes back to Mickey's face. "I heard you won in Cheyenne."

Smiling wide, she unbuttoned her jacket. "Yeah, and yesterday in Grand Junction, too. Now I can pay my rent!"

She stretched her arms wide and back. Jeff noted the improvement in her range of motion—her shoulder must be healing. He also registered the pull of purple silk across her breasts, and the barest hint of lace underneath.

Remember the deal. Shoving fantasy aside, he loosened his tie and cleared his throat. "So, what's next?"

Mickey crossed her legs, and the short skirt rode about halfway up her thighs. "How's the setup for livestock coming? What do we have so far?"

His temperature soared. Was she doing this on purpose? Doubtful; Mickey didn't play those games. No, he knew where to place the blame for his hyperactive libido. The past ten days without her, after the few they'd shared, had been a taste of the desert he'd thought he wouldn't have to cross twice. Living alone again took effort. Where before he'd felt comfortable and satisfied with his house and his life, now everything seemed dull. Empty. Barren.

"Jeff?"

He looked over to see that she'd been waiting for his answer. Dragging his mind away from what couldn't be changed, Jeff made his report. He'd secured some positive feedback from the ranchers he worked with, including Dex Hightower. "Dex has a couple of bulls that should be in the national finals this year or next. Have you got some cowboys who can ride them?"

Crossing her arms over her chest, Mickey gave him a haughty stare. "*Cowboys?* Why not some women to ride those bulls?" Then she broke down with a laugh. "Yes, I have some cowboys. A couple of the top riders, as a matter of fact. Plus my friend whose son, Stevie, was sick—he was the first one I asked and he said yes right away. We're gonna have a great show."

Jeff nodded, and silence fell. He wanted to keep her talking, wanted to make the moment last, but this was obviously not the place. The restaurant's staff bustled around them, clearing the room, making it plain that the time had come to leave.

Mickey seemed to pick up the hint at about the same time he did. She looked over at with a sheepish grin. "I guess we're in the way, hmm?"

Standing, Jeff pulled his jacket closed and fastened the button. "Yeah, I suppose we should clear out. Do you need help packing up your gear?"

Mickey eased back into her shoes with a groan. "That would be fantastic." They worked in silence for the few minutes it took. Jeff carried the heavy boxful of papers and promotional materials, and she gave him a grateful grin. Her ribs weren't actually quite as healed as she let on.

Then they were standing in the parking lot, under a gray sky threatening rain. And just like inside, Mickey couldn't think of a way to end it...because she really didn't want to say goodbye.

Going back to her single, detached life had been tougher than she would have believed. Not that she was alone so much, since the kids at camp rarely let her out of their sight from dawn until bedtime. And she and Laurie had a million details to talk over for the show. Her time and attention were always in demand.

But something had shifted. She no longer felt quite so...comfortable in her independence. The two hours she'd spent in her empty apartment, picking up mail and the clothes she needed for her performances, had seemed like a sentence to solitary confinement. She kept listening for a friendly whistle, kept expecting someone to walk in with a joke, or an argument ripe for the picking.

To put it bluntly, she'd missed Jeff like hell.

And now he was here, looking polished and yet somehow a bit of a rogue in his black, Western-cut suit and narrow tie. She remembered the deal, yes; she knew they had agreed to stick to business. Still, that had been her idea. Couldn't she back down...just a little bit?

"Do you have to hurry back?" She hoped he would assign the breathless quality of her voice to the effort of stowing the slides and projector behind the truck seat.

When she turned around, his smile was waiting. "No, not really. I took the day off and left the guy in Buffalo on call. What do you need?"

"Oh, nothing." Mickey swallowed hard, tried to sound casual. "But I was thinking...I have a meeting with my sponsor tomorrow morning, and I don't really want to go back to spend the whole afternoon staring at the TV in my room, and I thought—"

"Mickey?" Laughter rode in his voice.

"Um, yeah?"

"Where would you like to go?"

All dressed up as they were, and with the weather not really conducive to outdoor activities, the choices seemed limited. They ended up in Denver's Museum of Natural History, a place Mickey had never visited. After Jeff insisted on paying their admission, they walked past the gift shop to escalators that would take them up to the exhibits. And that's where all hell broke loose.

Children. Everywhere. Every size and shape and color, running loose, walking in lines, being carried. Some wore matching T-shirts proclaiming which day camp they came from, some hung on to a mom's hand or sat atop a dad's shoulders. The whole scene was a kaleidoscopic advertisement for kids.

Jeff took it all in stride, laughing and grinning, redirecting the little ones who collided with his knees, holding serious discussions with intense eight-year-olds focused on the characteristics of dinosaurs.

"You think, like, they slept standing up?" inquired one young afficionado, staring at a long-necked model.

Leaning his elbows on the low partition separating them from the beast, Jeff gave the question serious consideration. "I'd say it would be impossible to get your head up off the ground, once you laid it down."

"Maybe they used a rock as a pillow."

"Or a treetop—softer."

"Yeah..."

Mickey turned away. The boy by Jeff's side sported the same look she saw every week on the kids at her camp—oversize shorts, sloppy sneakers and socks, and a slightly wrinkled T-shirt advertising a famous mouse. He looked healthy, happy, carefree. Nothing about him should have gripped her heart the way it did, nothing he'd said had been remotely emotional.

But the sight of Jeff in communion with a boy who could, without any difficulty, have been his son—*their* son—clawed at her like a wildcat. The blond head bent so close to the darker one—two "men" in deep conference together over something as serious as a dinosaur skeleton—only painted her a complete picture of the damage she'd done, the joy she'd denied herself and Jeff by running off the way she had. If she'd stayed...if they'd gotten married and settled down...if she hadn't been so incredibly selfish—

"Where's the fire?"

She hadn't realized how fast she was walking until Jeff's grip on her elbow slowed her steps. Fighting for composure, Mickey took a deep breath before turning to face him. When his eyes widened, she knew she wasn't hiding anything very well.

"Mickey? Are you okay?"

A woman who rode raging broncs when every muscle in her body screamed in pain could surely fake her way through this, too. "Sure!" She flashed him a showstopper smile and made a point of consulting her museum guide. "What should we see next?"

The gem area was quieter, since most of the kids apparently preferred dinosaurs to rocks. But even here there was an excited murmur as little hands left frosty palm prints on glass cases and wide-eyed faces reflected wonder at the bright minerals on display.

One person, however, appeared completely uninspired by the accomplishments of Father Time and Mother Nature. Mickey's gaze kept returning to a thin, tall girl who leaned sullenly into a corner. Something about the child's build, about the way she held herself, conveyed the impression of a person more at home on horseback than on her own legs.

"Lee Ann, get over here!" The call came from across the room—a woman with three children arranged in stair-step ages around her. "Look at this diamond!"

The girl only shrugged, and turned more deeply into her niche. Her mother, clearly exasperated, marched over. Shamelessly, Mickey listened in.

"I didn't bring you here to sulk, young lady," the woman announced. "Why can't you enjoy yourself?"

A roll of her eyes conveyed Lee Ann's perspective. "I want to go home."

"We will, honey, but this is a special trip, just for you. Can't you have fun?"

"I don't want to look at some old rocks."

"What do you think you want to do?"

"I want to go home and ride. You wouldn't let me yesterday because of the rain and this morning because we were coming into town for this. And Spirit is going to be just as fresh as anything because he hasn't been out in two days. I want to go home."

A whisper came over Mickey's shoulder. "Sounds like somebody I knew once upon a time."

She nodded, acknowledging Jeff's comment. Lee Ann bore a strong resemblance to the girl Mickey had once been. The same lanky hair and build, the same drive to ride and perform. It was like looking in a mirror.

Lee Ann's mother, though, wouldn't stand for this nonsense. "Well, no ten-year-old girl needs to spend her whole life in a barn or on a horse. Certainly not on her birthday." She grabbed at a listless hand and pulled the resisting girl to join her brothers and sister. "Now you just come along and cooperate, or you won't be riding today, either. In fact, it'll be next week before you sit down in a chair, let alone in a saddle!"

Mickey stood stock-still, staring, as a chunk of memory fell into place. Ten years old today, July 8. Lee Ann would have been a tiny baby ten years ago, all soft and pink and cuddly, the light of her mother's life. Darkness crept in from the edges of the room as Mickey's vision tunneled, narrowing to focus a decade back to the day Lee Ann had been born.

On the same day another baby died.

Jeff watched Mickey's face lose all its color; for a second he expected her to faint dead away. But she gathered herself with a visible effort, took a step away from him and then stopped.

When she turned, her expression had frozen into an artificial calm he'd never known her to wear. "What do you think? Have we seen all there is? Maybe the weather has cleared up and we can walk around in the park for a while.''

He wasn't about to argue with her, not when she had that blind look in her eyes. This wasn't the place to talk about it, anyway. He'd get her somewhere private, and then he'd find out what was wrong.

Outside the museum, they followed a sidewalk around the corner of the building to the top of a long flight of stairs leading down to the grassy spread of City Park. Mickey seemed barely aware of where she was going. She took the first step, staggered, and would have tumbled all the way down if he hadn't caught hold of her shoulders with both hands.

She crumpled out of his hold into a crouch on the step, her head down on her knees. Jeff looked her over, making sure she was physically okay, then dropped down beside her. Leftover storm clouds chased across the sky during the long silence it took her to recover.

He felt her sit up at last, and turned his head to watch as she raked her fingers through her hair, loosening the braid and freeing a few light strands to be caught by the wind.

When she sensed his stare, she looked toward him and managed a smile. "Hi."

Jeff didn't intend to be put off. "Want to tell me what that was all about?"

She took an audible breath. "No big deal. I skipped breakfast—nerves. I didn't eat lunch, too busy wheeling and dealing, I guess. The combination suddenly hit me in there, and I felt a little sick. I'm fine now."

He didn't believe her. Oh, he believed she hadn't eaten; Mickey always tended to run on pure energy, and had to be reminded to take in fuel. But hunger didn't account for that look in her eyes. Something had hurt her. Bad. And she didn't want to tell him what it was.

She ought to know better than that by now. Deal or no deal, he wasn't going to let this one slide. Still, to keep from scaring her off, he decided on an indirect approach. "Well, then, you're due for some food. Let's find a place for an early dinner."

Mickey acquiesced easily enough and directed him to a Tex-Mex restaurant she'd liked in the past. She even let him order her a margarita to go with the chips and salsa. He hoped the alcohol would loosen her up.

It seemed to. For the first time he heard the tale of those ten years, of the path she'd climbed to the top, and some of the people she'd met along the way. He listened closely to the names of the cowboys she'd worked with, and couldn't restrain a surge of satisfaction when none of them seemed very important romantically. Visions of Mickey and another man had tortured him nightly for the first year, and at intervals ever since. Jeff was glad to think he'd wasted that time.

But nothing she said could account for this afternoon's reaction. And no amount of cautious questioning seemed to bring out the answer. He finally decided the indirect approach wasn't working worth a damn.

Still, he waited until she finished her drink. "What happened this afternoon, Mickey?"

She slurped the last of the icy tequila and looked up. "I told you. No food."

"That's what you said. Now tell me the truth."

"Come on, Jeff. That's all there is." Her shrug tried for indifference. "Low blood sugar, they call it. I've had a hell of a day."

The signs of evasion were there to read. She wouldn't

meet his eyes, couldn't hold back the flush creeping over her cheeks and throat.

"You were fine until we got to the museum with all those kids," Jeff insisted. "What—"

"I was fine until my system figured it couldn't handle another hour without something to work with! Give me a break!"

When she started sliding out of the booth, he thought he'd driven her off again. She stood over him, sliding her purse strap over her shoulder. "You're the medical man here. Think about your basic physiology course while I go to the rest room. You'll figure it out." A brisk turn on her heel, and she was gone.

Mickey reached the ladies' room and slipped inside the door before sagging against the wall, reserves totally depleted. Her shaking hands and swirling head could be the result of low blood sugar, or too much tequila on an empty stomach.

But not her aching heart.

She should have known better. She should have remembered the date, should have realized that being with Jeff on today of all days would make everything just that much worse. And then to take him to a museum, where there would be kids, where she could see exactly what she'd missed...

Damn it, she should have known!

And how could she explain? How in the world could she look into his face and tell him what she'd done? Tell him about the baby they'd made together? About the life so full of promise, so precious, so fragile, so very new? And how her stupid pride, her stubborn arrogance, had destroyed it?

"Are you all right, dear?"

Mickey looked up out of her hands into the concerned

face of somebody's grandmother. A coolness on her cheeks made her realize she'd been crying.

"Can I help you? Is there someone I can call for you?"

Dear God. "No...no, thank you. I'm okay." Pulling in a ragged breath, Mickey straightened up. "Really. I'm fine." She ripped a paper towel out of the dispenser and mopped her cheeks. "See?"

The grandmother tilted her head in skepticism, but left anyway. Mickey turned to the mirror and stared at the wreck of her face.

"You can't go out there like this. You can't let him see what you're thinking." She ran cold water onto the towel and plastered it over her forehead, her cheeks, on the nape of her neck. "Get a grip, or you'll make everything worse."

She'd never known fear like this. No fifteen-hundred pound bronc could skew her heartbeat this way, make just breathing an act of will. She didn't want to face him, didn't want to have to admit what she'd done to the man who had a right to ask. Ten years of hindsight—and the revelations of the recent past—had only sharpened the edge of this particular blade. If she told him now, the last fragile link between them would be slashed forever.

But there was more to consider than simply her cowardice. Jeff didn't deserve the pain of knowing. He would find a woman someday, someday soon, who would give him the family he wanted. Finding out about that long-lost child would only cause him sorrow without purpose. Mickey wanted to spare him that, at least.

How? If she went back out, he would press her for an answer, one she couldn't—wouldn't—give. The temptation to run stampeded through her. She could walk out, get in the truck, and be out of Denver before Jeff realized she was missing. No explanations necessary—until the next time she saw him. And since they were working together on the show, that next time would be in the very near future. Not to mention the fact that she'd be leaving him stranded...

Again.

She couldn't do it. This time she had to face him, had to somehow get through without telling him that part of the truth. She didn't know how, only that she would.

Thankfully, for once she'd brought makeup with her, in case she needed to touch up before the luncheon. By the time she'd finished, she thought the repair job good enough. The dim lighting in the restaurant would do the rest. A couple of deep breaths and she opened the door, her story straight and her face, she hoped, giving nothing away.

When she slid into the booth, their dinner was waiting, considerably cooler for the delay. "Oh, Jeff, I'm sorry. You should have started eating."

"No problem." He set down his beer, made a tent of his hands and pinned her with his gaze. "Are you going to explain?"

Mickey put her fork back on the table, taking a minute to align it precisely next to her plate, then her knife and spoon alongside. She knew what she had to do, if she could just avoid saying anything to make him suspicious.

"Yes, I'll explain. I'm sorry—I've been trying to sandbag you to keep from talking about it. But...but being with all those kids today made me, well, made me realize what we could have had, if I hadn't run away. We...we wanted a family, and we m-might have had one or two or even three children by now if...if I...'' She let her voice trail off, dropped her eyes to the enchiladas congealing on her plate. The aroma made her want to gag.

The silence from the other side of the table made her shake. When she looked up, Jeff had leaned against the seat and was watching her with an almost calculating expression on his face.

Typically, he said the last thing she expected. "That was part of the decision you made when you left, Mickey. Didn't you realize it?"

She stifled the sigh of relief that rose from her chest. He'd taken the bait. Allowing a hint of irritation into her voice, she prepared to fight. "No, I didn't. I didn't think at all, as a matter of fact. I just knew I had to get away."

"But, later..."

"Later, I had enough to do just getting a life and a career started on my own. I didn't have time to think." The story hung together pretty well, she thought. Mainly because it was the truth. Or most of the truth, anyway.

And Jeff seemed convinced. His shoulders relaxed suddenly, and the grim line of his mouth broke up. "Yeah, you never did look too far ahead, did you? I can see that this afternoon could have been pretty rough, when I think about it. Is that why you work with the kids at camp?"

Damn his insight. "I guess so. I never thought about it quite like that before. Are you going to eat your dinner?"

With her hunger well-advertised, Mickey couldn't afford not to eat. She managed half of the platter by the time Jeff had finished. While he went to the rest room, she had what remained of the food taken away. She'd even paid the bill paid before he came back.

He lifted an eyebrow in question as she signed the slip.

"I owe you one," she reminded him. "For old times' sake."

"Sure."

The ride to pick up his truck went smoothly, despite Denver's rush-hour traffic. They talked—chatted, really—about the area and the weather and the ride Jeff had ahead of him. When she pulled up beside the Suburban, they sat for a moment in the quiet.

Then Jeff turned in the seat and took her hand off the wheel to cradle it between his palms. The friction of his callused skin against hers ignited a slow burn deep in her chest.

"We lost a lot, Mickey." His voice was low, obviously restrained. "There's no doubt about that."

"I'm sorry," she whispered as tears stung her eyes. Had she ever said that before?

"Me, too." He lifted his gaze from their joined fingers to her face. The pain in his eyes seared her soul. How much worse would he feel if he knew it all?

His hands tightened painfully around hers. Mickey bit her lip to hold back a gasp.

And then he let go and reached for the door handle. "I'll call you sometime next week," he said, stepping down from the truck. "I expect to have pretty much everything lined up by then."

She blinked, at a loss, and then caught up. "Good. If we have any problems, we'll let you know. Thanks for coming today. Having you here made a difference."

"I was glad to help out. Take care." With a two-fingered salute, he swung himself into the Suburban and drove out of the parking lot.

Mickey followed more slowly. She held back every thought, every impulse, until she'd bolted the door of the motel room behind her. Still not daring to think, she slipped off her jacket and hung it over the chair, then unfastened the skirt and laid it on the table. Linen wrinkled so easily, and she hated ironing. Always had.

Finally, with nothing else to do, she sat down on the bed in her slip and blouse, wondering how to keep from breaking into little pieces. An answer occurred to her, one she fought as long as she could. Wasn't it too late for this? After ten years of self-imposed exile, what right did she have to expect anyone's help with her problems?

None. But she picked up the phone anyway, and dialed the California number from memory. Her mother answered on the first ring.

"Hi, Mom. It's me."

"Mickey, sweetheart, how are you? *Where* are you?"

She eased her legs up onto the bed and leaned back against a pillow. "I'm in Denver."

"On a Monday? Are you finishing up after a show?"

"No show this time. I had a meeting." She explained about the Camp Crazy Woman Rodeo. "We were looking to hook some sponsors, and I'm pretty sure we succeeded."

"You always could talk your way around a room, Mickey. It took every ounce of your dad's will to hold out against you sometimes. And I know I probably gave in too often."

Mickey closed her eyes and smiled. "Funny, Mom, it didn't feel like that to me."

"It never does, sweetheart." Laughter threaded

through the bright voice. She paused, and then said, "I talked to Jeff a few weeks ago."

"I know. He told me."

Another pause. "And Roberta Fender called me last week."

"Will wonders never cease?"

"She said you'd been staying in Jeff's house." After three daughters, Ruth York didn't have to change her tone to imply a question.

"For a few days, that's all. I took a bad spill and he made me come home from the hospital to his house, to get some real rest. I'm back at work now."

"You won't be seeing him again?"

It won't make any difference either way, the damage is already done. Mickey sighed. "As a matter of fact, he's handling the stock arrangements for the rodeo. He was down here today for the sponsor meeting. I imagine we'll be running into each other every so often now that I've moved back. Wyoming's a big place, but there aren't all that many people to fill it up."

"He was always there to help you out, wasn't he?"

Oh, damn. "Yeah, he always was."

"Well, he invited me up to see him, when we talked, and I told him I'd think about it. Maybe I'll come for your rodeo. I'd love to see you again, and your camp and your kids. What did you say the date was?"

"The third Friday in August." She listened with half a brain to her mom's tentative plans while the other half wondered *one more time* why she'd ever thought she had to run away. This comfort, this acceptance, was part of what she'd lost. Jeff's trust, her family's support…and, of course, a baby's life. She'd thrown it all away.

Good job, cowgirl.

"That sounds like it might work," her mother was saying as Mickey came back to the present. "I'll leave a message on your answering machine at home when I know more. I'm so glad you called, sweetheart, I've been wanting a chance to get away and this sounds like a perfect vacation."

"Mom?" She could tell the truth now, though. Her mother had lost a baby, the only boy. She would know the heartache and understand. What a blessing it would be to share the burden...

"Yes, Mickey?"

She dragged in a deep gulp of air. "I'm sorry."

"Sorry for what, sweetheart?"

"I—" Mickey blew out the same breath. She couldn't do this. Couldn't possibly lay an extra sorrow on her mother's shoulders. "I—I don't think I apologized, not really. I just wanted you to know that I realize how wrong I was to run away, to...to wait so long to let you know where I was. I'm really sorry I put you and Daddy...and Jeff...through all of that."

"Oh, Mickey." The tenderness in her mom's voice soothed like a warm hand resting on her hair. "We all knew that, sweetheart. But it's good to hear you say it. Thanks."

Tears gathered behind her closed eyelids. She blinked them back so she could end the call calmly. "Thank *you*, Mom. I'm looking forward to seeing you in August. Take care, okay?"

"You too, sweetheart. Give Jeff my love."

"Bye."

She replaced the receiver carefully as scalding tears leaked onto her cheeks.

Forgiveness hurt like hell.

Mickey curled into a ball in the middle of the bed, hiding her face in her hands. And then, safe from prying eyes, she let misery take her down.

CHAPTER TEN

MICKEY WAS STILL struggling to climb out of her despair when she got back to camp the next afternoon. She parked behind the barn, hoping for a few minutes alone with Clem and Thunder, a chance to ground herself in the animals and absorb their unconditional support.

But as soon as she opened the door, before she got both feet on the ground, she heard the war cry.

"Mickeymickeymickeymickeymickeeeeee...!"

It's showtime! "Karenkarenkaren!" Then thin arms came hard around her waist while the cap-covered head burrowed into her ribs.

"I'm so glad you're back." Karen squeezed tighter, then looked up. "Can I ride now?"

"Whoa, there!" Mickey put her hands on the girl's shoulders and pushed her far enough away to look into her eyes. "Where's everybody else this afternoon?"

"They're all swimming. But Laurie said you'd be back and so I waited for you and now you're here. Can I ride Clementine?"

"But, Karen...are you sure you're ready?"

Karen nodded. "My daddy took me to a carnival this weekend, and they had pony rides and I did it! Four times! And now I'm ready to ride a big horse. Can I? Can I?"

Confidence was all well and good, Mickey thought,

staring at Karen's shining face. But sitting on a pony walking a circle at a carnival was a long way, literally, from the view atop the back of a full-size horse. Karen had never come close to Clem outside the stall. She wasn't thinking, right this minute, about the size difference.

Still, such enthusiasm could take her over that hurdle, if she let it. "Sure," Mickey responded to the pleading in the gray eyes. "Let's see how Clem's feeling today."

Karen danced ahead of her into the barn. At the clunk of Mickey's heels on the ground, the horses poked their noses over their gates as if they'd missed her, too, and she took the time to pet each one. Clementine snorted softly into her hand, looking for carrots. "Sorry, sweetheart, I didn't bring anything with me this afternoon." Love was so easy, with horses...

An impatient hand tugged at her shirt. "Come *on,* Mickey. Let's ride!"

Mickey pulled in a deep breath. "Settle down a touch, Karen. We need to do this slowly, for you and for Clem. She's been sick, remember?" No one had ridden Clementine since Jeff had treated her three weeks ago, but her knee looked good and Karen's light weight wouldn't pose a real risk. "Let me get a bridle and bring her out of the stall."

When the gate swung back and Clementine stepped out, Karen lost some of her enthusiasm, just as Mickey had expected. "Gee...she's big, isn't she?"

"Isn't it great that such a big animal can be so gentle? Remember how she takes the carrot from your hand?" Karen nodded, but looked less convinced. Mickey smiled. "Let's go outside... You first, okay?"

With undisguised relief, Karen turned to skip down the aisle and into the sunshine. Mickey followed, lead-

ing Clementine and watching the animal's gait for signs
of lameness. But Jeff had done a good job, as usual—
the horse moved easily and eagerly outside. Mickey tied
her to a post on the opposite side of the corral from
Karen, then went back in for the saddle and blanket.
When she came out again, Karen was standing in the
same spot, looking even less certain.

"You know where the helmets are, Karen?" The girl
nodded, saying nothing, her eyes fixed on Clementine's
swishing tail. "Go find one that fits you nice and snug
while I saddle this lady for you."

Giving Karen every opportunity to change her mind
in private, Mickey turned away, set the saddle on the
fence, and pulled the blanket off her shoulder to drape
over Clem's back. She heard the thud of sneakers as
Karen ran through the barn, a pause, and more footsteps,
slower this time, as she came back. The girl was scared
to death...and determined to do this anyway.

Mickey tightened the girth and gave the cinch a final
tug. She walked around behind Clementine to see Karen
standing at the door to the barn. "Are you sure?"

The girl hesitated, standing as still as a statue, her
face pale in the shadow of the helmet brim, her gaze
focused inward. Then she swallowed. "Yeah," she
said, taking a step forward, and then another. "I'm
sure!"

"Okay." When Karen came close, Mickey held out
her hand. She wasn't surprised to feel the girl's fingers
cold and trembling. "I'm going to lift you from behind," she explained, drawing Karen closer. "I want
you to grab the saddle horn, lean forward and throw
your right leg over. Got that?"

The white helmet nodded.

"Good." Mickey drew Karen up to Clementine's

side, stepped behind her and set her hands on the narrow waist, praying that the first mount would go smoothly. She didn't know if Karen had enough stamina to try twice.

She cleared her throat. "Ready?" Karen managed another nod. "One...two...three!"

It was as easy as lifting a feather pillow. Karen floated up and over, her small hands reaching... reaching...catching at the saddle horn. She flung her leg out straight, knocked Mickey's hat off, then threw her foot across the saddle to Clem's other side. Another second of wobble and she was seated firmly in the saddle.

Mickey looked up, grinning, into a face green with excitement...or was it simply fright? "Okay?"

"Okay," the girl whispered.

"Hold on to the horn. I'm going to adjust the stirrups." She kept a hand on Karen's thigh, for reassurance, and checked the length of the strap. Thank goodness she'd guessed right. "Let's put your foot in here. Good. Now, I'm going around to the other side..."

There was no way she could keep touch with Karen as she changed sides, but she went in front of Clementine, ducking under the horse's head so Karen could see her without moving. Clem sidled just a bit, more of a shift in weight than anything else, as Mickey came up on the other side. "Here I am."

She closed her hand on Karen's calf, with a mental wince at the difference in feel between the solid muscle on this side and the prosthesis that replaced the left leg. Shaking her head, she eased the right shoe into the stirrup. "There you go. Now you want to take hold of the reins."

But instead of loosening, the girl's knuckles whitened on the saddle horn. "I can't." She swallowed. "I'll fall off." And then, as Mickey looked up, she said, "I want to get down. Now."

"Karen..." Panic blazed in the round eyes. A single tear materialized and wandered across Karen's pale cheek. Mickey knew it would be cruel to force her any further. "I'll help you down." Stepping in, she held out her arms. "Lean over, sweetheart. I'll catch you."

The light weight came down in a tangle of arms and legs. Then, without a word and before Mickey could say anything, Karen jerked out of her hold. Sliding sideways on hands and knees under the corral fence, she stumbled to her feet, scurried down the dry grass on the hillside and headed across the clearing toward the cabins. After a minute, the slam of a screen door echoed across the silent sky.

Mickey propped an elbow on Clementine's back and covered her stinging eyes with her hand. Her chest ached with sadness for Karen. They still had time this summer, though, to conquer the fear. Mickey wouldn't let Karen down, and she wouldn't let her quit.

That girl *would* ride in the Camp Crazy Woman Rodeo.

And she'd love it!

IT DIDN'T SEEM to make a difference how long it had been since he'd seen her, Jeff realized. Ten years...two weeks...watching Mickey was a spectator sport that never bored him.

He could have stood there all day in the shade of the camp barn, watching her put up a fence. Kneeling on the ground, positioning a post, her concentration was total. She hadn't seen him arrive, so he took the chance to study her as she worked. She wore a red tank top for coolness in the dusty heat of the afternoon, but sweat glistened on the well-defined muscles of her brown arms, in the curve of her throat and the valley between her breasts. His body tensed at the sight, and he knew he'd better calm things down while he still could.

"Hey, Mickey."

She turned her head quickly at the sound of his voice. "Jeff! What in the world are you doing up here?" Hands on her knees, she pushed herself to her feet and came toward him. "You're just about the last person I was looking for on a Saturday afternoon."

Stripping off her work glove, she extended a hand and he took it, trying to feel friendly, feeling just about everything else. Holding her hand recalled those few minutes in her truck in Denver and the strength of the connection he'd felt with her then. The potential of that link had monopolized his mind more over the last few days than he cared to admit.

He wrenched his thoughts back to the present. "I got your message about calling you here this weekend to talk over the rodeo. Since I had the day free, I decided to head up and compare notes. We've got just under four weeks to get this show together."

She grinned, and stepped past him into the shade of the barn. "Don't I know it. But I do believe everything's working out."

He settled next to her on a bale of straw. "You straightened out the mess with the fairground in Sheridan?"

A long swig from the water bottle on a nearby crate delayed her answer. "Yeah. They thought we wanted the whole weekend, and they had Sunday booked. One Friday night was no problem."

"You've got a full roster of riders?"

"You bet! I'm having men and women's bull riding, bareback and saddle broncs. I've already got a commitment from a couple of the leading cowboys, and the top three women in all three events—"

"Including you, I assume."

"Of course."

"Do these cowboys know the women will be riding rough stock, too?"

"I've told them. Separate events, on the same program. Nobody does it that way on the professional circuits, but I've always hoped we could change that someday. Maybe this'll be a start. And the kids from the camp are gonna try barrel racing."

"How about the little girl I met—Karen, right? Is she learning to ride?"

Her shoulders, golden brown with a delicate spray of freckles, lifted in a sigh. "Not yet. We ran into a snag, I let her try too soon. I got her up on Clementine, but she was spooked, and I haven't been able to get her to try again."

"That's too bad. She wanted it so much."

"I know." In Mickey's whisper, he got a sense of how much the girl's fear bothered her. But then she straightened up and shook it off. "Anyway, Laurie did get the insurance companies to extend our coverage until after the show, so we can get through the summer, anyway. If we make enough money, next year will be set, too."

"Is the show insured?"

She nodded. "Between the individual riders and the fairground itself, we're pretty much covered."

"If it was that easy to begin with, this whole shebang wouldn't have happened."

"I think that would be a shame."

"Yeah."

A comfortable silence fell between them. Jeff let his mind drift, let the soft sounds of the horses, the distant rustle of the breeze in the pines, ease him into peace. This feeling, this confidence in the ultimate goodness of the world, was what Mickey had always given him. He couldn't believe he'd lived without it for so long.

He couldn't believe he was considering trying to ask for it again.

Before he was ready, she stirred. "If I don't get up, I'm going to fall asleep. If I fall asleep, the fence won't be built and I'll get in trouble. Guess I'd better go back to work."

Jeff watched her stand and carefully stretch, willing himself not to respond to the tilt of her hip and the supple length of her spine.

He focused his attention very carefully somewhere else. "Looks like you're all alone up here." That probably wasn't the best thing for him to have noticed. The possibilities...

Mickey took off her hat to mop her forehead with a bandanna. "Yeah, the kids leave on Friday and the rest of the staff takes the weekend off. I didn't have a show, so I said I'd stay to keep an eye on things."

"Could you use some help?"

He got the feeling he'd surprised her. Maybe she didn't feel quite as comfortable with this as he did. Maybe he could give her a chance to be. "I can stay and work with you awhile. It'll go faster that way."

Her white smile widened. "That would be great, if you let me give you dinner afterward."

"You're on."

They worked until the sun dropped far behind the

treetops, setting the posts for one side of the corral. Jeff discarded his shirt pretty quickly, and Mickey found herself more distracted than she wanted to admit by the smooth skin of his back, the play of muscles underneath as he lifted the heavy posts into place. His patience and good humor made the job easy, but she found herself more and more tongue-tied, failing to keep up with his light banter.

Whatever she'd said, whatever she'd thought, being friends with Jeff was proving a lot harder than she'd believed it would be.

Because what she wanted was not friendship at all.

She left him to the last post and went to wash up and start dinner. Staring into the small, crazed mirror in the staff cabin, Mickey gave in to a sarcastic laugh. "No wonder he's not thinking about anything but the job," she said. "You look like you've been dragged through a bush backward." Her hair was escaping in wisps all around her flushed and sunburned face, she was sweaty and dusty and tired. Not an image to inspire passionate thoughts in anybody's brain.

"Which is good," she reminded herself, changing into a shirt with sleeves and wiping her face and hands without doing much about the rest of the mess. "It'll make this easier if only one of us has to deal with lust."

On the way to the kitchen, she decided on a portable dinner. Tucking last night's leftover steak between thick slices of bread, she added a bag of chips, a box of cookies and a pair of apples, and packed the feast into her backpack. Grabbing a couple of canned drinks, she walked out to find Jeff stacking the tools in the barn.

"Good job, cowboy! Where'd you get to be so handy with a fence?"

He grinned as he shrugged into his shirt. "Some nice

rancher with a passel of daughters taught me all I needed to know. Guess he wanted to keep me away from those girls.''

The ploy hadn't worked. But Mickey didn't want to think about it. ''Well, there's a sink behind you, there. Wash up a bit and we'll have some supper.''

He turned around as directed, but talked over his shoulder. ''Is this a walking dinner? I'm about ready to sit down, if it's all the same to you.''

Mickey waited until he'd dried his face, then led him out of the barn. ''I like to take my dates out for a nice dinner,'' she said. ''None of this stay-at-home stuff. I've got a special table reserved at a very impressive restaurant.''

He followed her through the trees, up to the top of the ridge, then along the rim of the gully to where it widened as it joined Crazy Woman Canyon. With the air of a hostess seating a valued guest, she placed the knapsack on her table rock and flung out an arm. ''Voila!''

The tumbling, pouring sound of the water far below played like a musical theme, counterpointed by the wind stirring the trees, the evening song of insects and the homing calls of birds finding their rest. Jeff took a sandwich and settled his back against the rock. ''What a setting! I'd be here all the time.''

Mickey settled beside him, not touching, but not too far away to seem obvious. ''Whenever I get the chance. Some nights, after a really hectic day, I come up here to recharge. It's like magic—my own personal energy source.''

He turned his head and she met his gaze, warmed by the understanding she saw there. ''Thanks for sharing it with me, Mickey.''

She wanted to deny that she'd done anything special, to put the conversation back on a lighter footing, but she owed him more than that. So she just nodded and ducked her head to eat her sandwich.

The stars came out as they ate. The sky darkened slowly from blue to azure to indigo, and then the crystal lights appeared, one by one, as she and Jeff talked easily of whatever came to mind. It was the most healing, most restful conversation she'd known for a long ten years. Mickey savored it, treasuring the chance to feel this way with him again.

Full darkness crept up before they thought to stir. They'd been sitting in silence for a while, heads tilted back against the big rock as the night surrounded them. But a sudden bite to the breeze made Mickey aware of how much time must have passed.

"You're going to have a long drive on a dark road," she commented gently. "I shouldn't have kept you so late."

"No problem. I'm too comfortable to move." He shook his head slowly, sleepily, from side to side, and kept his eyes closed.

Now that she thought of it, the idea of Jeff driving late into the night on the mountain's twists and turns started to nag at her. Mickey sat up and tugged on his sleeve.

"Come on, Jeff. I think you should be leaving, or it'll be after midnight before you get home. I don't want your death on my conscience."

Casually, easily, he resisted her pull. Instead of getting up, he flung his arm out to the side and dragged her down beside him, holding her firmly when she tried to wriggle free.

"Sit down and be quiet," he ordered, still without opening his eyes.

She subsided against him, biding her time until she could catch him unaware, shake him up a bit. He really needed to get on the road...his safety was at stake...he owed it to himself...

He was so warm.

Heat radiated from his body and it raised her own temperature. Behind her head his arm was solid, relaxed, a perfect support. Under her cheek his heart beat steadily, measuring the infinite night with its regular pulse. His chest lifted on a breath, and then another.

Mickey brought her hand up to rest over his ribs, a move so natural, so instinctive, she hadn't realized she'd done it until she felt a break in that regular rhythm. And then an odd, violent slam as it resumed its usual pace.

She had literally stopped his heart, just by touching him.

Holding her breath, she let her hand glide, not far, just a short way across the front of his shirt, the muscles of his chest. Immediately the rhythm under her ear changed, became faster, less even. Her fingertip brushed his nipple, brushed again. This time his breath came as a gasp and his heart slammed into even higher gear. She felt tension in the set of his hip against her thigh.

Playing with fire, they called it. A compulsion as strong as any she'd ever known. Jeff was here, under her hands. She loved him, always had, and she couldn't be this close without touching him. Without tasting him. Mickey lifted her head, tilted her face to the moonlight, then blocked the brightness with the shadow of Jeff's head as she pressed her lips to his throat.

His whole body shuddered in response; his hand

tightened on her shoulder. She had the feeling she couldn't have broken away from him now if she'd tried.

Otherwise, he didn't move. She didn't want him to. His pulse beat against her mouth, against her tongue. He tasted of musk, of sweat and dust, of work. He tasted like Jeff, a memory she hadn't realized she still held until it came to her. She'd hungered ten years for just this taste.

Turning her body closely into his, Mickey sought more. The line of his jaw, the arch of his cheek, the hollow of his temple and the fair hair drifting there. A curving ear, and the realization that one of them had started trembling. She didn't know who. Didn't care.

Another turn, a lift, and she was astride his hips. Moonlight played over his face but left his eyes black, without even their usual glint. His hands had come to rest at her waist, and she knew the trembling was his, until she looked at her hands raking through his hair and saw that they shook, as well.

She brought her gaze back to Jeff's, waited for him to say something. But he only returned the look, with a serious cast to his countenance that defied interpretation. His mouth, with its full lower lip and well-remembered texture, drew her eyes. Bending, she met his lips with her own.

His lack of response stopped. He took the energy of her kiss and returned it, amplified a thousand times. Then Mickey lost track of his reactions, because her own were too consuming, too shattering to ignore.

"Hell, woman, you're burning me up." His words were a rush of breath against her cheek.

"I know." She whispered into his ear as he dragged her shirt out of her jeans.

"This isn't supposed to happen. We weren't going to

do this." He muttered it against her throat, then soothed the rasp with his tongue. His hands slipped gently around her ribs, his palms captured her breasts.

"I know." She arched up, fumbled with buttons and flannel. Her shirt fell open, then his.

"We're not going to stop."

Mickey placed her palms on his bare chest, felt his heart hammer against the heel of her hand. "I know."

He sealed the agreement with a kiss. A soft kiss of promise on her lips, a flutter of tenderness across her eyelids. Then the sweet, wet warmth of his tongue dragged along the column of her throat.

A surge of sensation took Mickey under, a flood of love and longing she had no chance of—no interest in—diverting. Here at the edge of the earth, under a blanket of stars, the only demands she would consider were Jeff's. What he wanted, what she could give him...those were the boundaries of the world.

"Talk to me, Jeff. I need to hear..."

The whisper sent a shiver along his spine. Jeff wasn't sure there was enough of his brain left functioning to form words, but what Mickey wanted tonight, Mickey would get from him. Only him.

He breathed in her warm scent from the valley between her breasts. "I want you. I need to taste you, drink you in..."

She trembled as he suited action to words, roughly exploring her soft skin with his mouth. Her arms wound over his shoulders, her hands cradled his head.

He lifted his face, claimed her mouth again with erotic, symbolic intent, making promises he definitely intended to keep. She opened for him, surrendered completely, and her humility almost distracted him from the laces on her boots.

Only seconds later, he had reached the limit. "Stand up," he commanded hoarsely.

Without hesitation, she did as she was told. He hooked his fingers in the waist of her jeans, kept hold as she straightened, and the denim, with the wisp of cotton underneath, slid down those long, strong legs. Legs that could hold to the back of a horse bucking like crazy underneath her. Legs that were going to do exactly the same thing for him....

His palms rode the smooth skin along the outside of her thighs as she lowered herself back around him. He watched, in a state of almost painful anticipation, as she worked on his belt, the button and zipper of his jeans. When she tugged, he lifted his hips to let her slide the fabric between them away.

And then it was skin against skin. The incredible silk of her bottom, resting on his legs. The warmth of her palms on his hipbones. The glimmer of tears on her cheeks as Mickey lifted her face to meet his stare.

"Jeff, I—"

"It's time, lover. More than time." He skimmed her waist with his fingers, pressed his palms against her lower back. She lifted in response to his pull, came closer, close enough, took him in her hand, then slowly...slowly...slowly sank down.

His breath left him in a long sigh. He had no thought, no feeling except a sense of infinite peace. Mickey curled to put her forehead on his breastbone, her hands at his waist. They had never been closer in their lives.

Jeff tilted his hips, rocking into her, and she responded immediately, tightening her knees and thighs. Again; this time she lifted her head, leaned forward to bring them closer, to draw him deeper. The clasp of her body around his drove the last shred of sanity from his brain.

His control disappeared at the same time. She felt too good, it had been too long. But he wanted to give her the ride of her life, more than six seconds of fury on some stupid horse, a lifetime's worth of excitement and danger and ecstasy in a few blessed minutes. He grabbed her bottom, pulling her down harder against him, grinding his hips up into hers. Not with anyone, and never with Mickey, had he felt such fierceness, such an edge of pure fury in love.

Jeff was angry. Mickey felt the violence in his shoulders as she held on, in the grip of his fingers on her skin and the hard thrust of his hips.

Well, he deserved it. He deserved every ounce of fury he felt and she would let him rage unchecked, would meet his force with her own. The explosion, when it came, would liberate them both.

CHAPTER ELEVEN

THE EXPLOSION, when it came, startled the forest around them into stillness.

They stumbled back to camp in a sort of trance, on legs weakened by passion and release. Desire nearly ambushed them again as they leaned against a tree, hands hungry and mouths fused, until a threatening rustle in the brush nearby suggested retreat.

Mickey groaned and pulled back. "Wouldn't this be better in bed?"

Jeff only let her go so far. Holding her close against his side, he resumed their forward progress.

"It couldn't get any better," he murmured against her temple. "Just more comfortable."

But then he set one foot inside the staff quarters and stopped in his tracks. "A single bed? A single *bunk* bed? You've got to be kidding!"

Laughing softly, Mickey pushed him into the moon-silvered cabin. "Take it or leave it, cowboy. That's all there is."

Pivoting quickly, he captured her hands and drew her with him as he backed across the floor. When he ducked and dropped to the bunk, a tug pulled her down across his chest. "I'm taking," he murmured, letting go of her hands to cup the back of her head and draw her close. "As long as you come with it."

She smiled against his mouth. "Count on that."

Jeff's shirt hadn't been rebuttoned, and now she skimmed it completely off his shoulders, wanting his skin under her palms, against her cheek, beneath her lips. Wanting as much of him as she could have, for as long as it lasted.

We're not thinking straight.

The warning flashed through her mind as Jeff pushed her back so he could drag her shirt over her head. They'd gone into this against all the rules they'd made, against plain common sense. Hell, she hadn't even remembered birth control until it was far too late. Mickey tried some vague calculations, made even hazier by the blaze of fire Jeff trailed across her hip as he eased off her jeans, and decided the slight risk was worth it. Lightning never struck the same place twice.

And then his tongue touched her, and she stopped thinking altogether. Only feeling was left as he took her soaring.

She came back to earth needing him still. "Jeff," she pleaded, pulling him up to look into his eyes.

"Want something, Mickey?"

She propped herself on one elbow. "There's a wicked gleam in your eye, Buchanan. What's up?"

Untangling their fingers, Jeff brought her hand into the heat where their bodies met. "Me, for starters. Can we do something about that?"

Her smile widened slowly, sensually, as her hand began to play. It was all the answer he needed.

Games. The games they came up with in that bare, chilly cabin, with only the moon for light, took them down a path they'd never traveled in the past. Jeff tried to remember, in the scattered moments when his thoughts cleared, if he and Mickey had ever allowed themselves such a bawdy, rowdy time in bed.

He came to the conclusion that they hadn't.

Oh, it had been good, he recalled during a brief respite while Mickey slept lightly in his arms. No other woman had ever taken him as far as this one could. He supposed that was one reason he'd never married any of them. A lifetime of settling for second best just didn't offer much hope for happiness.

But so intense. So serious. Maybe because they'd fallen in love as kids, because they were the first—the only—for each other, they'd taken loving more seriously than anything else in their lives.

And that could have been his fault, Jeff realized as Mickey stirred and, waking, let her fingers tickle along his ribs. Maybe he'd been so filled with a sense of responsibility, so convinced of his role as her mentor and defender, that he forgot to let laughter into their bed. Ten years had made a real difference...

In all ways except one. He still loved her.

He'd run away from the idea during the week Mickey had lived with him, ignored it that afternoon in Denver, brooded over it in the days just past. But as Jeff slid inside her again and saw her eyes widen and soften as their bodies fused, he knew it for the truth.

For him, for always, loving meant Mickey York. His life had never worked right without her; his home didn't have a heart without her there.

But he was sure Mickey wouldn't want to know that. So before he could confess his feelings, before she had to think up a way to answer that wouldn't hurt, he caught her mouth with his and let her take him on the ride of his life.

SUNLIGHT CRASHED across her face. Mickey woke up.

Her first reaction was relief. *He hasn't left yet*. Jeff

still surrounded her, curled around her back as she lay on her side facing the door of the cabin. By squinting she could read his watch on the wrist dangling over her shoulder. Almost eleven-thirty.

After a night like that, she thought with a mental smile, *we deserve to sleep late.*

But they couldn't stay where they were much longer. The camp staff always trickled back early Sunday afternoon to get ready for the campers coming in Monday morning. Unless she wanted to advertise last night's events, some reasonably quick rearrangements would have to take place.

Jeff's exhaustion could be measured by how easy it was to get up without waking him. He barely moved when she pulled the blanket over his shoulder, and only sighed when she stooped to brush his hair back from his eyes. Looking at him lying there in her bunk, all lean lines and bare skin and wicked impulses, made Mickey want to crawl in and start all over again.

No. Better not.

She took a shower, instead, alone. Only when she'd dressed completely and braided her hair did she dare come back to rouse Jeff.

"Wake up, Doc." She flicked his hip with the towel. He groaned, rolled to his stomach and buried his face in the pillow. "Come on, lazy. We've got another thirty posts to set today."

His head rocked slowly from side to side.

"We missed breakfast. Want some lunch?"

Another shake.

"Want me to send Laurie to get you when she arrives? That should give you maybe another twenty minutes to sleep."

One brown eye emerged from the pillow. "No."

"Yeah. She usually shows up about noon."

Cotton-covered foam muffled his reply, but Mickey could guess. "I left you some hot water. Make up the bed before you come out."

The next response wasn't muffled at all.

By the time Laurie showed up, a little later than Mickey promised, Jeff had settled at a picnic table with a tuna sandwich and chips. Mickey set down their drinks and seated herself across from him as Laurie strolled over.

"This looks nice," the director commented. "Social occasion or business lunch?"

Thankful for the bite in her mouth, Mickey held her breath until Jeff said, "Business, mostly. I came to see how the show is shaping up."

Without a blink Laurie launched into a description of her end of the arrangements, and soon she and Jeff were brainstorming on the final details. Trying to pay attention took more willpower than Mickey liked. She only hoped her tendency to lose track didn't show.

Other staff members started arriving at about two and soon drew Laurie's attention to more immediate camp concerns. As she bustled off, Jeff drew a deep breath. "Whew! She's hard to keep up with."

"Tell me about it." Mickey turned from watching Laurie disappear to find Jeff's waiting grin. "I told her once, when we first met, that she would make a great drill sergeant. Laurie said, and I quote, 'Been there, done that, got the T-shirt.' That's when I found out she'd spent eight years in the army. And she has a whole drawerful of olive-drab T-shirts."

Chuckling, he stretched to his feet. "I believe you. If she ever needs another job, tell her she can come run my practice."

After a few seconds his grin eased away, but he didn't shift his gaze. Mickey saw awareness come into his eyes, saw the whole incredible night play through his mind just as it had been playing through hers. Her breath caught. If she hadn't been sitting down, her shaky knees would have dropped her on her tail in the dust.

"Guess I'd better head back down the mountain," he said finally. "You probably have a million things to do."

"Um, yeah." But only one thing she really *wanted* to do.

"Can you get my hat? I left it in the cabin."

"Oh…sure."

Not just in the cabin. Perched atop her neatly made bunk, the gray Stetson practically crowed conquest. Mickey snatched it with a snort of exasperation and, for good measure, rumpled the covers so the bed would look normal. Her cabin mates would never believe she knew how to make hospital corners.

She caught up with Jeff as he strolled toward the barn and slammed the hat onto his head. "Of all the conceited, arrogant fools—" she muttered at him over his shoulder. "What are you trying to prove, anyway?"

He fished for his keys, reached the Suburban and opened the door without answering. A wave of heat blasted out of the truck and he took a step backward, almost on top of her. Mickey yelped. Jeff turned and caught her shoulders, then leaned back against the side of the vehicle, drawing her with him. She tried to pull away, but he refused to let go.

"Nobody's here, Mickey. Relax."

She stood still, but refused to relax. He didn't know how hard it was to stay separate, how tempted she was by the brace of his legs outside hers, the pull of worn denim across his hips and the strength she could feel in his hands.

How tempted…and how terrified.

"I'm not trying to prove much," he said in a low voice. "Just that last night wasn't a mistake, or a spur-of-the-moment fling. It meant something, Mickey. Something important."

Mickey couldn't say a word. A lie wouldn't work. Jeff always knew when she lied. But if she agreed, if she let him know how completely she loved him, how empty her life had been without him, she would have to say it all. Tell him about the baby, about the deepest and most dreadful of all her secrets. Break his heart, the way hers had been broken for the past ten years.

He read her silence for what it was. His knuckle lifted her chin, and the tears on her cheeks dripped over his hand.

"Mickey." Tenderness blended with frustration in his sigh.

Bending his head, he touched her mouth with his, quickly, softly. Closing her eyes, Mickey accepted the farewell without response. She was afraid to do anything else.

But he didn't pull away. His lips hovered over hers and then came back, firmer, more intent. On the instant, passion thundered between them as Jeff's arms swept her up against his chest and his hands caught in her hair. Mickey clutched at his shoulders, yielded her mouth and body with an abandon she couldn't control. If he wanted to take her there, she would let him.

An approaching car rumbled up the driveway. Jeff dropped his hands and let her step back. He drew in air as if to say something, but then just shook his head, pulled his hat down over his eyes and climbed up on the seat. She didn't even get a wave before he'd vanished.

Mickey waited a long time for sleep to claim her that night.

SLEEP BECAME more and more elusive during the next couple of weeks as the pace of arrangements for the show picked up. She spent her waking hours dealing with those, the kids, the camp and her usual rides. At night, she lay down in her bunk exhausted, only to find memories of Jeff stirring her mind and body to wakefulness. All the determined planning in the world couldn't help her evade the remembered heat of that night.

The situation got dangerous when she found herself falling asleep behind the wheel on the way to a show in Montana. She jerked her head up just in time to avoid a signpost, then came to a shuddering stop on the side of the road. Even a dose of adrenaline from the close call couldn't keep her awake. She opened her eyes an hour later.

At least the nap had given her the spark to finish the drive. She made Montana, made her ride and came in second. Not what she wanted, but the money paid for the trip.

There was nobody waiting for her when she pulled in on Monday morning after the long, tedious drive home. Not Jeff, of course. And not Karen, who hadn't been near the barn—or her—since the disaster with Clementine. Mickey walked stiffly through camp, saying hello to the kids at their various activities without seeing Karen among them. She'd just started to worry, when she caught sight of a lone figure leaning against the

fence around the pool, staring at the dust she was kicking up with her toe.

"Hi." As she came up, Karen half turned, keeping
her face down. Maintaining a few feet between them,
Mickey leaned against the fence, too. "What's going
on?" she asked the back of Karen's head.

In the long silence, she could hear the other kids
laughing in the distance. "Nothing," Karen said finally,
still stirring dust clouds up to her knees.

Mickey let some more time go by. "Clementine's
been missing you. She liked those carrots."

The girl in front of her just shrugged.

"And I liked it when you came to the barn to talk to
me while I worked." She hadn't planned to say that,
but she knew it was true. On a deep breath, she said
the rest. "I miss you, too, Karen."

Karen went completely still, for so long that Mickey
would have sworn she could hear the dust settling back
to the ground. She took a chance and took the two
strides between them, put her hand on Karen's shoulder.
Then she felt the trembling. And she heard the first big
sniff.

Mickey blinked against her own tears. "Karen,
sweetheart, you don't have to cry. It's okay."

"No, it's not." Another big sniff. "I...couldn't do
it. I can't."

"You tried, Karen. That's all that counts."

"I don't believe you!" She threw back her head, and
her cap came off. In the weeks since she'd come to
camp, her hair had grown in about an inch. It was soft
and shiny, the color of a new penny. "How can you
like me when I can't ride?"

Using both hands, Mickey turned her around.

"Whether or not you ride doesn't have anything to do with our friendship. Don't you know that?"

"But you're so brave." Karen lifted her pinched, splotchy, tear-streaked face. Her nose was running; she sniffed again. "There isn't anything you can't do. And I—I...I'm a coward."

Mickey stared at the girl, but it wasn't Karen's face she saw. *Jeff...*

The thin shoulders shifted under her hands. With a shake of her head, Mickey cleared her thoughts, then went down on one knee so that she was the one looking up. "I'm afraid, too, you know."

Short hair danced in the sunlight as Karen shook her head.

Mickey nodded. "Sure. I'm afraid of different things, that's all. Grown-up things. Everybody has fears, Karen. Your mom and dad, everybody. You can let those fears rule your life, if you choose." *Like I have, for ten long years.* She swallowed hard. "Or you can resist them and be a winner. That doesn't happen overnight. Winning takes time. But you're strong, and you could do it. If you really wanted to."

The stubbornness that helped Karen fight cancer wouldn't allow her to give in right away. Shaking her head, she pulled back, out of Mickey's hold. "Maybe." She whispered it again. "Maybe."

And then she was gone, running lightly back toward the camp, toward her friends. Or just away.

Mickey propped her elbow on her bent knee and rested her head in her hand for a minute, wondering if she had the energy to get to her feet. Wondering even more how in hell she could give such great advice...and yet be completely incapable of following it herself.

The question was doomed to go unanswered, as the

demands of camp life kept her hopping. If she were honest, she'd admit that she welcomed the activity, welcomed the chance not to think. Thinking only led her back to Jeff, to the past they'd shared and, from there, to the past he didn't know about.

Driving up to Idaho for a show, though, she decided he *had* to know. If Karen could be brave, so could she.

And then she pictured telling him, visualized the pain in his eyes, the shock in his face, the agony in his heart.

How could she do that to Jeff? As much as she'd already hurt him, Mickey knew she couldn't bring herself to deliver such news. Not in cold blood, as if it didn't matter. He didn't deserve this kind of pain. Driving sightless across the plains, fisting tears off her cheeks, she vowed to protect him from that ultimate wound.

And then wondered, for the thousandth time, if that wasn't just another selfish excuse.

Too exhausted even to argue with herself anymore, she drove into camp late Sunday afternoon two weeks before the Crazy Woman Rodeo, with about ten dollars in change left over from what she'd won in Idaho Saturday night. The buzz of the printer in the office caught her ear, so she stopped in to say hello to Laurie.

The boss looked up from her paper-blanketed desk. "You look good," she commented. "Get run over by a semi-truck? Or just a raging horse?"

"Neither." Mickey dropped into her usual chair and propped her boots on a box of printer paper. "I'm worn out. Thank heavens we've got less than two weeks to go on this show. And on the camp. I'm planning to hide out at my place for about a month afterward, just sleeping."

She meant it as a joke, but Laurie wasn't laughing.

"You know, that's the first time I've ever heard anything like that from you."

"I guess I'm getting old. Happens to everybody sooner or later." That didn't work, either. When she looked up, Laurie's concerned gaze hadn't shifted. Mickey closed her eyes and rubbed them, avoiding her friend's stare.

"What would you give up if you had to?"

She kept her fingers pressed against her temples. The dizziness she'd put up with all weekend had been joined by a headache. "What kind of question is that?"

"An honest one."

"For heaven's sake!" Cornered, Mickey reared to her feet...and then braced herself against the edge of the desk as the whole world started waltzing around her head. "Ooooh, boy."

Before she finished, Laurie was beside her, and helped her sit back down again. "I'll get you a cola."

Mickey didn't have the energy to say she doubted she could keep anything down. But, to her surprise, the soft drink did seem to make her feel better. Not right. Just better.

"Thanks. I'll live." The grin she sent Laurie got no answering smile, so she closed her eyes and put the cold drink can against her forehead.

"How long have you felt like this?"

"A few days. Must be some kind of bug. If I had a day to sleep, it would probably go away."

"When was your last period?"

Opening her eyes wide, Mickey lowered the drink. "Why?"

Laurie slipped into drill-sergeant mode. "Do you know?"

Fear curled into a tight little ball in her belly.

"N-no. Not exactly. But so what? I've always been irregular."

"It pays to keep track of these things when you're involved with somebody. Intimately."

"But I'm not—" Laurie's skeptical stare halted that evasion. Mickey swore. "How did you know?"

Her friend shrugged. "I've been expecting something to happen from the first day he came up here. You two belong together, like halves of the same whole. Only a matter of time, I figured...and I'm surprised your getting together took this long."

Mickey widened her eyes, wondering at how Laurie could know so precisely. "Watching you together that Sunday," the boss explained. "The way you didn't look at each other, the way one or the other would drop out of the conversation, going about a thousand miles away and having to be called back. It didn't take too much to figure out he'd been here all night."

Mickey felt her cheeks flush. "Well—"

"But the point is," Laurie interrupted briskly, "are you pregnant?"

The word seemed to vibrate in the air, louder than all the outside noises, more commanding than the hum of the computer and the whir of the fan. Pregnant. Again. Jeff's baby.

"Mickey?"

She took a deep breath. "Maybe. We didn't—I forgot..."

"Here."

Mickey lifted her gaze to see Laurie holding out a small white box. "What?"

"I bought this on my way up today. Use it."

Thanks to the wonders of modern technology, getting the answer took them less than five minutes. Mickey walked out of the bathroom and looked at Laurie across the office. "Yes."

The drill sergeant disappeared. "Oh, sweetie. What are you going to do now?"

Staring out the window overlooking the canyon, Mickey didn't answer. Her mind was a jumble of emotions, thoughts, sensations, none of which she could begin to sort out. Tears stung her eyes. She crossed her arms on the high windowsill and put her head down, hoping to hold back the tide.

She remembered her thought during that wild night with Jeff—lightning never struck the same place twice. *Wrong again!*

Without turning, she attempted to deal with Laurie's question. "What's there to do? Like I said, we've only got a couple of weeks left until the show. If the money comes in like we hope, maybe we can hire a couple of extra people to take care of closing up here, instead of doing it all ourselves." She did a quick calculation, unclouded by passion this time. "The baby should be born in April, so I'll be back up in time for next summer."

"What about Jeff?"

A world of knowledge spoke through Laurie's tone. She was the one—the only one—who knew the truth about the past, the one confidante Mickey had trusted with her mistake. And now that Laurie knew Jeff—not as a nameless myth, but as a man—she would understand just how difficult the entire situation had become.

Straightening, Mickey drew in a deep breath and turned around. "I can't hide," she stated flatly. "He'll come looking. And I won't run away again." She managed a ghost of a laugh. "I'm too tired to think about running to the bathroom, much less out of the state. I'm really trapped this time, I guess."

"Trapped, Mickey? It's his baby...and he loves you!"

"Until he finds out, Laurie. What do you think will happen if Jeff finds out?" They both knew she wasn't talking about *this* child.

A new voice spoke through the screen. "If Jeff finds out what?" Laurie, for all her usual aplomb, gasped as the man himself opened the door.

Mickey stood frozen. *Perfect. Just perfect.* Somewhere in the universe, somebody was laughing about this.

He stepped inside the office and let the door bump his shoulders as he crossed his arms and leaned against the frame. "Hey, Laurie...Mickey. Is there something I should know about?" As he looked from one to the other, his eyebrow quirked in question. "A problem with the show?"

Her gaze locked with Jeff's, Mickey was vaguely aware of Laurie's distressed clucking, like a flushed quail, as she fluttered by and escaped out the door. He straightened up to let her pass, then leaned again, without releasing Mickey's stare. She couldn't read his eyes.

It seemed important to say something. "Hi."

"What's going on?"

Her thoughts skittered away from such an ominous question, focusing instead on the man who asked. He looked really fine, as if he'd dressed for a special occasion. New jeans in deep indigo hugged his hips and thighs. One of his dad's trophy buckles cinched his belt. The dark blue and burgundy and gold of an Indian print shirt set off his tan. He'd trimmed his hair—would it still cover his eyes the way it had when she'd spent the night combing her hands through it?

Dear heavens. "What brings you up here, Jeff? You

picked a long trip for a Sunday-afternoon drive." She eased herself down into Laurie's desk chair. Maybe if she sat, he would, too.

He didn't. "I called and Laurie said you'd be in this afternoon. So I thought I'd see if you could get away for a couple of hours for some dinner. There's an inn not too much farther up in the mountains I heard recommended. But I get the feeling I interrupted something important."

"Well, yes and no. Nothing to do with the show, exactly. That's still on track."

"So that's the no. What's the yes?" His voice had gone deep with tension.

Mickey knew then. Laurie's last statement had come through loud and clear as Jeff walked up to the office. "You heard, didn't you? I'm pregnant."

A flash of elation lit his eyes, but passed quickly. "When did you find out?"

Not the reaction she expected. "Just today. I thought I was sick with the flu or something, but Laurie had other ideas."

He slipped his hands into the pockets of his jeans. It was a tight fit. "Should I apologize?"

Temper grabbed her throat. "For what? I seduced you, as I remember."

"A man should be responsible about these things. I assumed you were on the Pill."

The idea diverted her attention. "You what? Why would you assume anything of the sort?" Mickey didn't like the answer that occurred to her. "Thanks for the character reference, Buchanan. I'm happy to have an accurate reading on your opinion of my morals."

"I know the rodeo circuit."

"And you used to know me! I would expect some

degree of confidence after all this time, some element of faith—'' She didn't want to pursue that line of reasoning. "Maybe you think this baby isn't even yours? Should we get a paternity test?''

"Hell!" Jeff cursed himself more than her. The news had made hash of his every thought and he could barely keep his feet on the ground. Crossing the floor in two strides, he took her by the shoulders and drew her to her feet. "This is stupid. Let's back up. We spent an extraordinary night together and you're carrying my child. I think that calls for some serious talk, which is what I came up here to do anyway. Can you get away?''

She hesitated and that surprised him. Sure, she might still have doubts, but even Mickey couldn't ignore what had happened between them, and what it meant. These last couple of weeks had convinced him, if he'd needed convincing, that their paths had crossed for a reason that night in the diner. They'd been offered a second chance, and he'd come up here today to accept. Nothing so corny as a ring in his pocket—he'd learned never to make assumptions about what Mickey would do or say. But a proposal on his mind, definitely. And certainty in his heart.

He might have wanted to start their new life together without the responsibility of a baby, but he didn't mind in the least. The kids would have come along soon enough anyway.

When she pulled back, though, he lost all his bearings. "Mickey? What's the problem?''

"I don't think I can leave tonight, Jeff, that's all. There's always a lot to get together before the campers come in…and with the show coming up, I'm really up to my neck in details.''

He knew she'd been working hard. Maybe he could

take some of the pressure off. "What can I do to make things easier? Can I help you line up someone else to ride?"

She turned away and drifted over to stare out the cabin door. Her mind seemed to have drifted off, too. "Someone else?"

"Yeah, I'd be glad to make some calls for you. Just give me a list."

"Why should we be short a rider?"

"You're not going to perform. We'll need someone else."

Her head snapped around; her eyes flashed with temper. "What makes you so sure? Are you running this show?"

Jeff struggled for patience. "Any sane person would understand that you don't take chances riding bareback when you're pregnant. I would have thought even you had that much sense. Go ahead, Mickey, tell me I'm wrong."

She stalked as far away from him in the small room as she could get. "I'm not stupid, Jeff. It would kill me to lose another baby. But I would be grateful if, just occasionally, you'd let me decide…"

The words died away. Her face paled; her mouth tightened.

Jeff registered the hollow under his ribs where his gut used to be, a void now filled with only the echo of his pounding pulse. He counted the beats, waiting until he felt reasonably certain he could control his voice. Then he spoke.

"*Another* baby?"

CHAPTER TWELVE

HIS VOICE CRACKED on the second word. He repeated the question. "Another baby?"

The universe froze. Cold despair poured into her chest as Mickey contemplated the avalanche her hasty temper had led her into. Her worst nightmare had just come crashing into her life.

And her instincts, once again, screamed, "Run!"

She tried. Jeff had moved out of the doorway; she gave him no warning as she bolted across the room and lurched for the screen.

But before she could get out, he clamped one hand around her trailing arm and hauled her backward. With the other he slammed the storm door shut, using such force that the cabin shuddered. Then he had both hands on her shoulders, holding her in place.

His dark eyes glittered, his fury seethed around them. "Explain."

She couldn't think, this close to him. "Let me go."

"No."

She nearly wept at his refusal. How could it all be so wrong? How could something as beautiful as a child they'd made together provoke such chaos?

"Jeff—"

His hands didn't gentle. "You were pregnant? You walked out on our wedding knowing you were carrying my child?"

"No!" She brought her hands to his chest in supplication. "Jeff, I wouldn't do that. You know I wouldn't do that!"

Nothing about him softened. "What happened?"

She dragged in some air. "It was about six weeks later…I didn't even know I was…pregnant…until the bleeding started. When I realized it wasn't just…just the usual, I went to the hospital and…and they explained."

"Why didn't you tell me?"

"What was I supposed to do, call from Denver to let you know I'd had a miscarriage? I couldn't do that!"

"True, I might have been able to find you if you'd called."

It was a low blow. Mickey jerked away and nearly fell when his hands opened. She braced herself against the desk behind her. "Don't do this, Jeff. We can talk—"

"Can we?" Stabbing his hands back into his pockets, he tilted his head. She'd never seen his face with less color. "Just when were you planning to talk about this, Mickey? It's been almost two months since I ran into you at Emmitt's. It's been ten damned years since this happened. What's your time frame for telling someone he's lost a child?" He paused, his lips compressing into a stiff line. "Does your mother know?"

"No. Only Laurie."

He muttered a rude word. "You weren't ever going to tell me, were you?"

She couldn't lie any longer. "I didn't want to hurt you—"

His incredulous laugh made her wince. "Thanks for the concern, Mickey. I hate to think how I'd feel if you turned on me. Maybe you thought you'd keep this baby a secret, too…get rid of it before I found out so nothing would interfere with your career?''

She slapped him, the full force of her arm behind her hand. ''I don't have to take that from you. Get out.''

Jeff barely felt the sting; there was too much real pain. Questions pounded at him, demanding answers. What was she thinking? Why were they fighting? How had this scene turned so bad so fast?

But he shoved the details aside. Only one issue had to be settled now. ''I'll leave when I'm ready. We still have some talking to do. You're carrying my baby and, since I know about it this time, I intend to be there as the father.'' He ignored her gasp. ''I came up here today to ask you to marry me, and that's what I'm doing. I'd say the arguments are all on my side.''

Mickey backed across the room, shaking her head. ''We don't need to get married just because of a baby.''

Her denial burned like salt in an open wound. She wouldn't marry him, even to give their child a family…so much for his fantasy of happily-ever-after. But he wouldn't lose *everything*. ''That means you'll give me custody when it's born?''

Her jaw dropped. ''You're crazy! I'm not giving away my child!''

''Then there's only one answer.'' Jeff reached for the door handle, glad that his hand looked steady. Wishing his knees were. ''Let me know when you decide on a wedding date.''

He couldn't keep from adding, before he left, ''Take care of yourself.''

Mickey didn't have anything to say in reply.

If he passed anyone on his way to the truck, he didn't see them. He didn't see the corkscrew mountain road, either, or the trooper who stopped him for doing eighty-

five on the two-lane across the plains. Flying Rock went
by in a flurry of dust, and he didn't even know what
direction he'd taken out of town until he pulled a hard
right under the sign for the Triple A.

He slid to a stop by Dex Hightower's barn, only because running straight into it would have hurt some
blameless animal. While the dust settled and the growl
of the engine died away, he searched for a spark of
energy to get him out of the truck and into the open air.

The only impulse he could find was rage. Pounding
his fist on the steering wheel, Jeff propelled himself out
of the seat, slammed the door and started walking. Past
the barn, past the corrals and pens, out onto the open
plains under the white Wyoming moon.

Damn her. Damn her for all the years of emptiness,
for a decade of hurt and loss. They could have had it
all, and instead they'd had nothing. Because Mickey felt
threatened, because Mickey was too damned stubborn,
she'd denied them both a lifetime's happiness. Cost
their baby its life. Damn her.

His conscience reminded him that he'd been more
than slightly to blame. Fury trampled down the weak
protest.

If I'd known, he thought, *if she'd only told me about
the baby, I could have stopped her…we could have
worked it out.*

She claimed she didn't know until too late. Too busy
was more likely, he thought. Hell-bent on glory and the
chance to be a rodeo star, she hadn't noticed the signs
another woman would have picked up right away. He
couldn't even figure out how it had happened in the first
place. She'd gone off the Pill, he remembered, because
he was worried about the long-term effects. But they

were using *something*, he was sure. He'd have to remember to ask when he saw her again.

If. If he saw her again. He'd made some pretty unforgivable comments, and Mickey didn't forgive easily. This time, though, forgiveness didn't matter. On this balance sheet, he figured the debt was stacked pretty high on his side.

A baby. Dear, sweet God. Their baby.

Jeff swept off his hat and turned to face the west, blaming his burning eyes on the cold mountain wind. And when he closed them, he saw a picture of Mickey in some sterile emergency room in Denver, lying there bleeding and hurting and, *damn it,* alone. Losing a baby she didn't know she carried, without anybody there to hold her hand and dry her tears and tell her everything would be okay.

It twisted everything inside him to imagine that child, lost to them forever. And thinking of Mickey, all alone with her anguish, magnified that pain a million times.

I should have been there. Damn you, Mickey, I should have been there!

He didn't know how long he'd walked when the sudden flare of headlights coming over a rise caught him full in the face. Blinded, he stood still, figuring the best chance to avoid being hit was simply to stay put.

In another two minutes, Dex's truck stopped at his side. "Nice night for a walk," the rancher commented through the open window.

"I guess so."

"I saw your truck by the barn, thought you might have stopped in to look in on that cow." Though they'd lost the one steer, the cow he'd treated while Mickey stayed with him had started to recover and no other animals had been affected. Jeff knew he should have thought to check on his patient.

The tide of guilt surged higher. "Not…yet. I will before I leave."

Dex shot him a piercing glance, then opened the door and climbed out. "What's wrong?"

Jeff damned the revealing moonlight. "Mickey's pregnant."

"Congratulations." Walking around the pickup, Dex let down the gate and sat on the edge of the bed. "You two getting married?"

Jeff took the steps necessary to prop his elbows on the side of the truck. "Good question. At four this afternoon I thought so. Now…" He squinted at his replacement watch. "Five hours later, I have no idea."

"Did you ask her?"

"Told her is more like it."

The other man laughed quietly. "A certain lack of finesse there, Doc."

"You don't know the half of it." He explained the scene, and enough of the argument to let Dex in on the problem. "All these years, hell, these last couple of months, when we've been more or less together again, she never said a word. How I am supposed to forget that she lost a baby and wasn't ever going to tell me?"

Propping one booted foot on the floor of the truck bed, the rancher rested his elbow on his bent knee. "Guess that depends on what you want now."

Jeff blew a deep breath. "I want what I've never stopped wanting—Mickey. And our kids."

Dex took that in silence. After a while, he stirred. "You don't have too many options, do you?"

"I don't have any, that I can see. If you push Mickey, she runs, as hard and as fast as she can. The only thing that's keeping her tied down at this point is the camp rodeo. When that's over, she'll be gone. And I don't know if I can even slow her down.''

''She doesn't love you?''

''Ask a hard one, why don't you?''

But after his sarcastic reply, Jeff gave Dex's question some thought. A lot of the time he knew what Mickey was thinking before she had a chance to realize it herself. Not that she was predictable, just…familiar. So what was she thinking now?

That night at the camp…her hands and her hips and her mouth had all sent one message. She hadn't used the words, but the tone in her voice when she said his name, the sound of her sighs…

''Maybe,'' he said finally. ''But I don't know.''

''Well, that's better than knowing she definitely doesn't.'' Dex stood up, stretched out, then walked back around to the door. ''Mickey's not twenty anymore. Give her credit for having some sense. If she cares about you, and about your baby, she won't do anything to hurt either of you.''

He folded himself into the cab. ''Don't scare away the woman you love. Because you need her. And because,'' he said in a low, soft voice, ''once she's gone, your kid is out of reach, too. And you start wondering… You wonder how they are that night, you wonder what bedtime story they got, or if they got one at all. If the baby-sitter treats them right, if they have friends to play with. If they eat a good breakfast, if they wash their hands before dinner. You could go crazy sometimes, just wondering.''

Jeff had never heard him express the pain quite so strongly. He couldn't think of anything rational to say. ''I hear you'' was the most he could come up with.

Dex nodded. "Good." Like a retriever shaking off water, he seemed to lose the pensive mood. "You're about five miles out from the house, here. You want a ride back?"

"Sure...uh, no." He still had some serious thinking to do. "I think I'll walk, thanks."

The rancher tilted his head. "Suit yourself. We've got stew on the stove when you get there. And that cow is in a stall in the barn."

Grinning, Jeff pushed off the truck. "Right. I'll take a look before I come in."

With a tip of his hat, Dex gunned the engine and wheeled away.

Five miles under the stars wasn't really very far. Long before he'd come to any conclusions, Jeff caught the glow of lights in the near distance. The sounds of animals and men carried easily in the clear night air.

Back to civilization. Back to real life and the dilemma of the woman who had flayed him to the bone, the woman who carried his child, the one woman he'd ever loved. Maybe the only question, in the end, was how to get her back without begging.

Or maybe the only real question was, *Would begging work?*

CHECKING THE CINCH, Mickey issued her instructions.

"Grip hard with your knees." Jenny, a twelve-year-old battling leukemia, tightened up as ordered. "Right. Bend low, but keep your hands up. Jelly Roll knows just what to do." She patted the horse's smooth, glossy shoulder. "Let him show you." Looking up at the girl's face scrunched in concentration, she had to stifle a laugh. "Are you ready?"

Jenny nodded. Mickey stepped away and fished her stopwatch out of her pocket. "Go!"

With a kick of Jenny's heels, Jelly Roll took off into the corral. Following his instincts, he carried his rider on a smooth loop around the right-hand barrel, then headed without pause for the second. Taking another easy circle, he stretched out on the run for the top of the cloverleaf, with Jenny sticking like a burr to his back. Loping around one more time, he made the run back toward Mickey at slightly less than his usual breakneck pace, only slowing once he'd passed the corral entrance.

Jenny pulled him up slowly, turned around and trotted back. "What was my time, huh? What did I do?"

Mickey grinned as she walked over. "You did great! Thirty-two seconds...down more than five seconds from last week. Good job!"

"Is it my turn now? Is it?"

She looked down at the sprite who had followed her. "Sure, Davy. Let me get Jenny off and we'll get you going."

Davy took his run a little slower than Jenny, but still finished with his face beaming. Setting him down, Mickey looked at the six youngsters she'd been working with all afternoon, their faces shining with sweat and dusted with dirt, and decided a break was in order. "Pool time, guys. Go get your—"

A rumble of thunder interrupted, greeted by a collective groan. She revised her plans. "I guess nobody will be swimming today, huh? Sounds like movie time!"

Cheering, her crew of barrel racers streaked off to the dining hall with their assistant counselor while Mickey led Jelly Roll into the barn. She'd just reached his box when she realized she wasn't alone.

She glanced casually back over her shoulder. "Hi, Karen. How are you?"

Karen peeked around the corner of the doorway. "Okay. What horse is that?"

"This is Jelly Roll. I trained him for barrel racing a long time ago and a friend of mine rides him in rodeos around the country. I borrowed him back for the kids to practice on."

"He's short." She took two steps inside the barn.

"Well, shorter than Clementine anyway."

"Does he...bite?"

Mickey flashed her a grin and turned Jelly Roll around. "Only the food he's eating."

Karen managed a smile back. "That's good." She took two more steps, and then three, until she stood close enough to touch. And then she did.

Mickey bit her lip to keep from cheering.

"He's funny, isn't he, all brown and white spots?" Karen's thin hand stroked along the smooth neck.

"Yeah, but he's really sweet. Puts up with anything, as long as you give him an apple in the morning first."

"Is he the first horse you ever rode?"

"Oh, no. That was Duffy. My dad's horse. When I was a baby, my dad would hold me in his arms and take me around the ranch. I rode before I could walk." She looked at Karen. "It's always been easy for me, you know. I never had to try."

Karen swallowed. Her head lifted, and her gaze seemed to measure the distance from the ground to the top of Jelly Roll's head. Then she looked at Mickey through the dimness of the barn. "Do you think I could ride him?"

"I think you could..." Thunder growled again, closer this time. "But—"

"In the barn?"

The single aisle was plenty wide. "Sure. Turn on the lights."

Karen walked steadily back to the door and flicked the switch. Around them the horses stirred as light filled the big space. Then the girl turned and, her face set, came back to where Mickey stood. "I'm ready," she volunteered.

"Great." Mickey struggled to keep her voice calm. "You know how to get on, right?"

Karen moved into position without a word. Mickey touched her, and this time there was no trembling, as if Karen had decided she wouldn't give in even that far. "Okay. One...two...three!"

Afterward, Mickey wasn't sure if the propulsion that put Karen in the saddle came from her, or from the girl's determination. But with ease and grace, Karen slipped on top of Jelly Roll, and stayed there.

"Good!" This time she did have to adjust the stirrups; the other kids were taller. Mickey kept the reins in her hand as she worked, and Karen sat quietly, gripping the saddle horn.

Now came the tricky part. Mickey put a hand on Karen's knee. "Would you like me to lead him for you?"

Because Jelly Roll was so short, their faces weren't that far apart. Karen considered, her eyes focused inward. "That would be good."

"Fine." Mickey drew a deep breath, beginning to believe this might happen, after all. "Just relax. Let your body move with the horse. Don't work against him."

But at the first step, Karen jerked straight, her eyes wide. "Mickey—"

"Relax, Karen. It's okay." Another step; Karen opened her mouth to protest. "Please, sweetheart. Give it a try. You can do this. You know you can!"

Another step, and then another. Karen's hands tightened, her chin lifted, and her face was so white Mickey expected her to faint any minute. Walking backward, she slowly brought Jelly Roll along, her gaze glued to the rider he carried.

She reached the door, and felt the wind fresh and damp on her back. Was it her imagination, or had Karen relaxed a tiny bit? "Do you want to turn around and go to the other end?"

The answer came on a breath of sound. "Yes."

They took the turn carefully, and Mickey heard the sigh Karen gave when they were facing the other door. "Here we go."

She took this trip a little faster, at a real walk. And Karen adjusted, her body unconsciously picking up the rhythm of Jelly Roll's gait. Her face still looked scared. But her muscles were learning their lesson.

At the front door, Mickey glanced up in question. "Again," Karen decided. And grinned.

They made the circuit four more times. For the last one, Karen held the reins *and* the saddle horn, and Mickey led Jelly Roll with a hand in his bridle. She stopped him at his box, took the reins and tied him to the post. Then she walked over, put her arms around Karen and looked up into her face.

"You, my dear, have just ridden this horse!"

"I did, didn't I?" A wide smile split the glowing face. "Can I do it again?"

Mickey laughed. "Tomorrow, kid. Jelly Roll and I are worn-out, if you aren't."

For a second, Karen's lower lip came out in a pout.

But in obedience to Mickey's pull, she leaned over and slid easily off the horse's back. Mickey stepped back, giving her a chance to get clear of the animal, but Karen turned and went toward his head. "Thanks," she whispered near his ear, which flicked in response.

Then she came back to Mickey and, without a word, locked both arms around her waist and clung. Mickey held her close, swallowing against the knot in her throat, snuffling back tears. She couldn't have spoken if she tried.

"I wondered where you two had gotten to." Laurie's brisk voice broke them apart. "The sky's about to fall out there. Karen, you'd better get to the dining hall before you risk drowning."

"Good idea," Mickey said gruffly. "We'll watch you from the door. Run fast!"

But Karen hesitated. "Tomorrow?"

Mickey nodded. "Definitely. Tomorrow."

With her familiar, carefree grin, the girl streaked off. Laurie joined Mickey at the doorway to make sure she got safely inside. "You did it?"

"She did it. I just watched."

Laurie's curls bounced with her nod. "Yeah, sure. I believe you. Are the barrel racers ready?"

"I think so. They're having the time of their lives, anyway. And this morning I caught a glimpse of the clown acts the other kids are working up. The audience is definitely going to get their money's worth."

"No doubt about it. And how are you doing this afternoon?"

Mickey sank onto a hay bale, pulled off her hat and swiped her arm across her forehead. "Okay. Better than this morning, anyway." Mornings were getting hard to handle. She'd taken to keeping a box of soda crackers in her room in hopes that a square or two before she got out of bed would settle her stomach. Sometimes it worked. Today, it hadn't.

When she looked up, the boss's round face wore its worried look. "You could go lie down for a while," Laurie suggested. "They won't miss you until dinner."

"No. They're going to miss me *at* dinner. I've got a meeting down at the Triple A, remember? There are just ten days left until the rodeo—all the stock suppliers and handlers are supposed to show up for a final planning session. I need to be there." She glanced out the door at rain-spattered dust. "Even if I have to drive through a thunderstorm."

"That's right. I'd forgotten." Laurie paced across the width of the barn and back. "Will Jeff be there?"

Mickey shrugged, glad to be able to do so without pain. "Your guess is as good as mine. I haven't talked to him since last weekend." *Since he threw his proposal in my face and walked out.*

Laurie knew that detail. "You could have called him."

"There's nothing to say. After the show...after next Friday, I'll figure out what to do."

They backed away from the doorway as the sky opened. Rain came down in sheets as lightning danced across the tips of the trees. The horses stirred uneasily in their stalls.

"Are you going to marry him?" Nature's violence made a fitting background for that question.

"How can I?" Mickey stared out into the storm. "What chance is there that marriage would work, after everything I've done? He's got more forgiving to do than one man could possibly manage. I don't think even Jeff can handle this."

"He might surprise you."

"He might." She allowed an unwilling chuckle to escape. "He often does. But I owe him more than that, Laurie. Jeff deserves a woman who hasn't hurt him this way, who never would. One who doesn't keep secrets, or take off on her own stubborn path, leaving him stranded. I think he'll find her, now that everything is out in the open, and we've got each other out of our systems."

"But what do *you* want to do?"

Thunder rattled the tin buckets piled in a corner, adding clank to roar, and Mickey closed her eyes. A picture came to mind, unasked, of herself nestled into the sofa in Jeff's living room, in front of the crackling fire, with a baby in her arms. And she felt Jeff beside them both, keeping her close to his heart, at the center of his life.

On a deep breath she opened her eyes and realized she had to blink back tears. "It doesn't matter. I made my choice ten years ago. What I wanted then is what I've got." Focusing on the distress in Laurie's gaze, she pulled a grin out of her bag of tricks. "You, the best friend I could ask for. The campers here, sweethearts every one of them. And I've got another chance to be a mother to Jeff's baby—a kid who will, I'm pretty sure, keep me on my toes for the next twenty years or so. That's a pretty good tally, if you ask me."

They waited out the worst of the storm in silence, although Mickey could sense a herd of objections clustering under her friend's tongue. When the rain lightened, they made a dash for the office, and Laurie scurried inside.

Mickey would have left her there, but the boss put out a hand and held her back.

"How is it going to work," she asked, her damp gaze

solemn and concerned, ''when there's a child tying you together? Can he forget, when you share that bond? Can you?''

That thought had already occurred to Mickey. ''We'll work things out. Other people do. It's time I grew up enough to face Jeff, anyway. So now we'll share something more than just the past. Life could be a lot worse.'' She pulled her arm away. ''It already has been.''

''That,'' Laurie said in an irritated voice from behind the screen door, ''does not answer the question.''

Mickey held back her own temper. ''It's the best I can do. See you late tonight.''

Fighting a slick road and blinding rain on the drive down to Flying Rock, she allowed more of her mind than was really safe to tangle with Laurie's questions. The boss, of course, was right—Mickey had avoided giving an answer she knew all too well.

No.

No, she didn't think she would ever be able to forget. The idea of forging a relationship with another man and keeping Jeff Buchanan on the edge of her life made her laugh. She'd spent ten years trying to do just that, hadn't she? Yet the first time she saw him, the first time Jeff touched her, ten years had vanished, leaving her as much in love with him as she'd ever been.

If not more.

And so she'd be seeing him, sharing a child but not sharing his life. That situation promised more heartbreak and pain than she could contemplate. For about an hour after he'd stalked out last Sunday, she'd conjured up visions of the places she could go, calculated how far she could run, and how fast. Australia sounded good, she'd thought. They have rodeos in Australia, too.

But after the anger died, she knew she wouldn't go that far. No running away this time. That stricken moment when Jeff realized she'd been pregnant before, the white agony on his face...

Mickey couldn't face hurting him anymore. He deserved a chance to know this child. No matter how much it tormented her to see him without having him, she would make sure the baby was as much a part of Jeff's life as he wanted. And when he found someone to share his house and his life, she would rejoice in his happiness.

She would try, anyway.

The Triple A arrived sooner than she expected. The rain in the mountains hadn't reached the plains, although clouds had dyed the twilight black and shut down the wind. Mickey stepped out of the truck, not liking the scent of ozone or the close, edgy feel to the air. The drive back to camp tonight would be a wild one.

She did like the number of trucks parked in the yard, though, and the size of the crowd gathered in the great room of the house. Dex Hightower opened the door on her knock and welcomed her in. "How was the drive? Looks like rain up there."

Taking his hand, Mickey tilted her head back to meet his eyes. "Lots of it. You'll be getting some flooding, I think."

Releasing his grip, she turned to the man beside him. "How are you, Mr. Ross? I'm pleased we'll be using some of your animals Friday night. I hear they're top-level this year." She made the rounds, greeting each man she knew by name, trying to memorize the others when Dex introduced them. Ten years on the circuit had taught her the importance of remembering a face and a name.

The face of the man standing by the huge stone fireplace needed no effort of memory. "Hello, Jeff."

He nodded. "How are you, Mickey?" His dark gaze flickered over her. She wondered if he could tell that the waist of her jeans was feeling tight. She knew it was too early, knew she was just imagining it. Still…

"I'm great." She cleared her throat. "I'm glad you could be here." *I wasn't sure you'd come at all.*

"Anything I can do."

"Thanks." Sending him a small smile, she moved on. Whatever she might want to say to Jeff, now was not the time. She still had people to greet and a meeting to conduct. The handlers looked good, and the rodeo boss came highly recommended. The show would pull together just fine.

When the time was right, Mickey turned over the proceedings to the rodeo boss and Jeff, who between them had come up with the plans for handling the animals. Retreating into the background with the cup of milk Dex brought her, she found an empty spot on the hearth to sit and watch as the final details for her show fell into place.

He's tired. And tense. And unhappy.

She couldn't take her mind or eyes off Jeff. His shoulders looked tight, his stance lacked its usual ease. Even his voice seemed strained. No one would notice unless they knew him really well, but he was a long way from his best.

Way to go, cowgirl. Everytime you show up you hurt him more.

And this time, she didn't know how to end the pain. The stock men were deep into unloading details and pen diagrams when the front door blew open. A cowboy stood there, urgency broadcast by every line of his body. "Mr. Hightower here?"

"This way, Roy." Dex's deep voice carved silence out of the noise.

The crowd parted to let Roy through. He stopped in front of Mickey. "Jezebel's started foaling—"

She felt Dex relax. "That's good."

"And she's busted loose."

"What?" The sharp question cut through the resumed murmur of men's voices. "How?"

"Hank was tryin' to lead her in out of the storm. She caught him on the head with a hoof, he went down and before we could get her, she was out the gate and gone."

Dex didn't waste time on profanity. "Is Hank okay?"

Roy nodded. "Bleedin' like a stuck pig, but he'll be fine."

"Good." The tall man stretched to his feet. "Get a couple of men out there on horseback. See if you can round her up. I'm sorry, Mickey, gentlemen," he said, turning to the group, "but I'm going to have to find this mare. She means a little too much to me to let her foal out under a rock somewhere. Please make yourselves at home—"

"Hell's bells, Hightower!" It was Ben Ross, the man she'd met at the door and one of her dad's oldest friends. "We're all here. No reason we can't get this filly rounded up for you. This is too big a spread for just your crew. Right, boys?"

An orderly shuffle toward the door greeted his comments. In only minutes the pickups were fanning out over the range behind the house, their headlights spread like fingertips combing through the night.

As the last one parked in the straight-line drive, Mickey had to wait for everyone else to pull out before she could move. She had reached her truck when a hand fell on her shoulder. "Why don't you stay here?" She pivoted to meet Jeff's gaze. The darkness hid any clue to his thoughts.

For once, holding her temper took no effort. She didn't want a fight. "I know this ranch better than anybody here, except you. I could be useful."

"The storm's about to break." As he said the words, a raindrop splashed her cheek, and another her nose. Light flared in the sky behind his head.

"I'll be in a truck." Mickey hated this constraint between them. The muted tone of his voice, her reserved replies—she felt as if they were strangers.

"That's not necessarily safe." He hadn't lifted his hand from her shoulder. Mickey savored the warmth and weight.

"I want to go, Jeff. I can be careful. And we're wasting time."

"True." His fingers tightened for an instant, and then released her. She missed the contact immediately. "Come with me, then."

It wouldn't be easy. She didn't care. Five seconds later she climbed into the Suburban, he shifted gears and they took off into the night.

"Where do you think the mare would go?"

Mickey's question broke a silence that was anything but comfortable. Jeff glanced over, saw with relief that she'd put on her seat belt.

"Away from the storm would be my guess, which means east." He turned the wheel as he said it, steering toward the rougher terrain on the ranch. "Any other ideas?"

"Not yet." She sat forward, peering through the mud-spattered windshield. "Is the foal on time?"

"A little late, as a matter of fact. I checked yesterday, and thought she'd deliver soon. I haven't had a chance to look her over today, though."

He recognized the tree up ahead and the big dip it signaled a little too late. Without thought he put out his right hand and pushed Mickey back against the seat. "Watch out!"

The truck took the drop with the finesse of a Brahman bull under the rigging. Mickey tensed against his hand, the muscles in her belly going hard. They came up out of the gully and he braked, then turned in his seat. "You okay?"

Her eyes wide, she simply stared at him and nodded. Jeff realized he hadn't taken away his hand. Didn't want to.

But he did. Turning back to the wheel, he dragged in a deep breath and let up on the brake. "Let me know if you see anything moving."

Mickey didn't answer. Even as he scanned the horizon, trying to see a black mare moving against the black sky, he cursed himself for a clumsy fool. He shouldn't have touched her, not until things were straightened out between them. Just that brief contact had him aching to hold her, to love her, to make sure that she stayed a part of his life for as long as he could hold on to it.

And he had absolutely no reason to think that would ever happen.

Her formal stance when she'd greeted him today, her cool appraisal, made it clear that Mickey hadn't gotten over his bitter, scathing words. She hadn't by any means melted into his arms, begging him to make an honest woman of her. Hell, she hadn't even called him, in the week since he'd seen her, not for rodeo business or anything else. Her feelings, as someone once said, had been made perfectly clear.

And what did he expect? Ten years ago, he'd driven her into running away, cost Mickey her home and family and—he knew now—a baby. It must have taken most of that time for her to recover enough to come back, to forget the pain.

So how did he react when the passion they'd never been able to master got them into trouble again? He'd flung accusations and insults at her, as if the situation was all her fault. The fact that loving her and needing her and not being sure of her had unbalanced his reason didn't constitute an excuse. Mickey had a lot to forgive. He wasn't sure she ever could.

So he shouldn't presume. He shouldn't be sitting here wanting her, trying to think up some way to bring up their future and how they were going to share a child without sharing their lives. He didn't think it was possible, when just seeing her set his soul ablaze. But he would do whatever it took...

"Jeff! To the right?"

On reflex, he steered slightly, to point the headlights. Through the streaking rain he caught a glimpse of a drooping head and swollen belly. "Yes!"

He pulled up about twenty feet from the horse and opened the door. Rain poured in, and he cursed his lack of a coat. "Stay put," he yelled over his shoulder at Mickey.

Walking carefully, he talked to the mare as he approached. "Good girl, Jezebel. Yes indeed, it's a bad night to be out in the weather. And you're not feeling too good, are you, Jez? Gonna let me check?" Eight more feet and he'd be close enough to touch.

From inside the truck, Mickey watched as Jeff moved slowly toward the panicked horse, talking all the time. He'd had this magic with animals for as long as she'd known him. Nobody had worried about him in the corral with a bad-tempered brute. Using just his voice and his steady gaze, he could bring even the edgiest stallion under control. Mickey chuckled as she compared that talent with her own. She rode the wild ones, but Jeff tamed them.

Jeff got closer to Jezebel. The mare jerked her head up and whinnied. He stopped and talked to her until she lowered her head, then stepped forward again. Another two yards, and the trailing halter would be in his grasp.

Jezebel cried out again, in a voice Mickey could hear over the shriek of the wind, the tattoo of the rain. Only an arm's length away now, Jeff stretched out his hand, touched her flank, her shoulder. The halter hung only an inch from his fingertips, and he reached for it.

Lightning split the heavens, and the universe roared.

The mare screamed and lifted her front legs, pawing at the air. Jeff stepped back, out of the way.

Then, for some reason Mickey couldn't see, he lost his balance. In slow motion his feet flew out from under him. Arms flailing, he went down hard, on his back.

Jezebel reared again, hanging over the man on the ground like the black shadow of an avenging angel.

Mickey tore open the door and threw herself out into the rain.

CHAPTER THIRTEEN

JEFF WAITED for the bite of sharp hooves in his flesh.

But Jezebel wheeled on her hind legs, brought her front feet to the ground and raced away. Scrambling, he struggled to his feet on the slick grass, helped by hands on his elbow and back. When he looked around, he saw Mickey beside him.

He didn't waste his breath complaining. Holding on to each other, they ran back to the truck, flung themselves in and took off after Jezebel. The lightning came frequently enough that they could track her by the flashes, but each one shifted her course in a different direction. The truck reacted sluggishly as the ground went from dirt and grass to mud. Jeff wasn't sure how long it would be before they got bogged down completely.

"We're almost at the fence," Mickey said finally. "She can't get too much farther."

"What's out here? Any shelter at all?"

"No trees. Just that big wash…"

"Right."

He headed for the creek bed. Gouged out of the hard soil by spring floods coming down from the mountains, the wash stayed dry through most of the summer, a barren scar on the land. Its high banks, eroded through centuries, would seem adequate shelter to an animal panicked and in pain. But an animal wouldn't recognize the real threat.

They saw the flick of Jezebel's tail as she went over the bank at a shallow ford. Jeff braked, put the truck in park and reached for the CB-radio mike. A burst of static greeted his effort to broadcast. "Damn. The storm's screwed up reception. Time for plan B." He turned to Mickey. "You didn't listen to me before. But please, do what I'm asking now. Turn around and go look for a couple of people to help me. When you get half a mile away or so, use the horn, the lights, whatever you can to get attention. Bring them back here. And then stay in the damned truck. Okay?"

He'd never seen her so quiet, or so scared. Her eyes practically filled her face. Jeff lifted a hand to cup the curve of her cheek. "It's okay, Mickey. Everything will be just fine. I promise."

A big promise. But her face relaxed like a little child's. Her palm covered the back of his hand, she turned her face slightly, and he felt the heat of her mouth moving against his skin. His breath stopped.

And then started again when she drew back. "Good luck," Mickey whispered. "Be careful."

He didn't trust his voice. With only a nod, he stepped out into the storm.

SHE SHOULD HAVE argued with him.

Watching Jeff sprint through the rain, following the path Jezebel had taken, Mickey realized what a foolish task he'd assumed. All alone, in the middle of a storm, he proposed to track and catch a half-crazed animal and bring her to safety. When he disappeared over the bank of the wash, she barely stifled a cry of dismay.

Ready to chase and drag him back, she had the truck

door open and one foot on the ground before reason caught up with her emotions. Nothing she could do would change his mind. When Jeff believed something was right, he acted on his instincts, heedless of opposition. She couldn't argue him out of it, and couldn't overpower him. The only thing she could do now was to get him the help he required.

Quickly pulling her leg in, she slammed the door and slid over into the driver's seat, shifted gears and headed the truck back the way they had come.

A litany of reassurance tumbled through her mind as she drove. *He'll be safe. He knows how to find shelter if he needs it, knows to watch out for flooding and lightning and wind. He can handle Jezebel, he's trained and strong and experienced.*

He will *be safe.*

When the odometer registered half a mile, she braked and, wincing, planted her palm on the horn. With the other hand she flicked the lights, from bright to normal to off, over and over again, hoping her signal would catch somebody's attention.

And despite the din and the blinding brightness, she tried to follow, at least mentally, as Jeff walked along the running creek bed, his shirt plastered to his skin, his hair in his eyes, talking to Jezebel and coaxing her to trust him. Would his magic work again with the frightened mare? Could he overcome the storm and the panic and the pain and get her home?

It seemed like hours before a set of headlights crawled out of the darkness to stop by her door. Mickey rolled down the window, squinting against the pellets of rain as Dex's face came into view.

"Jeff's found her," she explained without waiting for

a greeting. "Down near the ford on the wash by the northeast fence. He needs backup."

Dex nodded once. "I'll radio some of the others. Send them on when they get here."

With a splash of mud, he was gone. In a matter of minutes three more trucks came by and she delivered the same report. When the fourth pulled up, bearing a couple of the handlers she knew by name, she figured she'd already followed Jeff's orders to the letter.

The message she relayed this time was her own.

"Stay here and keep signaling. There should be enough help up there by now, send the rest back to the house." Without waiting for protest, she wheeled Jeff's truck around and headed back to the wash.

She couldn't find them at first. The trucks she'd sent on had stopped almost a mile north of the spot she'd specified, and the men were nowhere to be seen. Turning the Suburban in a slow circle, she used the headlights to look for silhouettes. Where could they have gone? Had they already gotten out? Surely not so fast…

There. She caught a glimpse of moving shadows, two men running back toward the trucks from the north end of the creek. Scrambling down from the high seat, she ran through the rain to meet them.

"Where is he? What's going on?"

Roy dragged a coil of rope out of Dex's truck bed. "Damned horse backed herself under a bank at the deepest point. Won't move. Doc says the foal's got a leg hooked wrong and he's tryin' to bring it out. Hightower wants rope and blankets. Fast."

"Get in Jeff's truck. I'll drive you." When he threw her a dubious glance, she insisted. "He only took a light bag of equipment with him, he may need some of what's in back. Let's get closer."

The Suburban took the ruts and rises in the ground with a protest of creaks and groans and sputters. Mickey wasn't sure, when she finally shut off the engine, if it would start again. But she wasn't worrying about that now. Following the two cowboys out of the truck, she ran to the edge of the wash, located Dex's big shadow in the night and joined him at his post.

"How's it going? Where is he?"

He spared her a brief glance and pointed across the wash. "There. Under the cottonwood."

"Oh, God." The usually dry wash had become a full-fledged flowing creek, with about six inches of water rippling along the bottom in a yard-wide swath. A lone tree perched on the edge of a ten-foot-high bank, its labyrinth of roots the only support for a thin layer of dirt overhanging the creek bed.

And Jezebel had taken the shelter provided by the tree for her delivery room. Even in the dark, Mickey could see the flaring whites of the mare's eyes, the bared teeth. She couldn't see Jeff at all.

"Where…"

"Behind, trying to get the foal." Dex bit off his words as if each one hurt. "I promised my daughter that foal. But I don't want it at the cost of a man's life. Not Jeff."

"He'll be fine." She had to say the words, had to believe them. "He promised."

"Sure. If anybody can do this, Jeff can."

Whipped by rain, beaten by hail, Mickey stood peering through the darkness, trying to get a glimpse of Jeff. She'd never known such torture, never dreamed she would have to stand by and watch as he risked his life for an animal. There would be other horses, other foals. There was only one Jeff.

A strange feeling of recognition came to her slowly out of the night, a sense of familiarity, as her years of rodeo work flashed before her eyes. She had always known—at least until ten years ago—that she could count on looking up into the stands to find Jeff waiting, watching, willing her to win. Was this fear what he'd felt as she'd entered contest after contest, each holding the potential for serious injury or even death? Had Jeff dreaded her performances with the same stomach-churning terror she felt now?

It hadn't, Mickey reflected, started with her. His dad had taught his young son the traumas of rodeo competition, and Jeff had learned the lesson well. He'd nursed his dad through numerous injuries. By the time they'd met, Jeff knew firsthand all the risks of rodeo life.

And yet he'd stood by and let her follow her dream, had supported her every step of the way. If his caretaking had chafed her occasionally, if she'd felt constricted by his plans and his orders, well, how else was he to cope? How else could he have dealt with the danger of her chosen life than by trying to keep her safe as much as he could?

"I don't believe it!" Dex took a step forward, to the very edge of the bank. "He's got the foal!"

Below them, a figure stumbled out of the shadows of the overhang and dropped to his knees. In his arms, a darker form nestled, looking lifeless. Jeff put his burden down on the muddy ground and began to rub its chest and limbs.

"It's dead." Dex began to turn away. "We took too long."

"No!" Mickey grabbed his arm. "Look!"

The foal had started struggling. Jeff let go and

stepped back, hands propped on his hips, watching. A darker shadow appeared at his side, resolving under a lightning flash into Jezebel, come out to watch her off-spring start life. She stepped in front of the man, nuzzled her baby, prodded him on the rear. Finally, after enough encouragement, the foal propped its front legs up, gave a mighty heave and struggled gamely to its feet.

The spectators on the opposite bank let loose a muted cheer. Nobody needed to be warned what would happen if Jezebel spooked again.

Jeff looked over at them and cupped his hands around his mouth. Mickey could barely hear his words over the rush of water in the wash.

"Ropes...let's get...here."

The waiting men sprang to action. In seconds a line snaked across the wash, right into Jeff's expectant hand. He tied the end to Jezebel's halter, picked up the wobbly foal and together the three waded through the knee-deep water of the swollen creek.

Mickey knelt in the mud of the high bank. "You're crazy, you know that, Buchanan?" The rain had backed off into a steady drizzle, so she didn't have to shout. "Only a madman would deliver a foal in the rain."

He flashed her a grin. "Some females just won't do things the easy way. What can I say?" The smile faded. "I thought I told you to stay in the truck."

"Jeff," Dex interrupted, "the bank is gentler about fifty feet on up. Lead her there and we can get you out."

"Right."

Mickey followed the crowd, but a bit more slowly. Relief had crept into her bones, weakening her knees and making her aware of the chill of wet clothes, the drip of her hair. This ordeal couldn't end fast enough, as far as she was concerned.

Jezebel's head appeared above the top of the bank as Mickey arrived. Now that the pain of birth had ended, the mare seemed to feel cooperative, and she mounted the slope with a minimum of fuss. Dex stood for a few seconds talking to her. Mickey could hear a combination of affection and exasperation in his tone.

Meanwhile, Roy had joined Jeff down in the wash. The span of water had widened considerably, and they had only a narrow strip of bank left to work on as they wrapped blankets around the foal's middle and rigged a system of ropes to haul the animal up the slippery bank. When they were set, Roy climbed back up. Jeff stayed to steady from below as the confused, frightened baby began its bumpy trip to safety.

The foal arrived at the top. The first words Mickey heard were, "It's a colt!"

She started to grin. And then hesitated, trying to tune in a different signal. A subtle, insidious tremor was working its way through the heels of her boots, into her knees and belly and chest. No sound, not yet. Just that vibration, promising, threatening, warning…

"Jeff!" She turned from the crowd around the colt, stepped back to the bank. "Jeff, you've got to—"

He looked up at her. "Mickey, what's—"

They could hear it then. A menacing rumble, growing loud enough in just two seconds to drown their words. Jeff looked north to where the wash took a sharp bend toward the west, then turned back. Mickey read his lips as he shouted, "Get me a rope."

She turned. Dex was beside her, coil in hand.

The line shot out into the darkness, and Jeff caught it easily. Dex braced himself for the other man's weight.

Mickey grabbed at the rope in front of his hands and added herself as an anchor.

Jeff began to climb. His head appeared at the top of the bank and Mickey let out a shaky breath. For a minute she'd been afraid the night would go wrong.

Then the rope went slack. She fell back against Dex, who caught her even while letting loose a string of curses. They stumbled to the edge of the bank and looked down. Jeff had slipped in the mud, all the way back down to the creek bed. Standing thigh deep in the swirling water, he was knotting the rope around his waist this time.

Dex bellowed into the night. "Sanders! Johnson! Get over here!" The two men came running and grabbed the end of the line to add their support.

Mickey knelt again by the edge, trying to pretend her knees would have kept her standing. "He's ready," she called. The men began to pull.

A wall of water crashed around the bend in the wash. The thunder drowned out everything—rain, wind, thought. Black in the night, frothing like a rabid animal, the flood was upon them before they could take a second breath. For another instant she could see Jeff, watched him look toward the fury, saw him tighten his hands.

And then he was gone.

Filthy water washed by, coming within a foot of the top of the bank. Too frightened to scream, Mickey reared up and pushed her hair out of her eyes, trying to see through the rain and the night. Dex…

The three men on the line had been joined by more. Hands wrapped in the rope, they held firm against the water surging a few feet away. Jeff…

Mickey staggered to her feet and turned back toward

the wash, searching for Jeff. Gone. Crashing, thrashing waves, trash, whole trees churned by her, but only the tension on the rope in Dex's hands gave her hope that Jeff had hung on. And even if he had...he could be dead weight by now. Shoving a fist into her mouth, Mickey bit back a sob.

At the first easing of the tide, Dex gave a grunt and took a step back. And another. More than one of the men on the rope slipped in the mud and the wet, and twice they lost ground when a new wave rolled through. At some point someone came up behind Mickey and put his arms around her; she didn't know who. She was afraid to ask why.

But gradually the hauling process worked. A thatch she took for a ball of weed resolved into Jeff's hair, and then his shoulders, bare and scratched, emerged from the flood. By the time they got him all the way onto the bank, Mickey was down beside him on her knees.

"Jeff." Under the filth his face was deadly white, his body lay deathly still. "Dear God...please, open your eyes." She tapped his cheek with her palm, tried to find a pulse in his throat. He didn't seem to be breathing. "Jeff, can you hear me? Damn it, Jeff..."

JEFF CAME TO with a steady barrage of profanity in his ear. It took a minute to sort out the voice, and then he laughed.

Or, rather, choked.

"Lighten up, Mickey. I'm okay." His voice came out in a surprising whisper. He cleared his throat and tried again. "Somebody turn on the lights." Not much improvement in the sound. He must have swallowed a hell of a lot of water.

"No lights in the back of this truck, Buchanan."

Dex's voice came from his other side. "How do you feel?"

"Just great. I plan to run a marathon first thing tomorrow morning." Putting up a hand, he grabbed at the cloth swishing over his face. "That's enough, Mickey. My face is as clean as it's likely to get without soap."

"I'm trying to keep the blood out of your eyes, idiot. You've got a gash on your scalp a vampire could feast on for a week. You need a doctor and a dozen stitches."

She sounded worse than he felt. Jeff turned his head. In the dim light he could make out her white hands twisting a stained piece of cloth into a knot, and her white face, with tear tracks marking the dirt. "You're the one who needs doctoring, I think. You look like hell, Mickey."

"A matched set."

He ignored Dex's provocative comment, being concerned with inching himself up onto his elbows. The exercise proved that nothing was broken, though everything hurt.

"You should lie down," Mickey protested as he propped his shoulders against the side of the truck.

He ignored that, too. What was it he wanted to talk to her about? Oh, yeah. "And you should have stayed in the truck. You don't need to be out in weather like this."

Her shoulders lifted on a sigh. "I don't think you really expected me to stay away, did you?"

Reasonableness? From Mickey? "No, I guess not. But I would like it if you took better care of yourself."

"I know."

Her calm, her total lack of fireworks, worried him more than the wetting she'd received. If he'd believed he could move again, he would have put his arms around her. "Are you feeling okay, Mickey? Is something wrong?"

She dropped her gaze to her lap and the twist of bloodstained cloth. "I'm fine. It's just—I never realized..."

"What?"

Mickey looked up. As he'd expected, tears glittered in her lashes. "You could have died. For a couple of dumb animals, you could have died."

Jeff stared at her, confounded. An attempted shrug gave him a new set of aches. "I didn't, though."

"But you might have!" Her violent response stunned him. "You should have considered the risk before running off like that!"

Even after a good dousing, she could spark his temper. He fired off a shot of his own. "Just like you should think about the risk before you get on one of those broncs you're so crazy to ride?"

Their gazes clashed, held. He read concern in hers, and fury and...he didn't dare go further. Being wrong would hurt too much.

And anyway, Mickey wasn't ready to let go of the argument. "I've spent years running those risks," she informed him tensely. "I accepted them a long time ago."

"And I thought the lives of those animals and Dex's investment were worth the effort I put out. Give me credit for some intelligence, Mickey."

"Give me—give the rest of us credit for worrying about you, Jeff. There was more at stake out there than just money."

"There always is."

Into the quiet that followed his comment came their acknowledgment of what was at stake between them now—their past, their future, their child. Jeff waited for Mickey to make the first move, to tell him what she'd decided and where he would have to start picking up the pieces.

But she didn't say a word. They rode along in the dark for a long, silent time.

Eventually light sneaked in through the windows of the truck. He looked away from Mickey's face to realize that they'd come back to the ranch house. Beside him, Dex slid easily to the end of the bed. Once Roy came around and opened the gate, he jumped out and turned to offer Jeff his hand.

"Need some help?"

"I'm okay." Wincing, he shoved himself down and out. The bruises on his legs came to life as his feet hit the ground. Turning, he found Mickey had scooted herself over to perch on the tailgate, waiting for him to move. Jeff stepped back.

"Looks like the rain passed over," he commented, trying for some balance in an impossible situation. "It's going to be a nice night."

"Good," she said in a low voice, not looking at him. She eased her feet out and pushed herself off with her arms. "I've got a long drive back."

He didn't get a chance to argue about that. Mickey stood up, swayed and closed her eyes.

"Catch me, Jeff," she murmured. And then passed out, for the second time that summer, in his arms.

None of the ranchers and cowboys still present even tried to suggest taking her from him as Jeff shouldered his way into the house. He heard Dex say, "I'll get towels," as he laid Mickey down on the bed in his old room. The towels materialized on the chair against the wall, along with some folded clothes.

"Call a doctor," he ordered without taking his eyes off the woman under his hands.

"Sure." And then the door shut softly behind him, closing them in alone.

Fingers at her jawline, he checked her pulse, reassured to find it steady and strong, if a bit fast. A look at her pupils reinforced the impression that she wasn't in any real danger. The baby...he didn't know about the baby. Couldn't begin to guess. But Mickey would be okay as soon as he got her warm and dry.

Working quickly, he pulled off her boots, eased the wet socks off her feet and her jeans down her legs. He bit back a harsh comment when he saw the splotchy purple of her goose-bumpy flesh. Grabbing a towel, he stroked her softly, hoping to transfer some heat. Then, with the terry as a blanket over her legs, he started on her shirt buttons, his shaking fingers making every move a fumble.

Once he had her clothes off, he went for broke and removed her panties, as well. She lay there before him, vulnerable and unaware. He put every ounce of his will into blocking desire before it took possession of his mind.

But with his hands moving over her, drying, warming, he couldn't turn off his reactions completely. Built small, Mickey had never worn a bra. That, he predicted, would change in the next few months. Against his will, his gaze lingered on her breasts, and he thought he could detect the signs of pregnancy in a new fullness, a slight darkening of the peaks. When he rubbed the towel softly over her belly, he wondered if he only imagined the gentle swelling under his palm.

Too soon, he knew. Still...

Shaking his head, Jeff concentrated on practicalities,

blanking out even the simplest thoughts. By the time she started stirring, he had the tangles combed out of her hair and her body covered with Dex's big flannel shirt, a pair of wool socks and a blanket. The return of color to her cheeks rewarded his efforts.

But the sudden smile in her eyes when she focused on him felt even better. "Jeff? What…" She pushed herself up a bit, and he helped her arrange a pillow behind her shoulders for support. "Another rescue? You've had a busy night."

"All in a day's work," he deadpanned, forcing himself to take his hands away and step back. He wanted to grab her close and never let go. But she hadn't given him the right.

Mickey didn't seem to notice his reluctant retreat. "How are Jezebel and son?" she asked as a knock sounded on the door.

"Just great." Dex stepped into the room. "Curled up in the box they should have started out in, fast asleep. You're looking better," he commented after a thorough survey.

Then he turned to Jeff. "You're not."

Now that Mickey was awake, relief had drained him of nervous energy. He probably looked nearly as bad as he felt. "Thanks."

Instead of offering him a break, though, Dex simply took out of his hands the towels and wet clothes he'd picked up. "I'll shove these in the dryer and get you two some food."

Making a mental note to thank his friend for a world of consideration and discretion, Jeff turned back to Mickey. He found her plucking at the front of the shirt she wore. When she lifted her gaze, a red flush stained her cheeks and throat.

"This isn't...I'm not...you—"

Taking the chair beside the bed, he reached for her hand. "You needed to get dry. It was just me, though. Don't worry. How do you feel?"

The blush didn't ebb, but she returned his squeeze and gave him a grin. "Dizzy. Stupid."

"Any cramps? Nausea?"

Her easy smile faded. She slipped her hand away. "No. No more than I've been living with, anyway."

"Dex is calling a doctor. We'll get him to check you out. Just to be sure."

Mickey dropped her gaze to the bedspread. Jeff would be concerned about the baby; that only made sense. It also hurt like the devil. He'd undressed her, seen her naked, and all he could think about was whether the baby was all right. The message couldn't have been plainer if he'd come right out and said the words. The only thing he wanted to share with her now was their child.

Well, she wouldn't cry about her losses tonight. Later. And for a long, long time.

Meanwhile, she'd make sure he took care of himself. "That's fine, as long as you let him check out that cut on your head while he's here." Lifting her chin, she challenged him to deny her request.

For once he backed down. "Sure. I can do without this headache on a regular basis." His grin coaxed a similar response from her. For once, Mickey thought, they were agreeing on what was best for each other.

Another knock brought Dex back, this time with a tray of food. "Hope somebody can eat some of this. Those guys out there couldn't decide on what the best cure for a busted head and a dead faint would be, so they sent in all the options." He set the meal down on a table. "I'd say you two have figured that out already. I'll clear everybody out so the doctor can get in. Any last-minute instructions for the show, Mickey?"

Sipping the soothing tea, she shook her head. "I think everything is settled. Tell them all thanks and I'll see them down at the fairgrounds Friday afternoon."

"Right."

Sharing the meal with Jeff in silence, Mickey kept her mind empty and her eyes on her bowl of soup. If it meant no entertaining conversation, so be it. She couldn't string two words together that didn't begin, "Jeff, I love you," so there wasn't any use in trying. He didn't volunteer his thoughts, either. Silence really was the only answer.

The doctor from Buffalo showed up just as she finished eating. He was new to Wyoming, he told her as he poked and prodded and probed, so he knew nothing of her reputation or history. Mickey appreciated the anonymity.

"Well," he said as he straightened up, "I don't see any problems. Stress, shock, lack of food—sounds like you had good reason to keel over. Have you seen a doctor yet about the baby?"

She swallowed hard. "Um, no."

He nodded. "It's early yet. Do you have someone in mind?"

When she shook her head, he reached for his wallet and pulled out a card. "Obstetricians are thin on the ground around here, but I did more than the required rotations during training. I'd be glad to follow you if you're interested. Just call the office and set up an appointment. Within two weeks," he added with a stern look. "You need iron supplements, vitamins and a general checkup. Take care of yourself and your baby."

Mickey cleared her throat. "I will. I promise."

As he left the room, she heard voices…Jeff's, anxious; the doctor's, calm and brisk. The baby, no doubt. He wanted to know about the baby.

Turning to her side, Mickey blinked back a sudden hot wetness. She would not be jealous of her own child. Besides, whatever she suffered now, she knew, was no less than she deserved.

And the chance to bear Jeff's child again was a greater gift than she'd ever hoped to receive. If giving him up was the price, she would pay it.

Jeff came in a while later. She heard his footsteps in the hallway and the telltale squeak of the door hinge. By the time he bent over the bed, she'd forced herself to relax, compelled her eyes to close, urged her breathing into an even rhythm.

The ruse worked. "Sleep tight, Mickey." The whisper of his words tickled over her ear. A slight touch on her temple might have been his fingertips—or a kiss. And then the door closed.

She didn't sleep at all. Long before dawn, before Dex or Jeff might think of waking, Mickey pulled her clothes out of the dryer and dragged them on. Carrying her boots, she slipped out the front door and across the porch, wincing as her bare feet touched cold stone and then, colder still, muddy dirt.

A light came on in the window of her old bedroom as the truck engine rattled to life.

To look up, to see him watching, would be more than she could handle. Without turning her head, Mickey pointed the truck down the driveway and, with a spray of gravel, escaped into the dark.

THANKS TO AN EMERGENCY on the ranch of his farthest-flung client, Jeff pulled into the parking lot at the fairgrounds on Friday night a good four hours later than he'd planned. The Camp Crazy Woman Rodeo preparations were in full swing, and spectators had already started to arrive. Two different television stations had sent vans, and a radio announcer was broadcasting live from a booth beside the ticket counter.

"Some event," he commented to Laurie when he found her in the office. A regular rodeo secretary had volunteered to check in all the performers, but Laurie was supervising just about everything else.

"You can say that again!" She barely glanced up from the list she was checking off. "Mickey's gotten us so much attention, I won't be surprised if the governor shows up. This is an election year, you know."

"How's she doing?"

Laurie looked up with an innocent smile. "The governor?"

He just stared. The camp director grinned sheepishly. "Oh...you mean Mickey. She's okay. No major aftereffects from your little adventure. How about you? I heard you took a washing."

"That about describes it. But I survived." He'd fought his way through the last week minute by minute; now the need to see Mickey took him abruptly by the throat. "Do you know where I can find her?"

Absorbed in her paperwork, Laurie only shook her head. "She had interviews with the press lined up one after the other between five and seven. At seven she starts pulling together the Grand Parade and getting the kids set to perform. Show starts at eight. Your guess is as good as mine."

"Thanks a lot." He started for the door.

"Did you expect me to make it easy?"

He stopped dead, but didn't turn around. For a second, the hopelessness of the situation almost overwhelmed him. "I wish to hell *somebody* would," Jeff muttered. And then slammed himself out into the crowd.

The weather had smiled on them, providing blue skies all day and now a sparkling night with just a hint of autumn coming around the corner. Parents and kids, cowboys and cowgirls mingled around the concession area and underneath the stands. Jeff wove his way through them, looking for one person in particular. It was the story of his life, in a way—always searching for Mickey, never quite sure where she was or which way she would head next.

He saw her at last, standing with an elbow propped against a fence as a knot of photographers snapped pictures. Assessing her from a distance, Jeff decided she had, indeed, recovered. Energy and enthusiasm radiated from her smile, backed up by the neon purple of her silky shirt. The shimmer of her chaps was a familiar sight—he'd helped her pick out that purple and silver pattern when she'd joined the college team. No fancy boots tonight, he noticed; she wore her lace-up riding shoes. The ones that meant business. And spurs.

His heart slammed into his throat, and he beat it back. She wasn't that stupid. But just to check, he retraced his steps through the throng, pulled out his wallet and bought a program. Thick and glossy, it represented yet another of Mickey's professional contacts.

Flipping through, he reached the page featuring women's bareback. And there she was…Mickey York. Three-time world champion, paired up with Inevitable, also a world-championship winner. A full-color photograph and a list of Mickey's titles over the years. A write-up on the multitude of riders Inevitable had dumped in his career. A quote from Mickey about the last time she'd ridden this particular horse. "Two seconds" leaped out from the print. Jeff crushed the program closed.

Mickey was scheduled to ride.

CHAPTER FOURTEEN

PIVOTING ON HIS HEEL, Jeff strode toward the animal pens, needing time to get himself together before he confronted her. Every doubt, every misgiving he'd ever entertained about Mickey rose to the surface of his mind, mocking him for his faith and trust, for his belief in her and her ability to do what was right.

Surely if she cared about him at all, she could have put her career on hold. That she hadn't—*wouldn't*—must mean she had no interest in making him a part of her life. By riding tonight she was proving how little she valued his opinion. And if she went against his wishes and risked their baby's life for a moment of glory, what hope did he have that she would let him play any role in the child's future?

The caliber of stock they'd arranged for guaranteed that the rodeo vet had little to do but enjoy the show. Jeff made some spot checks as the hour for the start approached, but didn't try to find Mickey again. He didn't know what he would say.

Maybe he would just leave without a word. Maybe tonight was *his* night for running away.

Not yet, though. He'd made a commitment to the ranchers and the animals they'd donated, and he would see it through. Even more important, he cared about this cause, about these kids. He wanted to see them perform, see their faces as they enjoyed their special night. And so he headed toward the stands at a few minutes before eight.

"Jeff?" His name in a familiar voice penetrated the crowd noise. "Jeff Buchanan, are you just going to walk by me without a single word?"

He jerked his head around, saw a slight woman in a denim skirt and recognized her cap of silver hair. "Ruth!" In two strides he reached her and bent to pull her into a hug. "What are you doing here? I didn't know you were coming!"

She leaned back in his hold, smoothing his shirt over his shoulders. "Mickey didn't tell you?"

"Uh...no." Ruth York's soft hazel eyes narrowed, and he knew he'd let on too much. Time for a diversion. "We've been pretty busy. When did you get here? Where are you staying—and why isn't it with me?"

Her face lighted with a grin that reminded him of her daughter. "Roberta Fender asked me to stay at her house. I don't think you need an old woman hanging around, getting in your way."

"Old woman!" He pushed the thought of Mickey aside and managed a mock frown. "That's ridiculous. What about that date we were going to have? Are you saying I'm too young for you?"

She winked. "I'm really not sure you have enough energy to keep up."

"Well, we'll see about that." A trumpet blew in the arena, announcing the start of the show. "We'd better get inside. We don't want to miss the Grand Parade. Where are you sitting?"

But with a shake of her head, Ruth stepped out of the circle of his arm. "I'm waiting for Roberta. She went to the ladies' room. You go on, and I'll catch you at the party later."

The death of chivalry versus an evening spent with Roberta Fender...not a hard choice. "Okay, Ruth. Save me a dance."

Five minutes later, he dropped into the empty seat next to Dex Hightower. "Hey there. Looks like a great crowd."

The big man nodded. "Not many bare spots, and there's still a crowd out at the gate. I'd say Mickey's got herself a hit." Dex's dark eyes narrowed as their gazes met. "You don't look any better than you did when I pulled you out of that creek Monday night. What's wrong?"

Jeff lifted his arm with the program in it, discovered his index finger still marked the place. "See for yourself," he suggested, tossing the book into Dex's lap.

When his friend started to speak, Jeff stopped him with a raised palm. "No. I can't talk about it. Let's just enjoy the show."

As always, Dex took the rebuff in stride. "Well, then, let me introduce you to someone." He motioned Jeff to lean over. "This is my daughter, Allyson. Allyson, this is Dr. Buchanan."

A moppet with her dad's dark hair curling wildly over her forehead peeked at him. "Hi."

"Hi, yourself." *A little girl would suit me just fine.* "I'm glad to meet you, Allyson."

She sent him a snaggletoothed grin, and hid behind her dad's shoulder again.

Jeff looked at Dex and smiled. "Cute."

No hiding that look of fatherly pride. "You bet."

The announcer called them to attention. "Ladies and gentlemen, girls and boys, I'd like to welcome y'all to the first annual Camp Crazy Woman Charity Rodeo. All the performers and workers you see here tonight have donated their time and talent and prizes to make sure that the special kids who need this very special camp will have the opportunity to attend. All the stock and equipment has been donated, as well, and we'd like to thank each and every person who's here tonight for their contribution to such a worthy cause!''

"First annual?'' Dex shouted over the applause.

Jeff grinned. "Mickey always did think big!''

"And now, ladies and gentlemen, girls and boys, the performers of the Camp Crazy Woman Charity Rodeo will begin this great show with the Grand Parade, led by the organizer of this event, three-time world champion Miss Mickey York!''

The gates at the far end swung back and Mickey galloped through, to be greeted with a huge wave of applause. Her posture proud, her seat firm, she led the parade for her rodeo with every ounce of showmanship Jeff expected. The big gray, Thunder, reacted to the lights and the applause with the confidence of a seasoned performer. Together, they made quite a pair.

Behind them rode the little girl, Karen, and Jeff had to laugh when he recognized her mount as his old friend Jelly Roll, the horse Mickey had trained for barrel racing. Jelly Roll, named for his chubby belly as a pony, took his role seriously. His gait was smooth and polished, his head high as he carried Karen in a circuit around the arena. For her part, Karen kept her eyes on Mickey, copying every move she made. It was a great way to learn to ride.

And then came the rest of the performers, the other kids from the camp, followed by professional cowboys and cowgirls, big names every one. The colors, the lights, the music, the procession of animals and riders, all had been choreographed by Mickey with an eye to making an impression. Jeff could practically hear money clinking into the till. He spotted Clementine under one little boy, and smiled. Her knee had healed up just fine.

Mickey led the parade out, but the gates didn't close. After a moment, a quartet of horses returned, all of them ridden by children. The center rider—Karen, again, on Jelly Roll—carried the American flag. Flanked precisely by the other three, she made a circuit of the arena to the strains of a patriotic song. As the crowd rose to sing the national anthem, the cohort came to a halt in the center of the wide expanse of dirt. Jeff glanced around, toward the end when he had to wipe the tears out of his eyes if he hoped to see. He caught most of the rest of the audience doing the same.

And then it was time for the show to start. First event, men's bareback riding.

Jeff wasn't going to wait around for the women. "I'll see you later," he told Dex. "Look me up before you leave."

"Hey!" Dex shout stopped him at the edge of the row. "Mickey asked me to bring Jezebel and her colt for the kids to see. He's in the barn if you want to look in."

Perfect. "Thanks, I'll do that."

With the crowds in the stands, the concession area had emptied out and he made his way to the barn with no traffic obstructions. Although the lights were on, the interior seemed dim after the brightness of the arena.

He halted just inside the door, letting his eyes adjust.

Mickey looked up in surprise and irritation at the sound of a footstep in the barn. She'd hoped to be left alone with her thoughts for just a few blessed minutes now that the show was under way. But even here...

Then she realized who it was. Even across a hundred feet of dirt, she could recognize that silhouette with no trouble at all.

"Hi, Jeff."

He hesitated and half turned, as if he would walk out without speaking. But then he pivoted back and came down the long aisle toward her. "Hey, Mickey."

She couldn't believe how rough his voice sounded. "Are you still hoarse from the other night? Or did you catch a cold?"

"Maybe."

Maybe? What kind of answer was that to an either-or question? Before she could press him, he stepped up to the gate of the box.

"Is this Jezebel? Oh, yeah…hello, lady. That's a nice boy you have there. Did yourself proud, didn't you?"

His low, crooning tones vibrated in her chest, and Mickey felt herself begin to melt. Lord, she loved him.

"Dex brought them down for the kids to see. They want to name the colt Stormy, of course."

Jeff nodded without looking her way. "Trouble would be more appropriate." The colt lifted his long black nose from under his mother's belly and glared up at them. "Yeah, you are trouble, boy. You are that."

She was beginning to think he wouldn't talk to her at all, that her disappearing act Monday night had cut them loose for good.

But then he said, "The show looks like a real success. I'd say your money worries are over."

"I think so. We couldn't have done it without you, Jeff." Taking a risk, unable to stop herself, she put her hand on his arm. "You don't know how much I appreciate your ideas, all your help. I don't have any way to say thanks."

Under her fingers, his muscles tensed into rock. "Mickey, I—" At last his gaze lifted to her face. His eyes were dark pools of tenderness, anger, hurt. "Anything I have, Mickey. You know that."

And then his hands reached out and captured her shoulders, pulling her slowly, relentlessly to him. Mickey let herself be drawn, let her hands come to rest on his chest, then slipped them up, over his shoulders and around his neck as he brought her against his body. Without a sound, without a word, Jeff closed her in his arms. Dropping his face to the curve of her neck, he simply held on.

Home.

The word echoed in her head. Mickey drew in a sigh, breathed Jeff deeply into her lungs. She'd reached the center of her life, the only place she ever wanted, ever needed to be. His shoulder under her cheek, his heart against hers, the warmth of his thighs pressing her hips, these were the walls of her palace, a place of defense and haven and comfort. Given a choice, she would never willingly step outside their sanctuary again.

"Mickeymickeymickeymickeymickey...Mickeeeeeey!"

Oh no...not now. Mickey sighed. Jeff lifted his head as the patter of little feet got louder. On a deep breath, he took a step back and dropped his hands, his gaze holding to hers. She let her palms slide slowly off his shoulders, not looking away.

Then Karen burst into their end of the barn, followed by her parents. "Mickey, the ladies' bareback is getting ready to start! Are you coming? Are you? You can't miss it! Come on, Mickey!"

Mickey stared at Jeff, trying to convince herself that what she saw in his face couldn't be real, hoping beyond hope that it was. Before she could say anything, though, Karen's parents had come into the barn. Though the last thing she wanted to do was talk to strangers, she put on her professional face and turned toward the couple.

"Hi, Mr. Wheeler, Mrs. Wheeler. Didn't Karen do a fantastic job in the flag ceremony? I was so proud of her."

Mrs. Wheeler stood apart from the group, but Don Wheeler stepped forward and shook Mickey's hand. "You bet she did! She looked right at home on that horse." With his other hand, he hugged Karen to his side. "Way to go, kiddo!"

"Look, Daddy, this is the colt Dr. Buchanan saved. Isn't he neat?" Karen dragged her father to look in at Jezebel. With a glance at Mickey, Jeff joined them.

Karen's mother moved in front of Mickey so that she couldn't follow. "I can't believe you would let her ride alone like that, without any help. That was irresponsible, Ms. York. She might have fallen. The horse might have run away with her."

Mickey stared at her a moment. "You're right. Those things could have happened." Mrs. Wheeler gasped, and started to protest. Mickey held up a hand. "But they didn't. Because Karen has worked like the devil to learn what she can do, what it takes to control an animal. She wasn't afraid tonight because she trusts herself, and she trusts that horse."

"I thought you understood—"

"I do understand. I understand that you're worried, that you wish you could wrap her up in a blanket and keep her safe forever. You've been through so much, it's only natural."

Mickey stepped close enough to cover the woman's

tightly clasped hands with her own. "But life is risk, Mrs. Wheeler. Each person has to find their own balance between safety and adventure. For Karen, this summer, that balance came in learning to ride. She *needed* to ride, to succeed, to become the person she wants to be in her heart. I don't think you can argue that the confidence and pride she feels in herself can only do her good, whatever the future holds."

Karen's mother looked down at their hands; Mickey felt a warm tear splash across her knuckles.

"You have to trust Karen, Mrs. Wheeler. She knows what she wants, what she needs. Guide her, but let her go as far as she can. She won't let you down."

Jeff heard Mickey's words. A small, steady hope within his heart had insisted all along that she wouldn't ride tonight, wouldn't risk their baby. Now, despite the evidence to the contrary, the open tenderness he saw in her face as she spoke to Karen's mother assured him that he could trust her, as she'd trusted him when he'd decided to go after Jezebel in the storm. Loving someone didn't mean controlling their life. Real love meant a commitment to faith and hope, a belief in the strength of the person with whom you shared your dreams.

"Come on, Mickey! Come on!"

Mickey's gaze sought his, and clung, but with Karen dragging her backward toward the arena, she didn't have much choice. And she seemed to have trouble finding her voice. She lifted her hand, as if to wave. Then, hesitating, she brought two fingers to her lips, to blow a kiss.

"Mickeeeeey!"

Jeff tipped his hat. "I'll see you later."

With one last, long look, Mickey grabbed her hat off a hay bale and disappeared.

Jeff turned back to lean his arms on the top of Jezebel's gate. He didn't need to watch the show. What he
needed was to get his approach worked out, so that
when he got the chance, he could convince Mickey,
carefully, completely, that they belonged together. She
might still be skittish, might have some doubts. He
would take this time during the performance to marshal
his arguments, building a case so persuasive she
couldn't possibly refuse.

But the announcer's voice didn't pick up immediately. After a minute, the delay in the show became
obvious. Jeff waited, practically counting the seconds,
and listened to the absence of sound. With every moment, his uneasiness grew.

The crowd noises came to him muted by distance. He
heard the beginning of the chant without, at first, rec-
ognizing the words. Then the volume grew and, with a
sinking heart, he understood.

"Mick-ey! Mick-ey! Mick-ey!"

They were calling. Begging her to perform. Her kids,
their parents, the fans...not knowing what he did, why
should they expect anything less?

And how could she bear to disappoint them? She
might very well think one last time couldn't hurt...these
were her kids, they wanted to see her ride...Mickey
wouldn't want to disappoint the kids...

Jeff started for the far end of the barn, the one closest
to the arena. He wouldn't—couldn't—let it happen.
Maybe she would make it this time, get through without
losing the baby. But the possibility wasn't worth the
risk. They couldn't survive the death of another child.
He certainly wouldn't. And Mickey didn't need another
loss, another reason to feel guilty.

For her sake, for the baby's, for the sake of everything they could have together, he had to stop this ride.

Running, he made it to the door. The announcer's voice brought him up short.

"Ladies and gentlemen, before we get started with the ladies' bareback event, we have an announcement. On advice from her doctor, Miss Mickey York has turned out of the contest." A long moan from the crowd greeted this statement. "She apologizes and hopes you'll be sure to keep an eye out for when she gets back into competition. Meantime, she's asked if she could announce tonight's riders, and I think that's a great idea. Let's give her a big hand!"

Mickey's crisp voice came over the applause. "Thank you very much, ladies and gentlemen. Let me tell you, we have some dynamite women competing here tonight, and I have no doubt one of them will be the next world champion. Our performances start with…"

Jeff didn't hear the rest. And he was very glad to share the barn with only Jezebel and Stormy as he weathered his own very personal reaction to the latest miracle in his life.

THEY THREW A PARTY afterward, in the exhibition hall. All the performers and all the kids who were still awake came for soft drinks and snacks and a chance to celebrate. Jeff watched the action from his station by the door with a grin.

"Nobody needs alcohol to get high tonight," he commented to Laurie as she stopped in front of him.

"Definitely not me!" He'd never seen the cool, efficient camp director quite so stirred up. She seemed taller, even, as if her shoes weren't in touch with the floor. "I never dreamed we'd get this much response...the things we'll be able to do with the money..."

She drifted away, caught up in her dreams, and ran straight into Ed Riley. Jeff watched the sheriff grin as he steadied Laurie on her feet before she floated away.

Then Riley came over to help him prop up the wall. "Great night."

Jeff nodded. "I'm glad you came. Mickey did a fantastic job, didn't she?"

"Sure did. It surprised me that she wasn't riding, though. Did she get hurt again?"

"No." He didn't know how to tell Ed about the baby, so he sidestepped the issue. "She's okay."

When Jeff glanced over, he saw the sheriff grin. Ed tilted his head slightly. "You two back together?"

Quite a leap of logic. "Not yet. We've got some things to work out."

Ed straightened up and put a hand on Jeff's shoulder. "Good luck. Invite me to the wedding."

As Ed walked out into the night, Dex and Allyson stumbled out of the waltz they'd been trying on the dance floor.

"Let's do it again, Daddy. I want to dance on your toes again!"

Dex tossed a helpless look at Jeff and swept his daughter up into his arms. "Let's get something to drink first, sweetheart. And then I'll introduce you to Mickey York. How about it?"

"The rodeo rider? Really? Neat!" With a salute in Jeff's direction, Dex headed off toward the refreshment table.

And still Jeff kept to his place. He could see Mickey across the floor, surrounded by her kids and their parents, accepting hugs and praise and presents with a permanent flush on her cheeks and a light in her eyes. She deserved the spotlight, and the accolades. He wasn't about to intrude on her special night. And what he had to say needed privacy to be heard.

Even with all the commotion, Mickey could feel Jeff's gaze on her, warming her from the other side of the hall. Every time she looked up, she met his stare. He hadn't come close, hadn't said a word to her since those minutes in the barn. Whatever he was thinking, he hadn't shared it with her yet.

Anything I have, he'd said. What did that mean? It sounded suspiciously close to something she remembered hearing on a Saturday afternoon ten years ago...*to have and to hold, for better or for worse, for richer or poorer, in sickness and in health.* She hadn't said the words then. But she could make that promise with her whole heart today. There was nothing she wanted more. Would Jeff say the same?

Wishful thinking on her part, Mickey decided. Fairy-tale endings didn't happen in real life.

Not her life, anyway.

"Are you gonna dance, Mickey? Are you?"

She looked down at Karen, glued fast to her side, still wearing her flag-bearer sash. "I don't have a partner. Will you dance with me?"

"Girls don't dance together!"

"Sure they do—line dancing. Come on!" Grabbing all the hands she could reach, Mickey swept the kids out onto the floor. Nothing chased away the blues like a good fast round of boot scooting. She saw her mom standing nearby and pulled her into the dance, too; Ruth York loved a fast two-step better than just about anybody. By the end of the song, they were all breathless and laughing.

But eventually the distractions came to an end. Sleepy kids got packed into cars by parents still expressing an embarrassing amount of appreciation. Mickey, in turn, tried to thank all the departing riders who'd donated their prizes to the camp. Being the kind of people they were, most of them just shrugged and smiled before getting into their trucks for the long ride to tomorrow's rodeo.

With the last of them gone, Mickey walked through the quiet fairground, realizing that *she* didn't have to make that all-night drive, didn't have to pump herself up for a performance again for a long, long time. She could sleep late, for a change. Linger over breakfast, take an afternoon nap. Think about baby clothes and baby names.

Perched at the top of the stands, she stared out over the arena, thinking about the show, about the kids, the wonderful absence of deadlines and arrival times. This peace, this sense of fulfillment, must be what real life was all about.

"You look," a quiet voice commented, "like the cat that swallowed the canary. A person might be forgiven for believing tonight was actually a success."

She hadn't heard him come up. Stretching her arms wide, Mickey grinned even wider. "Oh, you could say that. I stopped counting when the insurance bills were paid. Who knows how much extra we earned—or even how we're gonna spend it? What a dilemma!"

Jeff dropped onto the bench below her and propped his arm on his knee. "Not many people could do what you've done, that's for sure. I've seen championship shows that didn't go off this smoothly. If you ever need a new career, I imagine there were a few people here tonight who would be willing to stake you in this one.''

''Ah, but I had a lot of help.'' Taking a deep breath, she brought her arms down, rubbed her hands over her jeans and then lifted her eyes to his face. ''Thanks again, Jeff. We couldn't have done it without you.''

His expression preoccupied, he shrugged off her gratitude without a reply.

''All we have to do now,'' Mickey went on, needing to fill the tense silence, ''is make sure all the borrowed equipment gets back where it belongs. And pick up the trash. Then life can get back to normal.''

Lifting his face, Jeff snagged her gaze with his own. ''Just what is normal, Mickey? What exactly are you planning to do now?''

He always asked the hard questions first. She hesitated, trying to construct the right answer. Was this the time, the place to get into such an important discussion? ''I guess I've got some changes to make,'' she started cautiously. ''Now that I've announced I won't be competing anymore—''

''I want to thank you for that.'' His serious brown stare held hers. ''I know what a sacrifice it is for you to give up riding, and I appreciate the way you put this baby's welfare ahead of your commitment to the camp and the kids, not to mention your professional goals. I can't tell you what that means to—''

Mickey wasn't sure she'd heard right. Or that she liked the message behind what she heard. ''I beg your pardon?''

He stared at her, his raised eyebrows registering surprise. ''What's wrong? I just wanted you to know that I understand how hard the decision was, and that I'm grateful—''

"Grateful?" She swallowed, trying to calm down before she hauled off and slugged him. "Just what kind of person do you think I am?"

Jeff stared up into her flushed face, aware that the situation had shifted suddenly, that the good feelings had gone up in smoke. Time to tread carefully. "I don't understand."

"You thought I would compete tonight?" Mickey got to her feet, so that he had to look up even more. "You thought I'd ride a bronc bareback, knowing I was pregnant?"

Well, why not? "You jumped on me like a wildcat that day up at camp, wouldn't let me help you find another rider." He pushed himself up and plowed his hands into his pockets. "You were wearing chaps and spurs. And your name was in the program. What else could I think?"

She cast an exasperated glance up at the sky. "Be reasonable, Jeff. That program was printed before I even knew I was pregnant. And I had to ride tonight in the parade. You could," she declared, her fists planted on her hips, "give me credit for a little common sense!"

Despite his best efforts, his temper snapped. "Your history doesn't exactly inspire confidence along those lines, does it?"

The dead silence with which Mickey met his comment made him wish he'd never said it. She looked him up and down, her eyes narrowed to dangerous slits.

"You think I knew, don't you?" In all the time he'd known her, he'd never heard quite that level of cold anger in her voice. "The first baby—the miscarriage. You think it happened because I kept riding, regardless. That I didn't care enough, that I took chances I shouldn't have, hit the dirt one too many times and lost the baby. That's what you think.''

All at once, Jeff doubted that this conversation would end the way he'd hoped. But he had to be honest. ''Didn't you?''

''No, damn you, I didn't! I—'' She pressed her clenched fists into her eyes. Heart pounding, he steeled himself to hear the rest. It took a minute and a couple of deep breaths for Mickey to get it out.

''I told you I didn't know I was pregnant.'' The explanation came out in a dry-as-dust voice. She dropped her hands and turned her head away as if she couldn't bear to look at him. ''I hadn't entered a show since before I...left. I was holed up in a dump of a room in Denver, trying to get myself together enough to go on with life after doing something so horrible I couldn't even look in the mirror. Not eating much, not sleeping at all. Barely able to drag out of bed because of the guilt and pain.''

She met his gaze then, and her eyes glittered with tears. ''I missed you, you know. It's not like I walked away smiling. I tore my own life apart. I went to hell.''

Jeff took a deep breath. ''Mickey—''

''Finally, I figured that since I'd ruined everything for the chance to be a rodeo star, I'd better get to it. I entered the show, a small one. And I got tossed. No big deal. I'd taken a thousand like it before. That's the price of winning the prize.''

She looked down at her hands, which were twisting in front of her trophy buckle. ''The doctor was kind, actually. She said she doubted there was a connection between the miscarriage and the fall. The baby's so small that early, so well protected, that unless I'd been kicked, which I wasn't, she really didn't think I'd caused it. One third of first pregnancies miscarry, she said. The baby might have been defective, no permanent damage was done. I could always have another.''

Her face, white and miserable, lifted. ''But I knew. If I had stayed home, let you take care of me, our baby would have lived. Would be almost ten years old now, as crazy about horses and rodeo as I was. Or else smart, like you, a real scholar. I betrayed you, I killed our child. I—''

Tears streaming down her cheeks, she whirled abruptly and headed down the bleacher steps.

''Mickey!'' Jeff reached for her hand, missed. He turned, stumbled, caught himself and started after her. ''Mickey, stop!''

Mickey only shook her head and quickened her pace down the metal risers. She had to get away, had to escape. She couldn't face this. Not now. Not ever.

Failure had been her enemy from the very first time she ate dust in her dad's corral and heard her sisters laughing at her. She'd sworn in that childhood moment to conquer horses, to win, to do whatever it took for the rest of her life to avoid feeling foolish and weak.

And what had running away from Jeff done but allow her to escape the failure their marriage might have been, if she'd sacrificed it to her career? What explained her staying away for ten years, except the desire to hide from the truth? To avoid admitting what a mess she'd made, and how she'd cost their child its life?

Again, Jeff called after her. ''What good will running away do, Mickey? How in the hell is it going to help this time?''

Astonished by the question, by his complete understanding of her thoughts, Mickey slowed her steps as she searched for the answer. If she ran away, she would put off facing what she'd done. Again. And the past would hang over her for as long as she allowed, forestalling the future and whatever happiness waited there.

Karen had found the strength to face failure, the courage to overcome that failure and win. Now, Mickey decided finally, her child—hers and Jeff's—deserved parents who could do the same.

She stopped. Turned. Looked up to find Jeff waiting right behind her, with every ounce of concern and confusion and...and...love?...he felt showing in his eyes.

Then the lights went out.

Night fell around them, star-studded, crisp and cool, alive with animal sounds and the whisper of the wind. Jeff could hear Mickey's rapid breathing, could feel his heart slam against his ribs in an agony of apprehension.

"Jeff?" Her voice was ragged.

"Let's sit down." He fumbled for her hand in the dark, smiled when her fingers gripped strongly over his own. A few sideways steps brought the edge of a bench up against his legs. Mickey followed as he turned and they sat down together. He heard her sigh as the peace of the night closed around them, like a huge room they had to themselves. They might have been all alone in the universe, with just the stars for company. He liked the feeling.

"It must be midnight," Mickey whispered finally. "They said the timer was set to turn the lights off then." He felt her shoulders lift on a deep sigh. "I'm sorry, Jeff."

He let go of her fingers, moved just far enough away to get his arm around behind her, and then pulled her tight against his side. "I have a suggestion."

"Yeah?" She dropped her head to its natural resting place in the hollow of his shoulder, an instinctive, homing gesture. And all at once, Jeff was sure this night was going to end just fine.

"Yeah." He dropped a kiss onto her hair and then cleared his throat. This needed to be said in exactly the right way. "I think both of us have apologized enough. We've said enough thank-yous, have felt guilty and shamed and angry as much as we need to for the rest of our lives. Why don't we move on?"

She rested against him as she considered the proposal. He sensed her resistance. "It could have been so different—"

He tightened his hold, squeezing off the words. "Sure, it could have been, Mickey. I could have been easier to talk to, ten years ago, less sure that my way was best and my word should be law. They call that arrogance, I think. And you—"

She twisted around to face him, grabbed onto his shoulders in an effort to shake him. "Don't blame yourself, Jeff! You were only trying to make things good for us, while I was going off on my own selfish tangent..."

Her voice died away as he pulled his mouth in an almost-laugh. "Thanks for making my point. We were both wrong. We were good at loving each other, but that wasn't enough to make a marriage work. We needed to grow up, to experience life outside the Mickey-and-Jeff framework. Outside the safety net we'd known forever. You were right when you reached for independence. I'm just sorry there had to be so much pain."

"But the baby—"

Jeff closed his eyes. Their lost child still hurt, and probably always would. Nothing would serve now but honesty. "I know. And maybe you're right. Maybe if you'd stayed home, if we'd gotten married, that child would be with us now.''

Mickey dropped her hands, hung her head. "And you can't forgive me for that.''

She *would* get the wrong message. "No. If you need to hear it said, then listen good. *I forgive you.* For running away, for the baby...all of it. The problem is—*you* can't forgive yourself, Mickey. And until you do, nothing is ever going to be right again.''

He could tell when she started to cry. Maybe it was the pregnancy hormones at work, but he'd never known Mickey quite so weepy. She brushed the tears away, only to have more fall.

Capturing her wet hands, he enclosed them with his own and used their joined fingers to lift her chin. "Mickey, it's done. I don't believe you could have changed what happened, whether you stayed or left, whether you rode or not. I do believe you would have done everything you could to save that child, just like you're taking care of this one. We've got another chance now. Accept the past. And let it go.''

Forgiveness. Acceptance. He saw the ideas flicker through her widened eyes like heat lightning on a summer night. Almost immediately, the lines in her face relaxed, and her mouth curved more naturally.

She took a deep breath, made a great effort. "I think...I think I could do that. Or at least make a start.''

"Good.''

That one word seemed to set a seal on the past. Feeling freer than she had in years, Mickey turned again and curled her back comfortably into Jeff's side. His right arm settled over her waist. His other hand drifted up and she felt his fingers outline the curve of her ear, the line of her jaw.

"I guess things could have been worse," she mused aloud as he traced the slope of her nose. "We might have discovered we were miserable *after* the wedding."

The wall of his chest rumbled with a chuckle. "I don't know if I can go that far, but I'm willing to give you the benefit of the doubt."

A warm fingertip pulled at her lower lip. Mickey bit it lightly, then touched it with her tongue. "Thanks."

"Anytime." His voice sounded slightly breathless. "So, now what?"

Good question. Mickey knew what she wanted, but did Jeff want the same thing? Could she risk finding out?

She sat up away from him. "As I started to say back there, I have to make some changes, I guess. No more rodeo this year—at least not riding. Camp is over, and the takedown can be done by hired help. Laurie and I have a lot of planning to do for next year. The baby should be born around the end of April, and then I...I—"

"Can I be there?"

The question sounded so humble, so meek, it brought tears to her eyes. She turned to look at him. "Of course. And we can work out an arrangement—"

"No."

"No?"

Swearing, Jeff levered himself up off the bench. Grabbing her hand, he pulled her to her feet and then the rest of the way down the steps. At the bottom he hopped to the ground, turned and lifted her gently, his hands around her waist, to set her in front of him, so lightly that Mickey felt as though she must be made of glass. And what he said next might very well break her into a million pieces.

But then he gathered her hands between his palms and held them against his chest. "We're talking around the real issue, here. So I'm going to get to the point. I don't want an *arrangement*. That's my child you're carrying. I intend to be part of its life, every day, every night. That means we have to get married."

She opened her mouth to protest, but he shook his head. "I am not marrying you because you're pregnant. I mean...I would, but that's not why."

His hands slipped to her shoulders and closed, drawing her closer, though not close enough. In the moonlit darkness, she could read the urgency in his eyes. "You and I belong together, Mickey. We always have. Yeah, we had some growing up to do, some learning to take care of. We've done that. And I, for one, know that there's nobody on this earth I need the way I need you. If you don't feel the same, I'm giving you this one chance to say so. After that, it's a done deal."

Smiling, she took the one step that brought their bodies into contact. Jeff's arms came around her, closed and made the touch intimate. Mickey could feel the tension in his muscles, gauging the importance of her answer.

She linked her hands behind his neck. "I've been wandering for ten years," she told him softly. "Never settled, never at peace, never home. You're my rest, my harbor. If you want me, Jeff, if you can forgive me ten years of hell, then I'm yours. I always have been."

"*If!*"

Jeff took a quick kiss, and another. And then he settled his mouth on hers with deliberate intent, rubbing softly, caressing slowly, as she melted against him. The welcome in Mickey's sigh soothed his last doubt. On a sudden surge of desire, he shifted his hands and lifted her against him, feeling her legs wrap around his waist as she parted her lips and invited his first possession.

The night's chill dissolved like mountain snow under a summer sun. With her hands roaming his back, her eagerness firing his own, Jeff could only think of removing the cloth barriers between them, of closing all the gaps and making sure, once and for all, that he and Mickey were one.

But then fatigue shivered through his arms, allowing a single icicle of sanity to pierce his brain. He drew back a fraction. "Mickey?"

"Mmm?" She tilted her head to lay a line of kisses along his jaw.

"I am not going to make love to you outdoors, standing up, in front of an entire arena of empty seats."

She chuckled. "No?"

Loosening his grip, Jeff let her slide down until her boots hit the dirt. The friction between their bodies did nothing to cool him off. "No."

He gave in to her seeking mouth for an instant, then captured her hands and pushed her away. Dragging her behind him, he headed for the exit.

"No," he said again on a deep breath. "Let's go find a motel room where we can be comfortable and private."

"No." This time Mickey pulled back, and stopped their progress.

Puzzled, he turned around. "No?"

She was wearing that smile, the one he knew meant trouble. "I don't want you in a motel room. I don't want you on the seat of your truck, or in an arena of empty bleachers." Releasing his fingers, she stepped close and laid her hand on his cheek. In the darkness, her eyes shone with the light of the stars.

"Flying Rock is kind of a long ride from here, especially at this time of night." The love in her voice rushed through him like a summer breeze, soft and warm. "But there's only one place we need to be right now. Take me home, Jeff."

Yes indeed. "Right, Mickey. Let's go home."

EPILOGUE

SIXTY SECONDS.

Fighting anxiety, Mickey put her watch down on the kitchen table and took a sip of tea. The contractions were lasting sixty seconds, coming every five minutes. They grabbed all of her attention now, and required the kind of managed breathing she'd been practicing for months.

This, she thought, *must be it.*

Two weeks early, of course. Trust her baby to arrive before its due date, in a rush to meet the world. Her mom had predicted this, remembered that Mickey herself had come ahead of schedule.

Like mother, like…? Would it be a boy or a girl?

Needing to move, she got up and walked to the sink to stare out into the night. Trust her baby to arrive in the middle of an April blizzard, with Jeff out on a night call and Laurie snowed in up in Sheridan. The doctor in Buffalo didn't answer his phone. She was beginning to think she might have to do this all by herself.

And she didn't like that idea one little bit.

There it was again, the now-familiar tightening low in her belly that predicted a contraction. Already taking her first cleansing breath, Mickey felt her way along the counter back to her chair. She was well into her measured breathing when a cold wind slammed through the room.

"Mickey? What's with all the lights at two in the morn—"

Jeff stepped in and stopped dead. Mickey lifted a hand in greeting, but didn't try to talk until the contraction had eased.

Then she smiled, aiming for nonchalance. "I'm glad to see you. Want to close the door?"

He kicked the panel shut with one foot, crossed the floor and dropped into a squat beside her. "Are you...is it...?"

"Yes and yes."

A deep breath brought the color back to his face. "How far apart are the contractions?"

She picked up her watch. "Hmm. That one was four minutes. They're getting closer."

He dropped his chin to rest his forehead against her thigh. "There's no chance of getting to the hospital."

"Don't think so." She closed her eyes and rested a hand on his hair. Would their baby have Jeff's hair?

"Mickey?"

She opened her eyes. "Yeah?"

"I didn't really plan to deliver our baby." The eagerness in his gaze was tinged with apprehension. "I just wanted to watch."

"You always get the easy part. Guess you'd better start looking at this as work."

He grinned. "Guess so."

"First, though, you're dripping snow everywhere. Take off your coat."

"Oh...okay." Like a sleepwalker, he fumbled out of the snow-caked duster and hung it on a hook.

"The water's still hot. Make yourself a cup of tea."

"Okay."

When the next spasm started, he was ready, and having him there made a real difference. With Jeff holding her hand, breathing with her, stroking her swollen belly to help her relax, Mickey felt completely in control.

And when she opened her eyes, Jeff had regained control, as well. "Let's get you more comfortable," he commanded. "Why are you sitting on a hard chair in here when you could be in bed?"

She let him help her up. "My water broke about three hours ago and I've been dribbling ever since. I didn't want to get everything messy."

"Dumb, Mickey. Messes can be cleaned. Come lie down." He supported her on the walk back to the bedroom, and got her feet up on the bed just as the next contraction started. "Deep breath. Now take it slow."

In between contractions, he helped her out of the flannel gown she'd slept in and into a short robe they thought might make things easier. When she needed to walk, Jeff's arm was around her for support; when she needed a drink, he held the glass steady. As the intensity mounted, he didn't break a smile when she gave in to the urge to swear. Instead, he let her wring his hand into spaghetti.

Along about dawn, Jeff went out to the truck, came back with the supplies he needed. Deliberately closing his mind to the possibilities, he laid out gloves, suture and anesthetic, trying to treat the birth of his child into his unassisted hands as just another veterinary job. He checked over the baby's supplies, too—a couple of soft blankets, the bassinet Mickey and her sisters had slept in, a little tub of warm water to wash off the debris of birth.

"Jeff..."

A glance at Mickey's face was all he needed to read the situation. He moved up to grip her hands. "Push if you need to, Mickey. Hold on to me and push. That's right. Push!''

It took another hour. And then Jeff let go of Mickey's hands, forced himself to let her labor alone so he could ease their child's way into the world.

"A girl!''

Mickey sobbed and fell back against the pillows. Jeff tied off the umbilical cord and carried the precious burden to the tub, where he made sure the water was warm before lowering the slippery little body into the gentle waves. As he stroked her arms and legs, her little eyes opened wide, gazed up at him. She gave a choked, struggling cry and took a deep breath. And then let loose a real scream.

Mickey heard it. "Jeff?''

Grinning, crying, he toweled his daughter off and wrapped her in a pink blanket. Then he knelt by the head of the bed.

"Meet your mom, little girl,'' he whispered, placing the baby in Mickey's waiting arms.

Her finger trembled as she traced the line of a very determined-looking chin. "Oh, baby…welcome.'' She looked up at Jeff, tears streaming down her cheeks. "So sweet.''

He leaned across the small bundle, found his wife's mouth with his. "You're a hero, Mickey. I love you.''

Mickey smiled and turned her attention back to the miracle in her arms.

Jeff's arms came around them both. "A penny for your thoughts?''

Mickey shook her head. "I'm asking at least a million.''

"You should have married a rich man, then.''

She leaned back to look up at him. "You aren't rich? Now you tell me!"

He grinned. "Sorry...better luck next time."

Nestling closer, Mickey only smiled. A perfect baby. A second chance. All she'd ever wanted, more than she could possibly deserve. Holding her daughter, sharing a home with the only man she'd ever loved, she knew she'd never be sorry again.

"Next time, nothing." She gave him a mock punch and a soft kiss. "I learned a long time ago how to hold on tight. Believe me, cowboy, I'm taking this ride all the way to the whistle!"